WHAT PEOPLE ARE SAYING ABOUT

I CALL MY~~SELF EARTH~~ GIRL

Earth Girl hauls you into ~~...~~ ~~...~~ph. The
interplay between fantas~~...~~ d future
flow seamlessly into an environmental story that we are all living
out now. A real tour de force that is inspiring, probable and
possible when lived through the main characters.
Stephanie Sorrell, author of *The Therapist's Cat*

Clear, clever, ethereal writing that draws you in from the very
first page. *I Call Myself Earth Girl* is a powerful novel I found
difficult to put down.
Danielle Boonstra, author of *Without Fear of Falling*

Now here is a book with a difference: the main character is a girl
who exists beyond time and has eyes made of pure light! *I Call
Myself Earth Girl* is an exciting read that packs a spiritual punch,
invites us to rethink quite a few of our perceptions – and pay
close attention to our dreams!
Imelda Almqvist, Painter and Shamanic Practitioner

Jan Krause Greene's debut novel is one of those books you just
can't put down. The story is compelling and the characters keep
you wanting more. Most readers will be inextricably drawn into
Gloria's dilemma quickly. The plot twists and turns its way to an
unexpected, but satisfying, finale. The moral heart of this
intriguing tale centers on difficult issues that don't have simple
answers. Greene's characters don't find the answers, but they
make you hope that someone will. After you are done, you will
keep thinking about it for a long, long time.
Julie Mancini, Founding Director of Literary Arts Portland

Einstein once said, "The intuitive mind is a sacred gift and the rational mind is a faithful servant. We have created a society that honors the servant and has forgotten the gift." The times are changing. The paradigm is shifting. The new emerging consciousness unfolding across the planet, felt by millions, is about remembering, tapping into and harnessing the gift of the intuitive mind and no character has yet to exemplify this zeitgeist like Earth Girl. *I Call Myself Earth Girl* is a modern *The Giver, The Phantom Tollbooth* with the speed of *The Never Ending Story*, but there is one difference: Earth Girl brings us a message for our world that may just prevent a nuclear war.

Christine Harmon, author of *Clueberry World*

I Call Myself
Earth Girl

I Call Myself
Earth Girl

Jan Krause Greene

Winchester, UK
Washington, USA

First published by Soul Rocks Books, 2013
Soul Rocks Books is an imprint of John Hunt Publishing Ltd., Laurel House, Station Approach,
Alresford, Hants, SO24 9JH, UK
office1@jhpbooks.net
www.johnhuntpublishing.com
www.soulrocks-books.com

For distributor details and how to order please visit the 'Ordering' section on our website.

Text copyright: Jan Krause Greene 2012

ISBN: 978 1 78279 049 5

A CIP catalogue record for this book is available from the British Library.

Design: Stuart Davies

Printed and bound by CPI Group (UK) Ltd, Croydon, CR0 4YY

We operate a distinctive and ethical publishing philosophy in all
areas of our business, from our global network of authors to
production and worldwide distribution.

To My Grandchildren with Hope and Love.

Acknowledgements

This is my first novel (unless you count the version of *Gone with the Wind* that includes my handwritten new ending which I used to replace the ending that I tore out because I didn't like it. In my version, Scarlet and Rhett live happily ever after, but I was only ten, so what did I know?)

I feel gratitude to so many people who have supported me during the various stages of the creation of this manuscript, and so many others who encouraged me long before this story was even so much as an idea. So I will start at the beginning.

Thanks to my parents for always believing in me and for providing a home in which laughter and love were ever present. During their 68 years of marriage, they taught me that laughter is the best medicine for just about everything. A special note of thanks to my dad who would have loved to see this day. He was the most generous and gentle of spirits who believed equally in Peter Pan, Santa Claus and the truth of mathematics. And for my mom, who at 97 read my book, said it was the "best book" she ever read, and the next day told me she couldn't remember what it was about. I am so lucky that she loves me enough to make that prodigious effort. She always told me, "You should write a book." I am glad I finished this one while she is still able to feel good about it. And, of course, my big brother, who always made me feel smart and funny and who has been there for me in ways both big and small.

Thanks to Punky for always believing in me and my schemes, my dreams, my silly games and my grandiose plans ever since we were nine years old. Her friendship made my childhood more joyful, my hard times more bearable and my good times sweeter. She has enriched my life in ways that I can't possibly describe. She was my very first reader and she read this story each and every time I revised it. Punky, for this and for everything over the past 55 years, I thank you.

Thanks to my college roommates who have not only listened for so many years to me saying, "I want to write a book," but who also encouraged me to do so and who understood when my life was just too full to be able to sit down and write. They were always there. They always will be. Thanks, my dear ones, for honoring my tears as well as my laughter and for those double rainbows!

Thanks to Judy who encouraged me years ago to get a job at a newspaper. "At least you'll be writing something," she said, and she was right. That simple step led to a newspaper column while raising my kids. Thanks also to Linda and Roberta who have been such stalwart friends and supporters throughout this whole process. It was my amazing good fortune to live across the street from all three of you.

Thanks to all those who were willing to read the manuscript at one stage or another. There are too many to list, but special thanks to Roberta and Kathryn who read the whole thing many times and always made it sound like I was doing them a favor. Your enthusiasm for each re-reading and your insightful comments helped me more than you know. Thanks to Ginny for understanding my heart even when I couldn't find my voice. Thanks to Amy and Pat who read it (I suspect) on behalf of Sherry, knowing how very much I miss her. Sher would be so happy for me if she were here. I know that somewhere in the light she is smiling for me.

Thanks to Chrissy who believed in this book's publication from the moment she finished reading an early version. She has helped and encouraged me in innumerable ways, opening as many doors for me as she possibly can. It is only because of her that I even know about SOUL ROCKS.

Thanks to everyone at John Hunt Publishing, especially Alice Grist for believing in me and this book. A special shout out to Trevor for answering all my questions about formatting!

Thanks to Julie M for so generously giving me just the help I needed at just the right time!

Thanks to Bob for his belief that this book will make a great movie.

Thanks to my sons, Halby, Jeremy, Karl, Neil and John. No mother could have been more blessed. You have enriched my life in ways that you may never even be able to understand. You have been my most profound teachers. You have brought me a depth of joy that I didn't even know existed until you were born. From all of you, and each of you individually, I learned that nothing matters more than love. Because you mean so much to me, your enthusiasm and support as I have been working on this book has been incredibly important to me. I thank you for all of your encouragement, but most of all for becoming the good and kind men that you are. You make me proud everyday.

Thanks to Julie, Jami and Autumn for being such wonderful daughter-in-laws who let me feel that I now have daughters as well as sons. You each have added so much joy and light to our family. Thanks for all the conversations (truly I am so glad to have daughter in laws who have the female appreciation for conversation!!) and all the understanding as I vented about various aspects of this book-writing process.

Finally, thanks to my husband, Tim, my ever enthusiastic cheerleader, my gentlest critic and my stalwart supporter in every aspect of my life. To have you in my life is a treasure beyond measure. I love your touchingly open heart and delightfully open mind. You have embraced the writing of this book every step of the way, providing not only insight and encouragement, but also really delicious meals! I could thank you for so many different things, but I will sum it all up by saying, "Thank you for being you and letting me be me. I hold your heart in my heart."

CHAPTER 1

Gloria Geist awoke from the dream overwhelmed by a feeling of dread. It was that same dream again and it left her feeling vulnerable, afraid and pregnant...very pregnant.

She did not want to have a baby. Not now, not at this stage of her life. She was 46 years old. She had a married daughter who was expecting her first child. She had come to terms with being a grandmother before she was ready. She didn't think she could come to terms with being a pregnant grandmother. Besides, her husband and daughter would be horrified. This couldn't be happening, but she was pretty sure it was.

She shivered with apprehension as she finally confronted her nagging fear. She went into the downstairs bathroom, locked the door and peed on the pregnancy-detection stick that she had hidden weeks ago. If her fear was confirmed, and those last few months without periods were because of pregnancy, she would have to tell Jared she was pregnant rather than menopausal.

Feeling faint, she stayed seated on the toilet and put her head down between her knees. She held the stick tightly between the thumb and forefinger of her right hand. She was going to give herself a few seconds before she looked at it again. Maybe she had read it wrong the first time. After all, it had been years since she used one of these.

As the blood began to flow back to her brain, she was able to think more clearly. With the fingers on her left hand, she carefully counted back the months to the last time she and Jared made love. Not enough fingers on one hand. This was bad, really bad.

It didn't add up right. She didn't see how she could have conceived. Jared had been gone for a month-long business training right about the time she would have had to conceive if her missed periods were an indication of when she got pregnant. This didn't make sense. She decided to get to her gynecologist as soon as possible. She needed answers...and soon.

Her visit to the doctor left her with more questions, than answers. If her doctor was right about how far along she was, she would have had to conceive while her husband was out of town. This was a total impossibility. She shivered as she contemplated what this could mean.

As she walked to the parking lot, she began to feel off balance and out of it; the same way she felt after taking antihistamines. Her heart beat rapidly as she tried frantically to figure out how she could possibly be only three months pregnant. Maybe it would be better to walk. She headed towards Touro Park. A short walk around the perimeter might clear her head. What she really needed was someone to talk to, but how could she share this news with anyone? It would be devastating if it got back to Jared.

She sat on a bench and started to cry. Before she noticed, a man in a tattered pea coat, mismatched boots and a dirty watch cap sat down beside her.

"Hey, Curly, why the tears? What does a pretty lady like you have to cry about?"

She recognized him as soon as he started to speak. It was the homeless man whom she saw almost every time she went to the park. Most people thought he was crazy. She made a habit of greeting him and treating him with respect, even though Jared thought he might be dangerous. One day a few years ago, when her unruly hair was blowing into her face, he called her Curly. Ever since, that had been his name for her. They had developed a friendship of sorts, based on friendly greetings and her occasional gifts of hot drinks, gloves, sox and much-needed tissues. She figured she was one of the only people who treated him like a normal human being. She went out of her way to be kind to him. He often said to her, "Don't you worry. I've got your back," even though there was no reason to think she needed someone to have her back.

She wished he would leave her alone now, but knew that he

wouldn't go if he thought she was in trouble. Wiping away the tears on her cheek with the back of her hand, she looked at him intently.

"I know you can keep a secret. Right?"

"Hell yes, Curly. I can keep a secret. No one talks to me, and when I talk to folks they think I'm psycho. I'm your man for a secret. Just call me your secret keeper and I'll call you my secret weeper."

She considered his answer. Maybe he is crazy, but no one will believe anything he says about me.

"I've got a problem. I'm pregnant and..."

"Unplanned babies. Hmmmmm, there are lots of those in the world, Curly. Look at the stars, probably as many unplanned babies as stars in the skies. Did you know that we are made of stars?"

"Sure. I know...lots of unplanned babies but this one can't be my husband's," she said, tears beginning to flow again.

"Oh, well that's a different problem... Curly, I hate to tell you but you are in some deep shit. Cheating women, ummm, ummm, ummm...lot of songs been written about them cheating women."

"I didn't cheat! I didn't even have sex. I just...well...I think it happened in a dream," she said tentatively.

"And people think I'm crazy? That's a good one, Curly, but even a wacko guy like me can't believe that one. Unless, you are the Virgin Mary come back to life in the here and now. You aren't, are you?"

For an instant she considered the story about the Virgin Mary. She had never really believed this story, but for a moment she empathized with the Virgin Mary and what she must have gone through before she told Joseph that she was pregnant. She wondered when people started referring to Jesus' mother as the Virgin Mary, and that led her to wonder ruefully how people would refer to her. The Cheating Gloria? Maybe the Crazy Gloria?

"Hey, Curly, don't look so sad. Why don't you tell me the whole story? I'll figure out an answer. You know that when I look through a window, I always see things no one else can see," he said.

"I don't want to disappoint you, but the only reason I am telling you any of this is because I know no one will believe you if you ever repeat it," she said.

"Yeh, I get that. That's for true. Go on, tell me how you got yourself in this fix, Curly."

"I don't even know and I sure as hell don't know which will be harder, telling my daughter that I am pregnant or telling my husband I am pregnant with a baby that is not his."

"That one is easy, Curly. Telling your husband is gonna be harder for sure. Whoooeeee, that's gonna be a hurtin' time."

"You're no help. You don't even believe that I didn't cheat on Jared. But l didn't. You know the beginning of menopause does weird things to a woman's cycle and people have change-of-life babies. My periods have been kind of random lately."

"Maybe I don't need to know all the woman stuff details about this," he interjected.

"But, it's important. See, if I wasn't pregnant and my periods were regular, I would be just about due for my third period since Jared's business trip. According to the doctor, I am fourteen weeks pregnant. That means I got pregnant while he was gone. But that's impossible."

"Sure is impossible if he's the daddy," he added

"We didn't even have sex for months before he left because of his back sprain, and before that I got poison ivy on my legs, and that was gross. So if I figure back to the last time we actually made love, I would have to be at least six months pregnant, and the doctor says I'm definitely not."

"Ummm, ummm, that's a mystery."

"God knows what he thinks about why I kept insisting that I had to be farther along. He probably thinks I'm having an affair.

Like that would ever happen."

"Curly, you got a world of trouble here. I got to think about this before I see an answer. I'm gonna go look through that window there…that one, the third one over…that's the one. I think you best go home and face the music now. Get it over with."

As he walked away, Gloria considered her options. Maybe she should stop for a cup of coffee before going home. She just couldn't walk back into her house, knowing she was pregnant and that she literally did not know how she had conceived. It made no sense to her. Worse than that, it scared the bejeezus out of her. As she ordered a large latte, she pushed the hair off her forehead. Her temples were covered with sweat and her thick, curly hair was beginning to clump in moist bunches.

She had so much to figure out, so many questions she needed to answer. The list made her head throb. She really wanted to call her best friend Sheila, but Sheila was also her sister-in-law. She just couldn't take the chance that Sheila would tell Jared's brother. She sipped her latte tentatively, wondering if it was still okay to drink coffee. She hoped it was because giving up coffee would be even harder than giving up alcohol.

Alcohol. Oh my God, how much wine have I had in the last three months? She needed to get a grip. Most of all, she needed to figure out how to break this news to Jared. How could she tell her husband she was pregnant and the baby was not his, but not to be upset? How could she make him understand that she had not had sex with anyone, and yet she was pregnant? It made no sense to her. How could she expect him to believe it?

Would telling Melanie be any easier than telling Jared? Probably not. No matter how the baby was conceived, Melanie would not be happy to hear that she was going to have a sibling the same age as her own child. No point thinking they might grow closer because they were pregnant together. No way. Melanie would be at best incredulous and at worst very hurt and angry.

The more she contemplated telling her husband and daughter, the more convinced she became that there was no upside to telling them. She was in an impossible situation that made absolutely no sense to her. If she was having trouble believing it, how could she expect Jared and Melanie to believe it?

Despite her worries about how Jared and Melanie would react, the question that caused her the most distress would surely be the hardest to answer. *Does this pregnancy really have something to do with that dream? Could I possibly be the girl in the dream?*

For the past few months, Gloria had been plagued by a recurring nightmare; a nightmare so real and so graphic that she had begun to wonder if she had tapped into a past life. Each time she had the dream she felt more connected to it. But the realization that she was actually pregnant with a baby that could not be Jared's shocked her into believing that she was truly linked in some mysterious way to the girl in the dream.

Every time she woke up from this nightmare, about a young girl who was raped, she felt an intense desire to help her. But now, with her inexplicable pregnancy confirmed, she felt trapped and afraid.

The dream was always exactly the same. It was a narrative told by a young pregnant girl in a hospital. The girl always began the story by referring to her celestial life, but the story was about her earthly life. The dream always ended with the girl in a hospital bed, being told by a nurse, that she was pregnant. Every time Gloria had this nightmare, she woke up just as the girl was learning that she was pregnant. Each time she woke, she wondered if she felt a stirring inside her womb.

She had this same dream so many times during the past three months that she could recite it from memory. Now, as she sat bent over a half-empty cup of coffee, she reviewed the dream yet again.

CHAPTER 2

I call myself Earth Girl because I chose to live on earth, even though my celestial life was one of peace and beauty. I didn't know what to expect when I came back to life on earth, but it surely wasn't this. After all those years drifting in the world of light and air, I wanted a sense of place. I wanted to be anchored to a body that lived in a certain place and a certain time. I didn't realize when I volunteered to go back that I should have chosen the place and the time. I imagined the earth would be as it appears from the heavens, a place of bright beauty and abundant energy. But, the earth I returned to is a dying land, where green and blue have been replaced by brown and grey; where life itself seems to be painful and difficult; where cruelty is part of survival and only the fittest survive. Yet, once I took my earthly body, this desolate land became home, and as all human beings do, I became attached to it and I wanted to stay.

I hardly remember the first years of my earthly life before the awful things started to happen. I know I lived with my mother and father and little brother. I think we were happy, but I don't really remember much about our life before the terror began. Why is it that I can't remember the peaceful times? Sometimes I wonder if there ever really were good times, or if I just hope that there were. I remember hiding, running and looking for someone to protect me. And I remember when the woman found me. I was afraid of her at first, but she gave me food. I would have done anything for food back then. Even risk dying. My will to live was so strong that it made food the most important thing, the only thing, the one thought that compelled every choice. So even though I knew she might kill me eventually, I went to her readily when she offered me food.

Of course, I didn't plan to stay with her for long; just long enough to eat and sleep and think about what I should do. When she told me she would protect me from everyone, I didn't really trust her, but I knew I needed her. The first night that I slept next to her, I was drawn to the warmth of her body. I had been so cold, so hungry, so frightened, and now I was warm and full. I didn't even care if I was safe. That night was the first time I dreamt of the girl with the golden eyes. She was holding me and crying.

"I have chosen you," she said.

Then her face turned into a pool of water and her eyes floated on the water. They looked like golden balls of light. I reached for them, but no matter how close I came to them, I could never quite pick them up. When I woke that morning, I tried to remember every detail of the dream.

That same morning, I asked the woman who had rescued me what her name was. She said it would be safer for both of us if I didn't know her name. She told me to call her "my friend" if anyone ever asked about her. From then on, the name I used for her was My Friend.

Back then, I didn't remember my celestial life. I had lost my connection to it. But every once in awhile , when I looked into the sky, I felt as if I had once known how to fly. When I told My Friend that I thought I had once flown, she said, "Everyone wishes to be a bird when they look at the sky, but birds never wish to be humans when they look at the ground."

I had also forgotten my previous life on earth. It took a long time for me to remember that I had been here before. Sometimes I would have a glimmer of recognition. I would feel a strong connection to someone or some experience, but then it would pass out of the reach of my conscious mind. Even if I wanted to bring it back I was unable to. It was just beyond my grasp. It made me feel a longing to connect to something, or someone, but I could never figure out what, or who. It left me feeling empty, yet yearning. It made me believe, deep in the part of me that has feelings with no words to express them, that I am part of something. But, that was all before the things happened that made me realize I had lived on earth before. So, when I met My Friend I did not really understand who she was. Nor did I really understand who I was. It seemed the only clear memory I had was of the horrible things that happened to my family when the war started.

My life with her settled into a simple routine. I began to feel safe.

Too safe, in fact. I began to feel so secure that I became careless about following her rules. Each night she would leave me for a few hours. I didn't know where she went, but she always came back with food. Sometimes, I was sure she had found it in a garbage pile, but I didn't care. During those first weeks with her, eating and being protected were my only concerns. She didn't ask much of me...just that I make no noise and use no light while she was gone. Not that we had much light; just the flashlights that she found.

In the beginning, I was so afraid that I wrapped myself in her tattered blanket and lay perfectly still until I fell asleep. I would even try to breathe so shallowly that no one could detect my breath if they came upon our hiding place. It took many days for me to memorize the exact sound of her footsteps so that I knew it was she approaching. Until I was sure, my heart would begin to race with fear and I would begin to shake. I was so afraid of being raped and beaten again. I had watched my mother die after she tried to protect me from them.

I tried not to think about my mother and what had happened to us. But the memories of that night seemed to haunt me. I wasn't sure how old I was when it happened, or how long I had been on my own, running and hiding. I had lost all sense of time. I only knew that I had to make sure no one ever found me. I knew the men who killed my mother would hurt me if they ever found me again. And I knew that there were many more like them. They hated us and wanted to kill all of us. They had started with the men in our community, dragging them out of their homes while pointing guns at their heads. My little brother and I watched as my mother ran out after them, screaming and begging them not to kill our father. When she came back in, she held us close to her and said that she would not let them hurt us. She said that she knew our father would be safe because he was a good man and God would not let such evil people win out over us. But while she held us, I could feel her shaking and I could smell her sweat. It had a strong, pungent scent. It was an odor that I had never encountered before. Soon I came to know it as the smell of fear.

I couldn't sleep at all that night. I listened for my brother's breathing to relax and when it did, I knew he had finally drifted into sleep. But I couldn't sleep. The sound of my mother's muffled crying kept me awake. I tried to figure out how to help my father, but nothing came to my mind. If I couldn't help him, I told myself, I would devote my life to protecting my brother. He was too young to understand about war. I would try to keep him from even knowing what was going on. I would tell him our father was safe, no matter what I knew to be true.

The next morning my mother told us that we must pray for our father and all the good men that had been taken by the enemy. We must pray for our men to be safe and to defeat the enemy. We must pray for God to wreak vengeance on our enemy.

"What does vengeance mean?" my brother asked when we were finished praying. My mother, who I had always known as gentle and kind, replied, "Vengeance means doing worse to them than they do to us. If they kill our men, we must kill their men and their children. We must leave them with nothing. Not even hope."

My brother looked confused. "If God wreaks vengeance on them for killing our men, will our men come back to life?"

"No, they will still be dead, but their deaths won't be in vain. God will take more lives from them than He takes from us and that will mean we have won the war." When I heard these words, I knew that my mother had already lost hope. She would never ask God to kill anyone if she wasn't overcome with grief and fear.

My brother sat silent for a few seconds, and then he said, "I guess I don't understand war. What good does it do to kill everyone?"

On the fourth day after they took my father, some of them returned. They said they needed food. My mother tried to refuse to give it to them. One of them, a tall man with thick hair and a scruffy beard, laughed. "So you think you can stop us?" he said. "We take what we want and we leave what we don't want. Right now we want food. Another time, it may be something else. Maybe you, or maybe her," he said, pointing at me.

The bearded one came back that night. I could feel my heart

10

pumping frantically when he pushed open the door. He grabbed my mother by the arm and pushed his body against her while he caressed her cheek with a dirty hand. She pulled away from him. He laughed cruelly. "You think you are being a faithful wife, perhaps. What good is it to be faithful to a dead man? Better for you that you be faithful to me. Then you won't have to worry about losing your son too."

My mother's face turned pale. Whatever fear she had first felt was transformed into the instinct to protect her son. "Please, don't hurt him," she pleaded." I'll do what you want."

"I thought you would see it my way," he laughed. "No point losing a husband and a son."

I felt weak and sick. The floor seemed to shift under my feet. I didn't know what was going to happen, but I knew that it was bad.

"Take your brother and go out back," my mother said in a strangely calm voice. "Don't come back in until I come to get you."

"Let them stay. They might learn something," the bearded man hissed, as he ripped open my mother's blouse. "Leave, leave now!" she screamed at me. With one swift blow to the face, he knocked her on the floor. "I say they stay."

I didn't know what I should do, but I was too frightened to leave her alone with him no matter how much she wanted us not to see what was happening. As the man undid his pants, I tried to shield my brother by holding his face close to mine. I stared into his eyes, hoping that he would see only me. Two thoughts kept running through my head. My father is already dead. Please don't let him kill my mother.

When the man was finished with my mother, he left quickly. She was lying on the floor crying. Her lip was bleeding and her clothes were torn. She told us to leave her alone. I wanted to help her get up, but I knew she didn't want us to see her. I kept thinking about the prayers we had said, and I knew that not one had been answered. They had killed my father. Now they had hurt my mother. It was time for God to wreak vengeance.

After my brother fell asleep that night, my mother told me that she had to explain some things about men and women to me. She told me how babies are made and also that sometimes men do the same thing to hurt and humiliate women. She told me that when they do that it is called rape. She told me that I had to be very careful not to let anyone rape me. She said that when you are raped, it ruins you. She said it would be worse than dying and that I should do everything I can to get away. But, she also told me that if I couldn't get away and some evil man raped me, it would be his sin, not mine.

After she told me about rape I kept thinking how it didn't make any sense for God to design people to make babies a certain way and then make bad men want to hurt women that same way. I wondered if God wreaked vengeance on men who did that by having other men rape their wives and daughters. The more I thought about it, the sadder I was. My father had been killed. My mother had been raped and someday I might be too. I couldn't understand what was happening. At least my brother had not been hurt. I wondered if some day he would have to rape someone to make up for what happened to our mother. That thought made me even sadder than I already was.

The next day, the bearded man returned with two other men. I could hear their footsteps as they approached. I was filled with dread. When the bearded one saw me, he told me to help him take off his shoes. The other men stood by the door watching. I didn't want to touch him, but I was afraid not to. I knelt on the floor to untie his shoe. My mother was standing back against the wall, holding my brother close to her. She was shaking and my brother was crying. As I bent over his foot, the man pulled my head up and told me to unzip his pants.

My mother ran towards us saying, "Not her. Not her. Take me." He looked directly at her and yelled, "Shut up!" Then one of the other men grabbed her and covered her mouth with his hand. She must have bitten him because he let out a yelp and then knocked her to the ground.

The next thing I knew I was on the floor too. The bearded man was pulling at my underwear and I knew it was going to happen. I tried to get away. I even thought that maybe God would let me die right then and there so that I didn't have to be raped. I didn't want to be ruined and I didn't think I would mind being dead. Then my mother jumped on top of him and started punching him and hitting him. I think the other men were laughing. The bearded man pushed himself up and my mother fell off his back. I thought that maybe I wasn't going to be raped, but then I stopped thinking about me because he got on top of my mother and kept punching her face. It was too horrible for me to watch. I wanted to save her but I couldn't move my arms. Then I realized that one of the other men had grabbed me. I struggled to get away, but he wouldn't let me go. The bearded man was raping my mother. She wasn't struggling at all. She wasn't even moving. Then the man who was holding me, pushed me down and raped me. I don't remember anything about it. I just knew that I was being raped and that I hoped I would die.

But my mother died instead of me. After they left, I went over and lay down beside her. Her face was all swollen and she was sleeping. She never woke up. I cried and cried until I fell asleep. When I woke up I was filled with panic. I called for my brother, but he didn't answer. He was gone. I didn't know if they took him or if he thought he had to go wreak vengeance. I hoped that he had managed to hide from them and that he was running away to a safe place where there was no killing and no rape.

I wanted to bury my mother, but I didn't have anything to dig a hole with and I didn't know if it would be a sin to bury her without a funeral. It made me feel like tearing my eyes out when I looked at her battered face. I finally decided to roll her up in a blanket and push her body under the bed. It seemed mean and wrong, but I didn't know what else to do. I told myself it was like a grave, only indoors. I knew it really wasn't a good way to be buried, but I kept telling myself that it was. After I rolled her up, I felt bad and I unrolled her so that I could wipe the blood off her face. It was already crusted and hard, but I gently washed it off. Her body felt so cold and empty that it made me scared. Just before I rolled her up again, I remembered her wedding ring. I took it off and put in on my ring finger. It was too big, so I put it in my pocket. I knew it was all I would ever have left of my mother.

I decided that I should say prayers before I pushed my mother's body under the bed. I didn't know exactly what prayers to say. I knew she would want me to pray to God to wreak vengeance on the men who killed her. I said the meanest prayer I could think of. I prayed that God would send men to rape and kill the wives and mothers of the men who killed my parents. I prayed that God would make sure their daughters were ruined, just like me. And I prayed that my mother and father would watch it all from heaven and be happy because they didn't die in vain. It didn't feel much like a prayer to me because I didn't use words like "mercy" and "lamb of God" and "forgive us." Just to make sure it was a real prayer at the end I said, "Thy will be done, amen." Then I kissed my mother even though she was all rolled up in a blanket and I pushed her under the bed. When I was done, I didn't even feel sad. I didn't feel anything at all.

I waited all day and all night for my brother to come back, but he never did. I didn't want to leave because I thought I would never see him again if I left, but I knew that I had to leave if I didn't want to be raped again. I decided to leave something for my brother in case he came back; to show I love him and to give him hope. The only thing I could think of was my mother's wedding ring. I wanted to make sure he would notice it, so I tied it to the door with a piece of cloth that had been ripped off my mother's blouse by the man who killed her. Leaving my mother's ring there was so hard. It was the only thing I had to keep her with me, but I thought my brother might need it even more than me. He was younger and he still used to sit on her lap sometimes. He wasn't grown up at all yet. I felt as if I had grown up a lot ever since they took my father away.

CHAPTER 3

Gloria clutched the coffee cup so tightly that her fingers hurt. The dream was too upsetting. She could not finish it. She had to get outside in the fresh air. Covered with sweat, she grabbed her pocketbook and ran out of the coffee shop.

Gloria could barely drive home. Her mind was flooded with thoughts about Earth Girl. She did not want to be connected to her. Yet, she was unable to convince herself that she was not inextricably bound to her. No matter how she tried to dismiss it, this pregnancy put her in touch with a part of herself that she had never known before; a part of her that had always been there without her even being aware of it. It was as if she now had two identities.

She was the Gloria before she began dreaming about Earth Girl and the Gloria that she had become because of the dream. The pre-dream Gloria had her life in control. She knew who she was and what she wanted and she was very certain that she did not want to share her identity or her uterus with anyone. The Gloria who had the dream was torn between two realities: the one that told her none of this could be possible, and the one that she could not escape because of the baby inside her womb...the baby that she believed was Earth Girl's baby, not her own.

As soon as she got home, she crawled into her bed and pulled the covers over her head. Her hands trembled as she hugged her pillow. She was determined to return to the person she had been before the dream. She would force herself to stop believing this nonsense. She would take a nap and take control of this dream once and for all. Perhaps by concentrating as hard as she could, she would convince herself that her own pregnancy was just another part of the nightmare. Then she would wake up and realize with relief that she was not pregnant and it had all been an alarmingly realistic dream. Life would return to normal. It had to. She couldn't go on this way.

If she could just magically get things back to the way they were before she started having these dreams, she would never again complain about her mundane life...dull, boring, predictable would become her favorite adjectives. If only she could end this whole nightmare and her pregnancy through sheer force of will. If only she could talk to Jared about what she was going through.

She wanted to tell Jared about the dreams, but she didn't want him to think she was going into some menopausal crazy lady stage. Ever since she began missing some periods, she had been extra moody, rather weepy and sometimes downright sad. She had seen this in other women, and she had thought they could have avoided it if they tried. Now that she was experiencing these same symptoms, she realized that it wasn't a matter of choice. Perhaps, this was why hormone therapy was widely prescribed. Of course, she admitted to herself, there were plenty of women who went through all the stages of menopause without any symptoms at all. She just wasn't one of them. *I wonder if I tell Jared that I'm having dreams from a past life, will he think I need medication or will he entertain the idea that it might actually be a possibility?*

This, of course, was not her biggest dilemma. Her real problem was how to tell him she was pregnant and that it was not his baby. Gloria had never lied to her husband. She didn't want to start now. So, until she figured out what to do, she really couldn't tell him anything.

She and Jared had been married for 21 years. It seemed to her that as soon as they got home from their honeymoon, they had settled into an easy, comfortable life together. They had developed some habits that hadn't changed in all those years. Even though she knew some of her friends would be bored to death by starting and ending each day the same way for over twenty years, she found it reassuring that every day started with her making coffee, and each day ended with Jared checking the locks on the doors. Simple rituals, but they created a feeling of stability no matter what was going on in their lives.

During these years, they had experienced the numerous highs and lows of married life. New jobs and lay-offs, pregnancy and miscarriage, the thrill of a new home and the relentless demands of home ownership, passionate love and bored dissatisfaction, feelings of incredible closeness and painful distance, new friends and old friends, births and deaths and, most of all, the vicissitudes of parenthood. Through it all, she made the coffee each morning and Jared locked the doors each night. When they were too sad, too angry or too worried to talk these simple habits kept them grounded, reminding them that this too shall pass.

Jared was a practical, down-to-earth type of guy. Even his appearance said "solid, reasonable, trustworthy." He was always well-groomed and dressed conservatively. Gloria sometimes envied how well he was aging. His steel-grey hair made his eyes look even bluer. He was still muscular, if not as lean as he used to be. His slightly crooked smile could still melt her heart.

Gloria's most noteworthy physical attribute was her dark, thick, curly hair. But her appearance changed with her mood, as if her hair and clothes were props that she could use to express how she was feeling. Even her hazel eyes shifted from brownish to greenish depending on what she wore.

People had often said that Jared and Gloria were the perfect example of "opposites attract." He was short and compact. She was tall for a female and willowy. He was well-organized, disciplined and hard-working. She was something of a romantic, an idealist who was never really satisfied with the world as it was. She described herself as "spiritual, but not religious." Jared wasn't into spirituality, mysticism or metaphysics. He was much more interested in the here and now.

She was pretty sure what his reaction would be if she told him she was having dreams about a past life. If he thought she was losing it, he would want to find a way to help her. If he thought she was indulging in a silly whim, he would probably just ignore it and wait for it to pass. That would be okay with her. If only she could tell him about the dreams without telling him that she was pregnant.

Gloria tossed and turned, unable to stop thinking about Earth Girl. Despite her fervent desire to never think about her again, Earth Girl's story took over her consciousness.

CHAPTER 4

Once I left the house, I wasn't even afraid of the men who took my father and killed my mother. I didn't care if they killed me too now that I was ruined. But I didn't want them to rape me again, so I tried to hide whenever it was daytime. I don't know how long I hid in the woods, but eventually all I could think about was food and water. At first, I didn't know how to find food, but I watched the little animals. I tried to eat the same things they ate. I knew they ate worms, but I didn't want to. I saw them eat things that fell off trees. I think they were acorns and some kind of berry. I didn't want to eat them either, but I got so hungry.

When I tried them, they were hard to eat and bitter, but I was starving. I decided to just swallow them whole. Then I got a bad stomach ache and I threw up. I didn't feel like I could even walk, so I just leaned against a tree trunk and waited for the pain to go away. I don't think I ate anything else for a long time. I just sat there and sometimes I fell asleep. I couldn't tell the difference between day and night. I had dreams of women crying and men standing over them laughing and kicking them. In my dreams, the women were really little, like little puppies and the men were giant size. They could step on two or three women with just one foot. Most of them had mean, scary faces, but some of them had nice faces. I hated that dream and I hated the nice faces most of all.

When I couldn't stand sitting there any longer I started walking. I felt like all I really cared about was getting water to drink. I was so thirsty. I couldn't think of anything else. I knew that there was a lake not far from where we lived. I didn't think we were supposed to drink the water from it, but I thought it would be better than nothing. When I got near the lake, I saw people and I didn't know what to do. I didn't know if I could trust them or if they would hurt me. I thought that if I could get close enough to see a face I might be able to tell if they were enemies or friends. Then I saw one of them had a gun. He looked like he was aiming at the ground. I thought maybe he was killing an animal. I stood perfectly still and waited to see what would happen. Then I heard the noise of the gunshot. The man bent over and he started grabbing around. I moved a little closer to see what he was doing. Then I realized that it wasn't an animal he shot. It was a man and there was another dead man next to him.

I almost screamed, but I remembered that I had to be quiet all the time now so that no one could ever find me. I bit my tongue and kept watching. Then I had a bad thought. Maybe the dead men had been carrying water and food. I hoped that no one else would find them. I wanted to take the water and food for myself. I couldn't wait for the man who fired the shot to leave. I began to feel crazy, like I would run out and grab whatever I wanted, like I didn't even care if he shot me too.

Before I knew it I was almost right in front of him. I didn't know how I got there. I knew it was dangerous, but it was too late. He saw me. I started to run the other way, but my foot got caught in a bunch of dead branches and I fell. I could hear his footsteps coming toward me, but I didn't open my eyes. I just stayed as still as I could. I heard a gunshot, and that is the last thing I remember until My Friend found me.

When she asked me who I was, I couldn't even remember my name or how old I was. But I remembered what happened to my father and mother, and I knew that I was ruined and I had to live alone. Sometimes I thought of my brother and I imagined him finding my mother's ring and keeping it until he grew up and fell in love. I imagined him giving it to a beautiful girl and telling her that they were going to live in a special place where they would both be safe, because in this place no one ever had to wreak vengeance. But when I tried to think of my brother's name or what he looked like, I couldn't. I just knew in my heart that once I had a brother. Once, I even told My Friend what I imagined. "Keep that beautiful dream," she said. "It will help you during the dark nights."

At first when My Friend would go out at night to find food, I would be as still and as quiet as I could be. I was really too afraid to move and I would lie still, hoping to be safe until she came back. After she left and came back many nights in a row, I began to feel more secure. One night I turned on the flashlight and entertained myself by making shadows, but I began to feel guilty because she had told me never to turn on the flashlight while she was gone. When she came back early the next morning, she had fresh fruit to eat. She never told me where she got the food and I never asked, but I could tell that she was happy to bring back something so fresh and delicious. I enjoyed every bite of it. She smiled while she watched me eat. She even laughed when some of the juice dripped down my arm and I tried to lick my elbow.

Even though we seldom talked, I felt safe with her. I forced myself not to wonder if she was an enemy. I wanted her to love me. Sometimes, when she would come back, she would sit behind me while I ate whatever food she had managed to find. She would put her arms around my waist and rock me gently back and forth while she hummed. Her humming sounded like a lullaby to me, but I didn't recognize the tune. Once when she was rocking me, she put her face down on my head and I could feel her tears dripping down the side of my face. I felt like I should do something to comfort her, but I didn't know what to do. I just let her rock and cry. Finally, I said, "I'm sad too." She squeezed me a little bit and kept on rocking and crying.

One night while she was gone, I began bleeding. I could not figure out how I got hurt. At first I did not know where the blood was coming from. When I discovered that it was from the place where I was ruined, I felt ashamed. I didn't tell My Friend and I tried to hide it from her. But in the morning, she saw the blood. "Now you are a woman too," she said to me. With tears in her eyes, she helped me to clean myself.

Each day was pretty much the same, and so was each night, except that after the first time I turned on the flashlight I allowed myself to turn it on for a few minutes almost every night. I never told her and I was careful to put it back exactly where she left it. Then, one night, something awful happened. "You turned on the light," she hissed at me when she came home. "They know you are here. We have to leave *right now." I wanted to tell her I was sorry, but instead I started to cry. She slapped my face hard. "If you want to live, be quiet," she whispered in my ear. "Now follow me."*

She grabbed both of the flashlights and a satchel that she always carried. I never knew what was in the satchel, but I always assumed it was money. She seemed to know her way through the woods at night and she moved quickly. I couldn't see well and I kept getting tangled up in twigs and branches. One low branch was filled with thorns. As I brushed by it, it scraped my face and made it sting. But I forgot it almost as soon as I felt it because she turned around and pushed me down.

"Stay there. Don't move. Don't speak or they will kill us both," she said. Almost as soon as she pushed me, she started running away from where I was hiding. In a minute, I heard a man's voice. "Where are you going?" he asked. "Didn't you earn enough to eat tonight? Out looking for more?" Her voice was very low and I couldn't hear her answer. But his voice was louder.

"I heard a rumor that you are not alone," he said. "You know that they will be looking for a traitor like you. You must know that they know where you have your little hiding place. Do you really think no one knows where you hide? We let you stay because you gave us what we wanted. Why do you think we gave you our garbage to eat? We wanted to keep you alive. I still want to keep you alive. But the others don't trust you anymore. Shining lights, making signs to someone...you dirty little bitch." He stopped and looked at her, almost kindly. "Don't look so scared. Give me what I want and I will pretend I never even saw you. I don't care if you escape. You won't get far enough to make a difference. Lie down and keep quiet if you don't want them to find you. When I am done, I'll let you keep running."

He was only there for another minute or two. I didn't know what to do when she started to run again. Should I run with her, or should I stay and hide? I was shaking all over. I could just barely see her stand and look around. Then she started running through the woods. Running away from me. I knew everything that happened was my fault. I knew she would never come back because I had turned on the light.

I pulled my knees as close to my body as I could and I crouched down with my head on my knees. I wanted to cry, but I was too afraid. I tried to think about what I would do next. Should I wait until morning or try to run now? Maybe I should just go back and let them find me. Maybe then they would know I am just a kid and they wouldn't think she was sending signals. Or maybe she hated me so much for shining the light that she would tell them to come after me. Maybe she would even kill me if she ever saw me again. I knew I shouldn't care if I died. My mother and father were both dead and I would never see my brother again. I was ruined and no one would ever love me. I knew for sure that I really was ruined because I had betrayed My Friend by playing with the flashlight. Why should I even try to stay alive?

I decided I had no reason to try to survive. I would just stay there and close my eyes and wait for death. I hoped that I would fall asleep and never wake up again. While I was sleeping I dreamed of the girl with the golden eyes again. In my dream I was glad to see her. When she touched my face, I felt safe and happy and like nothing bad had ever happened. I wanted to stay with her forever. I reached to touch her face and she started to drift away, sort of like a cloud that changes shape and then disappears. I started to cry and I realized she left me because I was ruined. Then I woke up and I felt sadder than I had ever felt, even sadder than when my mother died. I promised myself that I would not eat or drink anything so that I would die sooner.

Chapter 5

Gloria was sobbing. In that moment, she wanted desperately to save Earth Girl. She knew what was coming next. The dream was always the same. She was torn between two worlds now, Earth Girl's and her own. She couldn't let these dreams take over her life. Forcing herself to sit up, she tried to smooth her matted hair. She had to get a grip. Jared would be home soon. She couldn't let him find her crying in bed.

By the time Jared came home from work, Gloria had showered, changed the sheets on the bed and begun to prepare dinner. She greeted Jared with a kiss on the cheek and a glass of wine.

"Don't you want one too?" he asked.

"Not tonight. I felt a tiny bit queasy today, so I think I'll stick with tea."

"Hope you're not coming down with something," Jared said as he headed toward the living room.

"Me too," said Gloria. "I do feel kinda tired."

She was finding it difficult not to talk about the only thing that was on her mind, so she suggested they rent a movie and watch it during dinner. As soon as it was over, she said she was sleepy and went to bed. This was not a lie. She was always sleepy when she was pregnant.

She had been pregnant with Melanie when they bought their house in Newport. It had been a dream of theirs to buy a house near the water. They could never afford a house with a water view, but if they were willing to buy something that needed some work, they could be near the water. They loved their quaint house on St. Anthony Street. It had character and a perfect little room for the baby's nursery. It was an easy walk to Thames Street and not too far from Touro Park.

After Melanie was born, Gloria enjoyed putting her in the stroller for long walks. She almost always ended up across the street from Touro Park, admiring the amazing trees on the grounds of the Athenaeum. By the time Melanie was ten, she had climbed every tree on the grounds at least once.

Although Melanie was 20, she still looked a lot like a ten-year-old tomboy. She had her father's compact build and her mother's thick hair, but not as curly. She wore it cut short. Her large blue eyes were framed by thick eyelashes. Like her mother, she seldom wore make-up, preferring the natural look. Her angular features were slightly softened by the weight she had put on during the first months of her pregnancy.

When Gloria woke up the next morning, she realized she had been dreaming about one of the trees at the Athenaeum. It was Melanie's favorite tree because the branches started so low to the ground and twisted and curved in all directions. If you stood in just the right spot, the branches appeared to form a hole about the size of a child's fist. Melanie used to pretend that if you put your hand through the hole, you would be transported to a mysterious land. In Gloria's dream, another little girl, one that she did not recognize, was sitting in the tree with her hand in the hole.

Gloria was surprised when Jared walked in the bedroom. She realized she must have really overslept.

"How was your workout?" she asked, trying to sound as if his answer actually mattered to her.

"Great! You look like you just woke up. Are you feeling okay?"

"I don't feel too good this morning. Must be a little virus I'm fighting off," she dissembled.

"Should we tell Mel and Roger to come tomorrow instead?" he asked.

"Maybe we should postpone just to make sure I don't have anything contagious. But I hate to wait. It's not every day your daughter tells you she's pregnant. I can't believe we haven't seen her since she called with the news. I can't wait to give her a hug and touch her belly."

As Gloria climbed out of bed, the thought that she might be sharing a pregnancy with her daughter brought on a wave of nausea. This couldn't be happening.

"I'm oddly excited about this too, even though I really wanted them to wait," said Jared.

"You'd think she grew up in the 50s... married and pregnant by age 20," Gloria quipped.

"True, but the thought of a little grandchild has a certain appeal," said Jared.

"Yes, it really does, Grandpa," she said playfully.

Gloria gave him a hug, while imagining what he would think of having a child and grandchild that were the same age. As soon as he left, she went back to bed. As she drifted off to sleep, she wondered why Melanie had waited until she was five months pregnant to tell them. Maybe she had feared they would tell her she was too young, just as they had when she had breathlessly told them she was engaged. Their reaction had hurt her feelings. Gloria still felt bad about that, and hoped that their reaction to her pregnancy news had been appropriately delighted, even though they truly did wish that Melanie and Roger had waited to conceive.

When she woke up, she began to feel extremely apprehensive about her own pregnancy. She felt as if she would never be able to cope with all that this pregnancy might mean. *Maybe I should pray. Of course, that will be a long shot...Oh dear God, this is Gloria. You haven't heard from me in, oh, about 20 years, but I never stopped believing in you. Oh, alright, maybe I sort of doubted your existence, but I really need you now if you're real.*

Okay, so prayer may not be my best bet. Gloria took three deep breaths. This had been her substitute for prayer, therapy, tranquilizers, and pointless arguments with her husband ever since she took those Yoga classes back in '98. Those deep cleansing breaths had worked pretty well for her in the past, but she seriously doubted that they could solve the problem of this pregnancy. If only she had found out sooner, she would have had an abortion. Maybe she still could, she thought. *Maybe it's not too late if I do it right away. That's what I'll do. I won't tell Jared. I'll find a clinic and go tomorrow. If I'm bleeding when I get home, he'll just think it's some menopause complication.*

An immediate sense of relief washed over her. She also felt incredibly sleepy even though she had just slept. This was the symptom that led her to believe she might be pregnant in the first place. She had been very sleepy when she was pregnant with Melanie, and during the short time she was pregnant before miscarrying when Melanie was four. She hadn't thought about that in a long time. Remembering made her sad, brought back a feeling of grief and loss that she had long buried.

Well, this is weird. All I want to do is end this pregnancy; yet, I still feel sad about losing that baby so many years ago. Life is so friggin' complicated. It's no wonder I'm so screwed up. I need to figure all this out...my past life and my present one. God, I better never say that out loud. I sound like a loon, and not the bird. The Crazy Gloria.

That was typical of Gloria. Even in her anguish, she couldn't resist making such comments, if only to herself. It was one of her personality quirks that had endeared her to Jared. He enjoyed Gloria's delight in her own sense of humor; her willingness to say things that were more corny than funny, and then to look delighted, as if she had made a hilarious joke.

She decided to stay in bed. She didn't expect to sleep for long, but left Jared a note just in case she was still asleep when he got home from work. "Still not feeling good. Taking nap. Wake me when you get home. Love, Glo." Despite her emotional turmoil, she fell back to sleep almost immediately. Her last conscious thought was how good it felt to be dozing off.

CHAPTER 6

While I lay there hoping to die, I heard footsteps. I knew for sure that they were not My Friend's. My heart began to beat fast and I began to shake. What if it was the man who found her? What would he do to me? I tried not to breathe, but he found me anyway. He stood and looked at me for a long time without saying anything. "Are you hungry?" he asked. I shook my head.

"You don't have to be afraid of me," he said." I will take care of you like I took care of her. I'll make sure the rest of them leave you alone. Now have something to eat." I shook my head again and rolled over so that he could not see my face. He sat down next to me and started patting my head. I wanted to believe that he was good, but I knew he couldn't be. Why would My Friend keep me hidden from him if he was good? He must be bad, like the man who killed my mother. I didn't care if he killed me, but I didn't want him to hurt me. I tried to think of a way to get away. He lay down next to me and rolled me over so that I was facing him. He touched my face gently and started to put his hands under my shirt. I pulled away from him, and he laughed.

"So you know what to expect," he said. "No point wasting time, then." He reached under my skirt and pulled down my underpants. I knew he was going to rape me. I was already ruined, so what did it matter? He got on top of me and put one hand over my mouth. I felt a terrible pain and I remembered what it was like to be raped. After he finished he stood up and he pulled me up too. He pushed his face into mine and said, "From now on, you are mine. I will give you food and water and keep you alive and you will give me what I want. When I get tired of you I will kill you, just like I killed her. You have no one to protect you except for me. If you try to run away, I will hurt you. I will keep you alive but if you ever try to leave I will hurt you every day because you are a filthy whore and you are lucky that I choose to take care of you."

Then he slapped my face hard and made my lips bleed. When he saw the blood, he wiped it with his hand, and then he grabbed my arm and started pulling me. "We're going back to your little shack. You can stay there by yourself and I will bring you food and protect you from the others. But if you ever try to leave I will find you and I will make you suffer before I kill you. You are mine now. Don't ever forget it."

I wondered if he really knew where our hiding place was. I thought maybe he was just trying to scare me. But he led me right back to it. We went inside and he gave me a canteen with water. I started to open it and he pulled it away. "Not yet," he said. "First, kiss me."

He pulled me close to him. I didn't want to kiss him, but I didn't know how to get away. I kissed his chin and he moved my face so that my lips were against his. He forced his tongue into my mouth. I thought he was going to rape me again, but he didn't. He just left me standing there. He turned around and walked out the door.

I was so relieved when he left that I started to cry. As soon as I realized I was crying, I remembered that My Friend had slapped me for crying. I realized that she was trying to make me strong. I stopped myself and started looking for food. I had a crazy thought. Maybe he left me some food as a gift. He might have hidden it for me to find later. I crawled around in the dark trying to search with my hands. I didn't find anything. So, I leaned against the wall and fell asleep.

When I woke up, it was raining. I was so happy to see the rain that I went outside and I sat against the shack with my face turned up to the sky and I opened my mouth wide so that I could drink the rain. Feeling the raindrops in my mouth made me even thirstier. I began to hope that my captor would come back soon. I began to think I would do anything for water to drink. I didn't care about being ruined, or hurt. As long as I could drink water, that was all that mattered.

When it started to get dark that night, I began to anticipate his arrival. I was waiting for him and wishing he would come. I hated myself for this, but I couldn't help it. I would do whatever he wanted if he would let me drink all the water in the canteen. When he didn't come I started to cry, but I had no tears. I hated him. I hated myself and I wanted to die, but I didn't want to die of thirst. I couldn't sleep at all that night. I made up my mind that as soon as the light came I would go to the lake and drink the water. I didn't care if it made me sick and I didn't care if someone found me and killed me on the way. I even hoped someone would kill me. But I knew I was not going to wait for water any longer.

Just as the sun began to rise, he came back. I begged him for water as soon as I saw him. I told him he could do anything to do me. I started to take off my underpants as I talked. He looked at me for a long time without saying anything. Then he opened the canteen and handed it to me. He let me drink all of it. Then he picked my underpants up off the dirt floor and handed them to me. He watched me while I put them on. He didn't say anything to me the whole time he was there. He just kept staring at me. I didn't know if he was angry or sad or sick. I didn't care. I just wanted him to keep bringing water and food. I was afraid to sit down, so I just stood there in front of him. Just before he left, he reached in his pocket and took out a piece of chocolate. He handed it to me and walked out the door.

I ate the chocolate really fast, but I threw up right after I finished it. I didn't know what to do. I could stay there and wait for him to bring water and food every day or I could run away and take my chances. I kept telling myself that maybe he was really a good man and that he was never going to hurt me again. But that didn't make sense to me because why did he rape me if he was really a good man?

I finally decided to leave. I was going to try to find good people somewhere, or I was going to die. I didn't care much which of the two happened. But leaving turned out to be a big mistake. I had barely left when he came back. He had food with him and a jug of wine. When he saw that I was trying to leave, he became very angry. He pulled me back to the shack by my hair and then he tied my hands behind my back. He showed me the food and the wine. He teased me by holding food near my mouth and then pulling it away. He drank the wine right out of the jug and then he held my mouth open and poured the wine into my mouth. I had never tasted wine before. It made me choke. He laughed and gave me more. I asked him for water and he laughed again.

"You could have had water and food today. You could have eaten *until your belly was full. But you tried to run away, so now you I will fill you up a different way." He pulled down his pants and pushed my skirt up over my face. Then he pushed me against the wall and raped me again and again. When he was finished, he said, "You won't be going anywhere with your hands tied. By the time I come back, you should be good and hungry." Then he pushed me down and left me lying there.*

I wanted to fall asleep. I wanted to forget everything that happened. I wanted to die. It seemed like the only way to be free. I tried to pray, but I couldn't find the words to say. I didn't even know if I believed there really was a God. How could a God who loves us make a world where people could be so cruel? I tried to make my mind go blank.

The next thing I remember I was in a hospital bed. I wasn't in pain and I wasn't thirsty. I didn't know how I got there, but I wasn't scared. I felt really safe for the first time since my father had been taken away. It seemed like everything else had been an awful nightmare. When a nurse came in and saw that I was awake, she started asking me who I was and if I remembered what had happened to me. I told her what I remembered. Then I started to cry. She took my hand and held it gently. She told me that the doctor would be happy to see that I was awake and that I could talk. Then, she told me that I was pregnant.

Chapter 7

Gloria's heart was pounding when she woke up. *I really am that girl.* This thought was followed by a flood of refusal. *No, this can't be. This is MY life, not hers.* Feeling as if she had been drugged, Gloria fell back to sleep. She began to dream of Earth Girl again.

But this time the dream was different. Earth Girl was no longer in a hospital bed. She was lying in the grass and looking up at two golden orbs in the sky. They emanated a bright golden light before falling into a pool of blue water. Earth Girl was joyful as she watched the beaming orbs splash into the shimmering lake, causing hundreds of glowing ripples to expand toward the shore. When the orbs disappeared beneath the surface of the water, Earth Girl felt a profound sense of peace.

It had been a beautiful dream and Gloria had not wanted to wake from it. She tried to remember the details, but she could not. Although most of the dream faded, she remembered the golden orbs falling into the water. The image made her feel at peace.

But this peace was short-lived. Gloria could not fasten the snap on her jeans. She stood sideways in front of the mirror. She was already starting to show. She put on a long sweater. How long would she be able to hide this? She had to do something. Soon. Luckily, Jared had a dinner meeting. She planned to be in bed before he got home. She wouldn't have to face him until morning. She could wear her robe until he left. She couldn't wait to go back to bed. Maybe things would seem better the next morning.

I could hear myself screaming as the doctor gave me a shot. "Please, don't kill my baby. Please, let it live. I don't care if I was raped. It's all I have. I can love it." Please, no! Please! I knew they were trying to help me, but I wanted the baby to live. I began to kick at the doctor. "Don't do this," I kept screaming. "Let my baby live. I'll find a way to take care of it. Please, stop!"

When Gloria woke, her heart was racing and she was covered with sweat. This was a new addition to her dream about the young girl. She felt both angered and frightened by it. Before she had the time to formulate a rational thought, Jared rushed into the room.

"What were you screaming about? It sounded like you were saying something about killing a baby. Melanie's pregnancy must really be getting to you. God, you look awful. Are you alright? You're dripping with sweat."

"I know. I think I was having a nightmare. I can't remember it now, but I feel like crap. I wonder if I have the flu."

As Gloria kept talking to Jared, she was trying to figure out her best course of action. Could Jared see on her face how trapped she felt? She didn't want to deceive him, but she wasn't ready for him to know about the baby, about her past-life dreams, about any of it. So, for now, she had to just pretend to be sick. After he left for work, Gloria sat at the kitchen table with a mug of coffee and two pieces of heavily buttered toast. She was eating jelly out of the jar with a spoon. As she licked the sticky remnants off the handle, she marveled that she could be so hungry and so sad at the same time. She had made a difficult decision during the night. She was definitely going to end the pregnancy. She needed to reclaim her life. As she looked through the phone book for abortion clinics, she wiped away the tears that trickled down her cheeks. She needed to find a clinic quickly. She knew she would get more results on the internet, but she was paranoid that somehow Jared would find evidence of the search.

She was going to tell him everything; explain all of it to him, but not until she was no longer pregnant. She wished she could go to her own doctor, but she couldn't imagine telling him that the baby was not Jared's...even worse...not anybody's. If she told him that she was carrying the baby from when she had been raped in a past life, he would probably have her committed. It sounded like lunacy to her and yet she believed with every fiber of her being that it was true. She had spent an almost sleepless night trying to convince herself that it wasn't so. There were a few explanations. She considered each of them.

This is Jared's baby. I am really six months pregnant and the baby is really small. I wonder what that means for its health? Actually, that is another good reason to end this pregnancy. Okay, most reasonable possibility and solution.

I am carrying someone else's baby but not from a past life. Somehow I got someone's sperm in me and it fertilized one of my last eggs.

Which sounded less plausible? Pregnant from a past life, or from the invasion of a mysterious traveling sperm that managed to get on her underpants and work its way up her cervix? Neither sounded like something anyone would believe.

A third alternative that she considered seriously for at least two hours was that she had lost her mind somehow; that maybe she was in a car accident, or had a stroke, or just went nuts and this whole thing was the wild delusion of a raving maniac. This was the scariest choice, because even though the other two answers meant that other people would think she was crazy, this choice meant that she really was.

She really wanted it to be Jared's baby. Dear, sweet, loyal Jared. He had always been there for her. She could count on him for anything. If it was his baby, she wouldn't be thinking about abortion. But no matter how hard she tried to convince herself that it was his, she just didn't believe it. She believed that it was Earth Girl's baby. She also believed that she must *be* Earth Girl if the baby was inside her body. She knew from her newest dream that Earth Girl wanted the baby to live and that made her feel guilty, but not guilty enough to keep this pregnancy.

"If I am that girl, what I wanted then was based on a whole different set of circumstances, and it definitely is not what I want now. It could ruin my marriage and my relationship with my daughter. If this is MY baby from a past life, no one in this present life needs to be part of this decision. I might have wanted a baby in that life because I was alone, and maybe God or the universe or whatever didn't let the baby be born because I would not have been able to take care of it, and, dammit, I can't take care of one now either. Not without giving up the life I'm living. It's too much of a risk. How could I expect Jared to ever believe me?" she said aloud.

Oh great. Now I am even making speeches to myself. I have to end this mess now. She rose from the table and picked up the phone. A few minutes later she was on her way to a clinic. She agreed to submit to the mandatory counseling; she agreed to think it over for 24 hours after the counseling session; and she agreed not to hold them liable if she was unable to conceive in the future. This last condition struck her as funny. *My problem is I seem to be able to conceive without even having sex. I guess I am a freak of nature. Not being able to conceive in the future is probably a plus in my situation.*

She was extremely anxious to get the next 24 hours over with and to have this all behind her. After returning home from her counseling session at the clinic, she couldn't think about anything else. She needed this abortion and she was counting the hours until she had it. Until then there was nothing to do except eat and sleep, hopefully without any dreams, and try to act normal for Jared.

After a mostly sleepless night, she arose the next morning and plodded sleepily into the kitchen to make the coffee.

"Great workout today!" Jared greeted her enthusiastically. "Best one in a long time! I lifted more than I have in years. I may be a grandfather soon, but I am not an old man yet. You feeling better? Any chance I might get lucky tonight?"

He gave her a playful pat on her fanny, and a longer than usual good morning kiss.

"I'm really in the mood today. Wish I could go into work late, but I've got a meeting."

Gloria returned this kiss, while secretly hoping that he had such a bad day at work that he completely lost the desire for sex. She would be in no shape for sex for at least a week, maybe more. She would have to blame it all on complications of menopause...the bleeding, the inability to have sex, the crying that she imagined she wouldn't be able to prevent. This was going to be the hardest day of her life, and she couldn't even tell her husband.

Jared went upstairs to get ready for work. Gloria stared into her coffee mug, unable to eat or drink. Just before Jared left for work, he came over to the table and gave her a hug.

"I've been thinking, maybe this working from home thing isn't playing out the way you thought it would. You seem down lately. Why don't you call the office and see how they feel about you going in a couple of days a week," he suggested.

"Yeah, that's probably a good idea. I'll call them as soon as I feel better."

"Shouldn't matter to them, right, whether you telecommute or not, long as you get those reports out on time, right?" he said.

"I said I'll call and find out as soon as I feel better," she said with an exasperated tone.

Jared didn't seem to notice that she was annoyed. He took her face in his hands and gave her a long kiss.

"Hold that thought 'til I get home," he whispered.

Of course she would hold that thought and it would depress the hell out of her. He was in the mood for romance and she would be sad, bleeding and sore. Plus, for the first time in days, she realized that she was way behind in her work. Telecommuting had given her flexibility about when she worked, and at what pace. She liked that. She often waited until the last few hours before something was due to finish it off. She worked best under pressure, or at least that was always her excuse for procrastinating. But now she was so preoccupied with her pregnancy that she had lost track of her schedule. *How possible is it to pull an all-nighter after having an abortion? I guess I'll find out.*

As her taxi pulled into the parking lot of the clinic, she was agitated by a mix of hope and fear. She wished with all her heart that having this abortion would make everything go back to normal. She had convinced herself it was the only solution. She was a little afraid that something would go wrong or that it would be painful or that she would have a slow recovery. But she figured she could make up excuses for all these things. She just needed to get it over with.

The nurse had just finished putting in her IV line when the doctor came in to introduce herself. Gloria found it comforting that the doctor was a woman. She had an urge to tell her that she might actually be six months pregnant, in case that meant she would have to do things differently, but in the end, she decided not to say anything. As the drug entered her bloodstream, she felt slightly euphoric. Her grip on the sheet loosened. She would let the doctors and nurses take care of everything. It would be over soon.

"Were there were any complications?" she asked when the doctor came to see her in the recovery room.

"No complications, other than your refusal to allow us to proceed."

"What do you mean? Did the medication make me combative?"

"Maybe, but I don't think so. I think the medication relaxed you to the point that your inhibitions were shut down and you told us what you really wanted. It happens sometimes. When it does, we can't go on with the procedure. It would be unethical."

"What do you mean? You didn't do the abortion? I'm still pregnant? I can't be pregnant. I wanted the abortion. I had the counseling. Why didn't you do it?"

Gloria was sobbing. Her heart was racing. It took every ounce of self-control not to scream at the doctor.

"As soon as your legs were in the stirrups, you began pleading with us to let your baby live. You said you would love it and take care of it. We tried to calm you down, but you were trying to kick me, and you kept saying, 'Please stop, don't kill my baby.' Under the circumstances, we couldn't continue. I'm sorry. The nurse will be in to help you dress. We've scheduled time with the counselor."

"I don't want time with the counselor. I want an abortion. I came here for a fucking abortion and that is what I want. Your drugs made me crazy, made me say crazy stuff, but I want, I need, this abortion. Please help me."

"The nurse will be right in. You can't leave until the meds have worn off. You do have someone who is going to pick you up, right? You can't drive, you know. Why don't you take this time to meet with the counselor."

When the counselor finally arrived in the room, Gloria was pacing and biting her lip. She couldn't stop crying long enough to say more than a word or two at a time. The counselor nodded understandingly and handed her tissue.

"I've seen this before," the woman said. "It's not that unusual. No reason to be embarrassed. Take a minute and then we'll talk."

Gloria finally pulled herself together. She shook the counselor's hand.

"Thanks for trying to help. I don't need counseling. It won't help. I would try to explain this to you, but I can't...and if I did you wouldn't believe it."

"Why don't you try me? I might surprise you. Everything is confidential here."

"What would you say if I told you I was raped?"

"I wouldn't be surprised. Do you want to talk about it."

"No, it happened so long ago that it's not worth even discussing."

"That distance you are feeling from the rape is a defense mechanism. The record says you are 14 weeks pregnant. That's not so long ago, but a rape can change your life so much that it seems like a whole lifetime has gone by. Do you want to talk about it? Not now necessarily, but I can make you an appointment with our rape crisis team."

"No. Thanks, but no thanks. This is different. No one could understand this situation."

"Gloria, you are feeling what so many women who have been the victim of sexual abuse feel. But you aren't alone."

"Well, that's for sure. I am never really alone. There's at least one other person sharing my life. Look, I know you are trying to help, but I'm out of here. Thanks. I already called a cab."

Gloria had the cab drive her directly home. No need to fill the prescriptions they had given her. What she needed was some time alone; time alone with Earth Girl.

CHAPTER 8

Gloria crawled into bed, wanting desperately to erase the last few hours from her memory. She pulled the covers over her head, hoping to find a few hours of oblivion. There was no reason to think anyone would bother her while Jared was at work. Since Melanie had married, the house always seemed too empty and quiet while Jared wasn't home. Today, it seemed like a refuge, or maybe a hiding place.

Her mind raced. Far from finding oblivion, she was overwhelmed with awareness. She was still pregnant. She couldn't believe that she had begged them to stop the abortion. Her last dream about Earth Girl had to be the reason.

"Somehow, my dreams about her are making things happen in my real life...my present-day life," she said aloud, as if she was a television detective solving a mystery for the viewers to witness.

She continued wondering if past-life experiences could control events in her present life. Maybe they could. *Maybe the weird inexplicable things people do; the things that seem to make no sense at all, are because of past lives.* This line of reasoning led her to start thinking about various sensational news stories that had captured the public's interest because they seemed so unfathomable. Most of them were about people who murdered their own children or parents, or felt they had been chosen by God to murder a president or other prominent figure. Could be because they were flashing back to a previous life? She knew that if their defense attorneys had tried to use this as a defense, she would have been the first to say that it was a ridiculous ploy to get a not-guilty verdict.

She had to admit to herself that she had no idea what was going on and she was scared. Scared of what might have been her past, but more scared of what might come in the future. The idea of having lived a past life was beginning to really frighten her. She dreaded the thought that this past life might really have control of her now.

Having a "normal" life had motivated many of her decisions. When faced with the choice of following her youthful dreams of fame, fortune and adventure, she had chosen convention instead. She wanted a husband, two children, a house in the suburbs, a fulfilling career (but one that was not too demanding) and a measure of financial security. Nothing over the top. Just "normal."

Gloria contemplated the life she had created for herself. *I managed to get almost all of what I wanted. I'm happily married, at least most of the time. I have a great house and a decent job that matters to me. And, of course, Melanie. I've really been so lucky. A good marriage, a healthy child, and enough money to feel secure. I got what I wanted out of life and I sure don't want to lose any of it now because of some crazy past-life experience. I just won't let that happen. I'm not sure how to get Earth Girl's baby out of my life, but no matter what it takes I will get rid of it.*

A moment of peace encompassed her as she decided that the first step was sleeping pills. A deep enough sleep and the dreams of Earth Girl might stop. Her next thought was of the baby. What would happen to the baby if she took sleeping pills? She asked herself if she even cared. She thought about it carefully. *I don't want this baby. I don't love this baby. IT IS NOT MINE. I don't know where it came from, or how it happened. I am sure I do not want this baby. There is no way I can have this child. No way.*

Suddenly, her momentary peacefulness turned to panic. All she could think of was how to end the pregnancy. There were other abortion clinics, but she had an eerie feeling that Earth Girl would show up at those clinics too. There was only one alternative left.

She looked at the clock. It was already past one. She would have to hurry. Grim determination motivated her as she went to the computer. She was amazed to find 9,080,000 entries in 2.5 seconds when she entered the words "self-abortion methods."

They all sounded dangerous: coat hangers, knitting needles, herbs that would make her deathly ill and prescription drugs that were intended for other purposes. Each of these methods was dangerous to the mother and even more dangerous to the baby, if it managed to survive.

She continued to comb the internet, hoping beyond hope to find a method that would definitely work and that would not endanger her own life. She had to make a decision quickly. Time was running out. The longer she waited, the more dangerous it would be. She didn't really have time to find the right herbs or drugs.

She walked to her bedroom as if in a trance. She looked through the closet for a wire coat-hanger. She couldn't find one. She had always hated wire hangers. When clothes came back from the cleaners on them, she always threw them into the trash. Her closet had only plastic and fat metal hangers. Not a wire hanger in sight. But she did have knitting needles; brand new ones that were still in their plastic wrapping. This struck her as a good omen. They were probably sterile, she surmised. Less dangerous than a coat hanger.

She struggled with packaging, trying first to rip it open with her fingers and then trying to tear it with her teeth. She began to cry. *Why is this stuff always so hard to open? It makes everything so much more difficult when you can't get the fucking wrapper off something you need.* She carried the knitting needles to the kitchen and poked at the plastic packaging with a sharp knife. When she succeeded in tearing away the plastic from the cardboard, an instant of satisfaction encouraged her to continue. She lifted out the light green knitting needle. Maybe she should boil it first. Fearing it might melt out of shape, she decided to douse it with rubbing alcohol instead. As she attempted to sterilize the needle, it occurred to her that she might need some alcohol herself.

Gloria never drank hard liquor. She hated the taste and the smell, but Jared liked whiskey and there was always some on hand. She got a large glass and poured herself a generous drink. She practically choked on her first sip, but forced herself to swallow it. She carried the glass of whiskey and the knitting needle to the master bathroom. Should she do this in the bathtub with water running, or on the floor with a towel underneath her? She opted for the bathtub.

As she ran the water, she continued to sip the whiskey. It burned all the way down, but it was not having the desired effect. Frantic with worry that it might not work, or that she might really hurt herself, she forced herself to take another large swallow of the bitter drink. It still wasn't helping. She looked at herself in the mirror, eyes rimmed with tears and cheeks pale with fear. *I might even die if I do this wrong.* But no matter how she worked it out in her mind, she had no choice.

She was pregnant with a baby from a past life. It wasn't Jared's, and he would never believe her. How could she expect him to? She didn't even believe it herself, but she knew in her heart and soul that it was true. She had lived a past life and in that life she had been raped, and now, somehow, she had that baby in her. There was only one solution. She had to get rid of the baby. She would deal with Earth Girl later. She would deal with guilt later. Right now, she had to act fast, before she lost her nerve.

She turned on the water and climbed in the tub. She put the needle down beside her. She wondered if the needle would float. Then she laughed, as she realized she was wondering if the needle she was going to jab into her uterus would float. *I can't believe I'm thinking about the needle floating. I must be nuts. I am nuts. No one would ever believe any of this.* She couldn't stop laughing, or was it crying? She couldn't tell the difference. *I must be drunk. I have to hurry and get this over with.* Gloria finished the whiskey with three huge gulps. This time the burn felt good. She began to relax in the warm water.

"I feel so sleepy. Better turn the water off," she said aloud, as she reached for the needle. A comforting drowsiness coursed through her veins as she spread her legs apart and began to insert the needle. She hoped that she could stay awake long enough to clean everything up after she was done.

"Ouwww!" she screamed. *That really hurts. I must have hit the wrong spot. I need to try again, but I don't think I can stand it.* The water in the tub began to turn a light shade of pinkish orange as she lost consciousness.

* * *

Melanie hurried from the obstetrician's office clutching the picture from her ultrasound. She couldn't wait to surprise her mother with the first picture of her grandson. She was imagining her mother's delight as she let herself in the front door.

"Mom, I've got a surprise for you. Mom, where are you? Upstairs? Hey, if you're taking a nap wake up. I have something special for you."

She waited a minute and then opened the door. The first thing she saw was the large drinking glass on the edge of the tub. Her gaze moved quickly to the tub and she let out a scream when she saw the bloody water. Her mother was slumped in the tub. Her head was resting against one of the corners. She was not conscious, but she was breathing. Melanie grabbed her cell phone out of her pocket and dialed 911. After she made the call, she let the water out of the tub and covered Gloria with a towel. She tried to revive her by gently slapping her cheek. Did Mom's skin always look so pale against the bright blue of the tub? No wonder Dad always hated the color of this tub. Then she burst into tears. *I have to call Dad. I hope she comes to before he gets here. He is going to fall apart if she is dying.*

The EMTs arrived just as Gloria was gaining consciousness. As Melanie explained how she found her, one of the EMTs noticed the blood stains and the knitting needle in the tub. She touched the other EMT's arm and looked at him knowingly. He nodded.

"What's wrong with her?" Melanie demanded.

Without replying they began to give Gloria oxygen before they lifted her out of the tub and onto the stretcher.

"Definitely been drinking, her breath has a strong odor of alcohol," the female EMT said.

Melanie reflexively grabbed the glass and took a whiff. To her surprise it smelled like whiskey. Had her mother been trying to commit suicide? She never drank hard liquor. She started to ask her mother what had happened, but the male EMT told her to save her questions until after they stabilized her. Seeming to disregard his own advice, he then proceeded to ask, "Ma'am, how much have you had to drink?"

Gloria could barely keep her eyes open. She raised her hand and made a gesture as if to answer his question. Then she closed her eyes again. The other EMT picked up the knitting needle and put it in a plastic bag. It was the first time Melanie noticed it.

"What's that? What was she doing with that in the bathtub?"

They ignored her question as they continued to work on Gloria. She was given an IV with glucose and her blood was drawn for testing. They were on the way out to the ambulance as Jared arrived. Jared left his car semi-parked at the side of the road. He rushed to Gloria's side and reached for her hand but it had an IV line in it. A look of shock passed over his face as he put his hand gently on her shoulder.

"What happened, babe? Are you okay?"

Gloria looked at him with drowsy eyes and turned her face to his hand on her shoulder. He lifted his hand and touched her cheek. Melanie took his other hand and squeezed it tightly. She had not given him any details when she left the message for him. She had simply said to come home immediately because Mom was sick and the ambulance had been called.

He turned toward Melanie and gave her a quick kiss on the forehead.

"She'll be okay, sweetie. She woke up with the flu yesterday. I'm sure it's nothing serious."

A wave of nausea overtook Melanie. She wasn't sure what to say to her father. How could she tell him that she had found his beloved wife drunk in a bloody bathtub? And the knitting needle...what was that all about? She decided to wait until they got to the hospital to tell her father anything. She glanced at her mother. Would she need a transfusion? Had she tried to kill herself with the knitting needle? It didn't make any sense. What was going on?

When they arrived in the emergency room, Gloria was wheeled into a small room separated from the other small rooms by a curtain that made three walls. Various medical apparatus hung on the fourth wall. Gloria noticed them as she was wheeled in. She imagined that the medical devices looked expectant and eager, as if they were hoping for an emergency requiring their use. This thought was quickly replaced with a moment of panic. *Am I dying?*

A young woman and an even younger-looking man hurried into her room. They immediately began packing gauze into her vagina. She closed her eyes and tried to think about what had happened. She could barely concentrate long enough to put it all together because a sudden wave of nausea overtook her. She had no control over her body for the next two minutes. Vaguely aware of nurses and a small pink kidney-shaped bowl, she had no choice but to allow her body to get rid of the whiskey in the only way it could. A series of violent abdominal spasms shook her body before the retching began. When the vomiting finally stopped, she lay back, gasping for breath. So much pain, so deep inside her abdomen.

With the awareness of this pain came the realization of what she had been attempting. Looking around her to make sure Melanie and Jared were not standing somewhere in the room, she asked the nurse if the EMTs had told her why she was brought to the hospital. The nurse nodded.

"A doctor will be in to examine you soon," she said. "Your husband and daughter will be allowed to see you before you are brought to the operating room. We are just waiting for the obstetrical surgeon to arrive."

Gloria was worried about what Melanie and Jared had been told. Did they know what she tried to do? Her heart was pounding inside her chest. By the time the doctor arrived to examine her and prepare for the surgery, she had lost consciousness again. She had no awareness of anything that happened until she awoke in the recovery room. She did not hear the doctor tell Jared that she was pregnant and had, apparently, tried to perform a self-abortion. She did not hear Melanie's refusal to believe that her mother was pregnant. Nor did she hear Jared tell them to save the baby. All she heard was the familiar voice of Earth Girl begging a doctor not to kill her baby.

When she woke up in the recovery room, the first thing she noticed was something that reminded her of a plastic clothespin on her finger. The second thing she noticed was Jared sitting in a chair next to her. He looked like he had been crying. Although fully conscious for the first time since passing out in the bathtub, she closed her eyes and pretended to sleep. She desperately wanted to avoid talking to Jared. *Did he know that I was pregnant and tried to give myself and abortion?* Not knowing the answer to this made it feel impossible to speak to him.

Numb from the waist down, she tried to assess her condition. There was no longer a searing pain in her pelvis and this was a relief. But she could feel Jared's eyes staring at her. There was no relief from the emotional pain of wondering what he was going through. With her eyes closed, she considered her options. She could tell him everything now and get it over with. He probably would be hurt or furious or both. She could try to explain about the dreams and how this baby belonged to the girl in the dreams. She could swear that she had not had sex with anyone but him and tell him how confused and scared she was. She could tell him that if he really loves her he would believe her and help her through this.

Jared really did love her, so maybe honesty was the best approach. But this story was almost impossible to believe. She would not believe it herself, if it was not happening to her. Heck, it *was* happening to her and she could hardly believe it. Had she lost touch with reality? Had she suffered some sort of psychotic break? But, if this were true, how could she be pregnant? This was the one fact that made Gloria believe she was still sane.

Her other option was to pretend not to wake up for days. Let them all worry about her so much that they wouldn't ask her to explain. If they did ask, she could pretend that she had lost the ability to speak. Maybe they would think she had been raped and the trauma had been too much for her. This would give her the chance to listen to what the doctors said about her condition. She would know if she was still pregnant before she had to say anything. This was the safest option. Keep her eyes closed and her mouth shut. Let everyone else do the talking. Let them come up with a theory. Whatever their theory, it would be more believable than the truth.

Feeling a little calmer, she dozed off. When she woke up, a nurse was taking her vital signs and putting a sanitary napkin on her. She had not worn one since Melanie was born. As the nurse, fastened the elastic belt around her, she realized how much she appreciated the person who had invented tampons. She kept her eyes closed in hopes of fooling the nurse, who was talking to her as if she was awake.

"You probably wonder if you succeeded in killing that baby. I don't know if this is good news or bad, honey, but that baby is still alive. And so are you. Don't know if you were trying to kill yourself too, but you're going make it. Thank God for that."

The nurse vigorously rearranged the sheets on Gloria's bed.

"Your husband is beside himself with worry. You got a good

man there. You better open your eyes, girl, and let him know that you are alright, because he is falling apart out there in the hall."

Gloria began to have heart palpitations, which registered on the bedside monitor.

"Okay, honey, it's okay. Didn't mean to upset you. Everyone is gonna be okay. You just need to save your strength now. You lost a lot of blood. I'll be in to check on you later. Everything's going to be okay. I promise," the nurse said quickly.

The nurse walked out of the room thinking about what an empty promise she had made. There was reason to think the baby had been injured, though the tests to confirm it had not yet been done. There was also reason to think that her patient had intended to kill herself as well as her baby. Most likely, everyone was not going to be okay.

Jared entered the room as the nurse left. He looked like a different person than he had 24 hours before. Normally, Jared was fastidious about his appearance, even shaving twice a day if he had an engagement in the evening. Now he had stubble on his chin, and his hair was uncombed. His clothes looked as if he had slept in them, but the truth was that Jared had not slept at all since Melanie's call. He had rushed home and then followed the ambulance to the hospital. He had not eaten or rested in 24 hours. Before leaving the hospital Melanie had brought him a cup of coffee and a package of Oreos from the vending machine. He hadn't touched either the coffee or the cookies, but he had the passing thought that his wife would probably like the Oreos when she regained consciousness…if she regained consciousness.

True to form, it had not even occurred to Jared to wonder how Gloria could be pregnant. He was surprised by the pregnancy, but his horror at thinking that she tried to give herself an abortion and his fears for her well-being overshadowed any other thoughts. He could understand that she would not want to have a baby at this stage of her life. He had to admit he didn't really want one either. But to not even tell him and to try to abort the baby in the bathtub...this he could not understand. Never in his wildest imagination would he have expected Gloria to keep a pregnancy from him, or to try to perform an abortion on herself. Something had to be terribly wrong.

Jared began to cry. At first, he was able to stifle the sound, but soon he was sobbing uncontrollably. His shoulders shook and tears streamed down his cheeks. "Please be okay. Please be okay. Please be okay," he kept repeating between sobs. Gloria couldn't take it any longer. She turned her head towards him and opened her eyes. Jared reached for her and began to cry even harder.

"Thank God! I was so scared. Don't worry, baby, you're going to be ok. Don't worry. Just rest."

Gloria's heart ached with guilt. It was obvious how much Jared was suffering. She wanted to comfort him, but she didn't know how. What could she tell him that would actually make him feel better? He was telling her not to worry and to rest. He was only thinking of how to make things easier for her and she knew that when she did finally tell him everything, it was only going to make things harder for him. Her heart began to beat rapidly again. She had the unbearable feeling that nothing would ever be the same between them. She had to fix this.

She reached for Jared and he took her hand. "I'm so sorry," she said softly. He bent over and started kissing her tenderly. Then he leaned down and gently put his head on her chest. His face was wet from his tears and his breathing was punctuated by deep uneven breaths every few seconds.

"It's okay, baby, it's okay. I would never be mad at you for getting pregnant."

Gloria tried to take comfort in his words, but all she could think about was how messy things were going to get when Jared finally figured out that the baby was not his. She had to tell him before he figured it out first. But not yet. *I'm just not ready yet.* Gloria caressed Jared's cheek. They were both deep in thought.

Their silence was broken by the arrival of an orderly with a dinner tray. Gloria took one look at it and began to feel a wave of nausea. "I can't eat yet. You have it. I need to go back to sleep," she said. Before he could object, her eyes were closed.

Jared realized that he was actually starving. Ordinarily, he would not be tempted by lukewarm, overly salty soup. But he was hungry and he didn't want to leave. After eating, he settled into the chair next to the bed and fell into an exhausted sleep.

Early the next morning an obstetrician came to check Gloria's condition. Jared waited in the hall. When the obstetrician left, Jared entered the room to find Gloria weeping.

"What's wrong? Are you in pain?" he asked.

"Yes, but it's not that. The doctor said that they have to do tests. They think I may have punctured the baby's brain."

Jared's shoulders slumped forward. He didn't know what to say. For the first time since arriving at the hospital, he felt a surge of anger at the whole situation.

"First you don't tell me you are pregnant. Then you practically kill yourself while trying to kill the baby. And now, we will probably end up with a handicapped child. That poor little guy…"

Jared stopped mid-sentence. He felt bad for saying what he was feeling. Gloria looked so miserable and she wasn't out of the woods yet. She was pale as a ghost and very weak. Feeling ashamed of himself for saying anything, he tried to make up for it.

"I didn't mean that. I guess I was just worried about him, or her. Didn't you know I would love this baby even though we didn't want another child? I just am so surprised that you wouldn't tell me. But, it will be okay. Once you get out of here, we'll start preparing for the baby, and we'll do whatever we have to take care of it if, no matter what sort of…condition, uh, injury…whatever, we'll deal with it."

Gloria didn't want to think about what she might have done

to this baby. This baby that wasn't even hers. She couldn't stand to think about it. It was all so bewildering and here she was, still feeling trapped and confused. She had tried to get rid of this pregnancy and failed. Now she would have to live with the consequences, whatever they were. Plus, now that the epidural had worn off, the burning pain in her pelvis had returned. And there was Melanie. Where was Melanie? Did she know too?

"Where's Melanie, Jared? Is she okay? This must have been so scary for her."

Jared wasn't sure how to answer, but opted for the truth.

"She's home. She was very upset by all of this. Finding you in the tub in a pool of blood...you can imagine how scary that was for her. And then to find out you are pregnant. She's...well, she's having a hard time processing it all. I think it might take a few days."

"Yeah, I get it. I need to talk to her. To tell her I'm sorry and that I didn't want to have a baby now; that I really wanted to concentrate on being a grandmother to her baby."

"Gloria, she'll get over it. You can tell her when you're stronger. The doctor told me you need to rest and get your strength back. I think you scared the doctors too. You lost a lot of blood. You had two transfusions."

"Jared, can I ask you something without you saying anything right away? Will you take a day to think about it before you give me an answer?"

"I guess so. I mean, I guess it depends. If it's anything I think is going to be bad for you, I am going to tell you that right away, but otherwise, ok."

"It's just that I want to know, Jare, if it's okay with you if we don't let them do any tests to see if the baby got hurt. I don't think I could stand going through the rest of this pregnancy knowing that I hurt her, or having you know it, either. I just want to start loving her before I know anything else."

"Why do you keep saying 'her'? Did they tell you it's a girl?"

"No, but I just know that it is."

Gloria could not tell Jared how she knew. She could not tell him that while she was sleeping the night before, she had dreamed of Earth Girl giving birth to a baby girl.

CHAPTER 9

Gloria had been home from the hospital for more than a week and Melanie was still not willing to speak to her. Jared had tried to convince Melanie that Gloria needed her support. Melanie remained steadfast. She was both hurt and angry and even she could not tell which feeling was stronger. All she knew was that she was pregnant with her first child and the day she rushed from the obstetrician's visit to show her mother the very first ultrasound of her beautiful baby boy, her mother had ruined it. Really, truly, ruined it.

She hadn't made a minor gaffe or a silly comment about Melanie being so young. She hadn't rushed out of the house in a hurry as if she didn't really care much about the ultrasound picture of her first grandchild. Melanie could have forgiven this. But, she could not forgive what her mother did. She got pregnant while Melanie was pregnant. That was bad enough. What grand-mother wants to have a baby of her own at the same time as her daughter?

But that wasn't all. She had tried to commit suicide and passed out in a bathtub full of bloody water. How was Melanie supposed to ever forget this? How was she supposed to forget that the day she wanted to tell her mother she was having a baby boy, instead of being greeted with hugs and tears of joy, she was greeted with a half-dead, drunken mother who had stuck a knitting needle up her vagina. Melanie knew she could never get that day back and transform it into the happy day it was supposed to have been. No, thanks to her mother, the day she found out she was having a boy would always be a day of horror.

Melanie repeated all this to Jared at least once a day because he was relentless in his attempt to get her to come see Gloria and to forgive her. He believed that if Melanie would forgive her Gloria would begin to recover. He believed that it was Melanie's anger that was making Gloria so nervous and unhappy. He even believed that Gloria would begin to love this baby if only Melanie would say she didn't mind having a sibling the same age as her own child. But Melanie wouldn't say it and Gloria seemed to be worse each day.

Jared had no way of knowing that Gloria was only slightly upset by Melanie's rejection; that actually she had barely thought about it because she was so worried about how to tell Jared the truth. He remained so preoccupied with her recovery that he hadn't even thought about when Gloria had conceived. When Gloria said that she needed to talk to both Melanie and Jared together he thought it was because she wanted him there to calm Melanie down. Actually she was so nervous about Jared's reaction to her incredible story that she wanted Melanie there to calm *him* down.

It was a brisk Tuesday evening when Melanie finally agreed to come to the house. Her husband, Roger, offered to go with her but Melanie wanted to do this alone. She did not want Roger to see or hear any of what might transpire. Her pregnancy had already been irrevocably tainted by her mother. Roger was her refuge and she did not want him to be part of this in any way.

On the brief walk to her parents' house Melanie noted the fading colors of autumn. She would always remember just how the clouds hung low in the Newport sky as she approached her parents' house. When you know you will be seeing your mother for the very last time you tend to remember everything about that day. Jared met Melanie on the sidewalk and embraced her tightly.

"Thanks, honey," he said, "this is really going to help your mom."

Melanie didn't say a word, but she did note that her father did not even mention her own pregnancy. He squeezed her hand and thanked her again. Melanie tried to smile. She knew none of this was his fault.

"Really, Mel, this is just what she needs."

"Yeah, okay Dad."

She didn't want her father to know that she had not come on a mission of forgiveness. As she walked in the front door she saw Gloria sitting on the couch. She was shocked at how bad she looked. Her father had not been exaggerating. Her mother was in bad shape. She looked pale and she had dark circles under her eyes. She looked as if she hadn't showered in days. Her hair was uncombed and matted against one cheek. Melanie had never seen her mother look even close to this bad, not even when she was suffering from a three-day migraine. Melanie was suddenly queasy. There was a pounding pressure in her chest. For a brief moment, she thought she might have a heart attack. But that thought was replaced by angry determination when Gloria asked Jared and Melanie to sit down so she could tell them something that she had been waiting for days to tell them.

"Oh this is how you think it's going to go," Melanie blurted, "you think you are going to lead this conversation like when I was a naughty little girl. Well, no way! Not this time."

Her voice was high and breathless. It was obvious to both Jared and Gloria that Melanie was furious. Before either one of them could react Melanie continued.

"I don't know why you decided to have a baby now, and I don't know why you changed your mind. But I am not going to let you ruin my pregnancy and I sure as hell am not going to let you anywhere near me or the baby. You can forget you even have a grandson. Just take care of your new little baby and forget about us. I hope this kid is everything you ever hoped for because it's pretty obvious I am not!"

"Oh, Mel, you know that's not true," Jared said.

Gloria didn't know what to say. She was stunned by Melanie's outburst. Melanie looked directly at her.

"I know you wanted me to go to college and that I am a big disappointment to you because I didn't do everything your way," said Melanie, as tears began to fall onto her red cheeks.

"Melanie, you've never been a disappointment to us. Not ever," said Gloria quickly.

"Yeah, right, Mom. I know you didn't want me to get married so young, but I never ever thought you would do this to me. I hate you, Mom. I never want to see you again!"

Jared rushed to comfort Gloria as Melanie was speaking, but Gloria rose and held out her hand with the palm up. She looked like a cop stopping traffic. She opened her mouth to speak and then she stopped. Both Melanie and Jared looked at her, waiting for her to say something. Finally, slowly, she began to talk.

"Melanie, I did not choose to become pregnant. I promise you that. I don't even know how I got pregnant...I..."

"Well, c'mon, let's be honest here. We haven't really used birth control as carefully as we used to, Glo," said Jared as he put his arm around her.

Melanie stood looking at both them with her arms folded tightly across her chest.

"Typical. Get on my case about an unplanned pregnancy, but don't mind your own store."

"That's not what I mean," said Gloria. "I really don't know how I got pregnant. It's so complicated and so crazy that you probably won't believe me, but I can't carry this around by myself anymore. I got pregnant without having sex with anyone. I'm going to tell you the whole story and that's all I can do. If you don't believe me, I can't help it. It doesn't make any sense to me either and that's why I didn't tell you before."

Gloria sat on the couch with a blanket around her shoulders and began to tell them about her dreams of Earth Girl, discovering she was pregnant, and knowing it couldn't be Jared's. She recounted the doctor's refusal to perform the abortion. Jared looked at her as if she was some strange creature he had never seen before. Melanie remained stonily passive.

By the time Gloria was finished with her story she was weeping openly. She reached for Jared's hand. He pulled away from her as if touching her would cause him physical harm. Melanie looked at both of them and realized that whatever she had come to say to her mother no longer mattered to anyone. At that same moment, she realized she still loved her mother and that she also pitied her. Her mother had lost her mind. She couldn't abandon her now.

Jared paced around the room without saying a word. His breathing became louder and his face turned bright red. He looked as if he was going to say something. Instead, he turned toward the wall and began punching it as hard as he could. Gloria and Melanie both screamed and pleaded with him to stop but he continued until his hand was raw and swollen. Then he walked out the door.

Melanie and Gloria hugged each other as they cried. What was happening to their family? Melanie's anger had completely dissipated because she truly believed that her mother had suffered a psychotic break from reality. She was shocked that her father would react so angrily when it was clear that Mom was certifiably nuts. For a moment she forgot about her own pregnancy. But with her stomach pressed against Gloria's as they continued to embrace, she felt a kick and then another one. Her immediate instinct was to point it out to Gloria. She had wanted to share her baby's kicks with her mom for weeks. Now she realized sadly she wasn't even sure which baby had kicked.

Gloria pulled away and put her hand over her abdomen. Then she put on her coat and headed out the door to find Jared. Melanie was right behind her. Jared had headed straight to Sambar on Thames Street. It was a restaurant with an international flair that also served as a friendly watering hole. He and Gloria went there together often for tapas and drinks. Now he was there to down as much whiskey as he possibly could without passing out. He would get as drunk as he could and still be able to walk the few blocks home. After the first stiff drink he didn't care whether he threw up, passed out, or dropped dead. What difference did it make? His wife had cheated on him, tried to give herself an abortion and then made up a preposterous story to try to get his sympathy. He didn't know who she was anymore and he didn't want to. She wasn't the woman he married. She was a cheating, lying, whore and he hated her.

Melanie guessed that her father would head to Sambar. He wasn't the first man to arrive at a bar with a busted fist and he wouldn't be the last. It was probably one of the best places to go if you didn't want a bunch of questions. She was pretty sure her father did not want to talk to anyone right about now. She peered through the window and saw him sitting at the bar.

"Dad, come on. Mom needs you. There's something really wrong with her."

"That's for sure. She's a liar and a cheat. Mel, I'm sorry to be like this in front of you, but I can't help it. Just leave me alone for awhile. I love you, Mel. Sorry I forced you to come over to see her. I didn't know she was going to act like we're both idiots. I can't believe she would do any of this. Right now I fuckin' hate her."

By this time, Gloria was standing behind Jared listening to him. She touched his shoulder. He turned towards her and lifted his arm so that her hand was forced off his shoulder.

"Leave me the fuck alone."

"I'm not lying, Jare. I swear I'm not lying. I don't understand any of this but I'm not lying and I didn't cheat on you."

The guys sitting at the bar tried to look as if they weren't listening. Melanie became acutely aware of her parents' public argument. She kept trying to get to them to leave. Finally the bartender, more than an acquaintance but not quite a friend, took matters into his own hands. He told Melanie to grab her mother and escort her out while he strong-armed Jared out the door.

"Sorry, folks, but not here, guys. This shit belongs in private."

Jared was barely feeling the effects of the shot of whiskey. He wanted to be much drunker than he was. Gloria was hanging on his arm crying and begging him to come home. They had never had a fight like this before and she wanted it to end. She could reason with him if he would just come home. He flatly refused and began walking in the opposite direction. Melanie ran after him. She used her one trump card.

"Dad, please do this for me. Not for Mom. For me. I need you both to get home safely. I'm pregnant, Daddy, and I can't take this. Please."

As mad as he was, Jared could not put Melanie through any more trauma. He put his arm around her shoulder and said, "I'll go home if you tell your mother to leave me the crap alone. I do not want to talk this out tonight or ever."

Jared did not speak to Gloria for the rest of the week. He got up, went to work, ate dinner out and came home. He watched television. He read. He slept in Melanie's old bedroom. Saturday morning he began to patch the hole he had made in the living-room wall.

"Can I help?" Gloria asked quietly.

"Yes, you can help. You can help by telling me the truth so that I can figure out how to get on with my life."

"I know you don't believe me. I don't blame you. All I can say is I am telling you the truth. I did not have sex with anyone other than you and I am pregnant and from my due date I became pregnant while you were out of town...I can't..."

"Stop saying you don't know what happened!" Jared interrupted angrily. "Stop saying I BECAME pregnant, as if you didn't have anything to do with it. You fucked someone and now you are pregnant. We both know that."

"Jared, you have to believe me. I didn't have sex with anyone. That's the truth. And the part about Earth Girl and my dreams is the truth too. Please believe me," Gloria pleaded.

"I don't know how you can expect me to believe this fairy tale. Next, you'll be telling me an angel came and told you to name the baby Jesus. Well I'm not Joseph and you're sure as hell not the

Virgin Mary."

Gloria's cheeks flushed. What could she say to say to convince Jared? Before she could even formulate a thought, he started yelling at her again.

"You cheated on me, and it would make both our lives easier if you would just admit it. By the way, does your lover know you're pregnant and that you tried to abort his baby? Maybe he's the one you should be talking to."

"I don't have a lover! There is no other man except for the man who raped Earth Girl," shouted Gloria.

"Why don't you just shut up about Earth Girl? I don't believe this crap and I never will."

Gloria sat down and put her head between her hands. After a moment she lifted her head and looked intently at her husband.

"Jared, I know you hate me right now and I know none of this makes any sense, but please just let me say this one more thing, please."

"Go ahead. Might as well get it all out now."

"I've been thinking about this a lot and all I can figure is that maybe in our past lives I was Earth Girl and you were the man who raped me and now in this life we are supposed to have this baby and raise it and make up for whatever happened then."

"That is the most ridiculous thing I have ever heard. What bullshit explanation do you have for Melanie? What supernatural past-life purpose does she serve in your crazy scheme?"

A vein on the middle of his forehead became engorged and began to pulse visibly. She had never seen this happen before and it frightened her. He grabbed the back of a chair with both hands.

"Please don't come near me. I might hurt you. I need you to go call the father of this baby and tell him that you want to move in with him or that he needs to put you up somewhere because you can't live here. As long as you continue to lie to me, you cannot live here. You made your bed. Now go lie in it, again!"

"But Jare, I..."

"And don't friggin' call Melanie to rescue you. She is pregnant with her husband's baby. She doesn't need all this shit."

Gloria stood her ground. She was hurt but she wasn't angry. She knew this was going to happen. How could she expect anyone to believe her? Her husband thought she was a liar and her daughter thought she was a mental case. There was no one to turn to; nowhere to go. So she was staying.

"I'm not going anywhere. If you don't ever want to speak to me again, that's up to you. But I didn't do anything wrong and I am not leaving. I thought you loved me but I guess that love is all gone because I am going through something you don't understand. Well, so be it."

Jared picked up the chair and slammed it down. He walked deliberately to the hole in the wall. He returned to patching the hole, acting as if he could not hear anything Gloria said.

"You can have our room. I'll move my stuff into Melanie's. I still love you and I don't blame you for not believing me. But I am disappointed that you truly believe I would betray you this way. I don't know what is going on, but whatever it is, it is ruining our lives and I am truly sorry."

Jared did not react. He continued smoothing plaster over the hole. Gloria walked over and stood behind him. She caressed his shoulders lovingly.

"I love you, Jared. I would never hurt you."

"Leave me alone. I can't stand to hear your voice."

With that, Gloria walked into Melanie's room and locked the door.

The next morning Jared went for a long walk. He felt as if he was trapped in a nightmare. He couldn't believe his wife was pregnant with another man's child. Yet even she said it was not his. As if this wasn't enough, because of her inability to work since attempting the abortion, she had lost her job. On Friday she had been fired by the supervisor of at-home workers because she had not produced any work at all in over two weeks. As mad as he was at her, Jared did not want her to lose her job. They needed the money. When they moved to the house in Newport they knew it would take two incomes to meet the mortgage. So despite everything that was going on, Jared was toying with the idea of getting his brother to save her job. Joe had pulled some strings where he worked to get her this telecommuting position in the first place. He could probably use his considerable status in the company to get her hired again.

Of course that would necessitate talking to Joe. Jared seldom spoke to Joe. Gloria and Joe and Joe's wife Sheila had a warm relationship. Gloria had introduced Sheila to Joe when they were all teenagers. After Joe and Sheila married, Gloria and Sheila's friendship had grown even closer. Gloria thought of Sheila as more than an in-law. She was a best friend who Gloria could confide in and go to for advice. Sheila had a Boston accent, a penchant for wearing clothes that made her look like a middle-aged hippie and a great big heart. She was one of Gloria's favorite people. The fact that their husbands barely communicated was hard on these two friends.

Gloria had been trying to get Jared to mend his fences with Joe for years. Joe was more than willing, she often told him, to let bygones be bygones. "After all," Joe would say, "we ain't getting any younger."

Gloria chided Jared about his relationship with his brother before every holiday and family occasion. "You two spent so many years being rivals while you were growing up. That's why it's hard for you to get past the thing with your mother. But, you gotta let that go. It's tearing you up inside."

Jared knew that she was right about this. As a matter of fact, before Gloria's mysterious pregnancy nothing had upset him more deeply than his difficult relationship with his brother. Although they were twins and had done many things together as children and teens, they had never been easy with each other.

There was always a sense of rivalry between them. Not a healthy rivalry that inspired each of them to try harder, but an unhealthy rivalry built on jealously. Their father had always pitted them in competition with each other and this left both of them feeling that their father loved the other one more. If they were girls they might have argued openly about this, but they followed in their father's footsteps and avoided sharing their emotions with each other.

As adults, they had forged an unspoken truce that allowed them to deal with each other at family functions, and occasionally to really enjoy each other. But there was always between them a difficult distance and an undercurrent of pain. For Jared the easiest thing was to just avoid Joe as much as possible.

When their mother died Joe had been at her side. Jared had been away on business in Asia and, even though he rushed home as soon as Gloria called with the news of his mother's heart attack, he had not arrived before she passed. He held this against Joe. Their mother had never regained consciousness after a major heart attack. When the cardiologist told Joe she was not going to recover and he needed to make a decision, Joe told him to pull the plug. Jared could not forgive Joe for this. For months after his mother's death, he would say to Gloria, "Why couldn't he wait until I got home? He didn't even give me a chance to say goodbye." Despite his hurt and anger he knew that he would have made the same decision as Joe. He would have chosen to end his mother's suffering as soon as possible.

The last two years of her life had been filled with pain and frustration. She had survived cancer by undergoing a year of radiation and chemo. Throughout the ordeal she tried to remain positive, but her sons and daughters-in-law could see the toll it took. She felt sick and weak most of the time. At the end of the year, she was declared to be in remission. The family celebrated and she tried to resume her normal life. When another lump appeared she opted to have it removed surgically. They all knew the cancer had metastasized and her chances were not good. Before the surgery she asked the family to gather round her bed. She told them she was not afraid and they should not be either. "Don't be depressed if things don't go well. You know how much I love you and love lives on. I will always be with you." She never spoke to them again. During the surgery she suffered a massive stroke.

Throughout the remaining year none of them knew how much she understood. But they sensed her frustration at her inability to communicate with them. She could not talk and could not take care of her most basic needs. She was confined to bed unable even to swallow. She was kept alive with the aid of a feeding tube, intravenous meds and sheer will. None of them felt entirely comfortable with the medical efforts to prolong her life. Both of her sons believed that she would not want to live this way. Yet they could not deny her life-prolonging treatment. So she lived for a year in this netherland between real life and real death. They both visited her weekly.

Her death was actually a relief to all of them. Yet Jared felt his brother had denied him the opportunity to say a last farewell. He had blown up at Joe on the day of the funeral and had avoided any interaction with him since then. Now he needed his help if Gloria was to get her job back. He knew he would have to talk to Joe and that he would have to make up some sort of story about what had happened to Gloria.

When Jared left for his walk, Gloria retreated back to bed. She was still feeling weak and extremely fatigued. She didn't know whether her symptoms were physical or emotional, but she knew that the only thing she really wanted to do was sleep. She grabbed Jared's undershirt. It was the one he was wearing when they had the fight. He had left it on the bathroom floor when he took a shower that night. The next morning Gloria picked it up, rubbed it against her face and brought it to Melanie's room. She could smell Jared's scent on it and she thought it would make her feel less alone. But as she held it close to her face this morning, she felt only longing. Longing to be held in Jared's embrace; longing to feel his tongue search for hers passionately as he moved his hands across her breast. She wondered sadly if they would ever make love again.

Unable to sleep, she looked around Melanie's room. It still looked like a teenage girl's room. She had thought about redecorating it after Melanie had moved out to live with Roger, but she never acted on it. Melanie suspected that was because they hoped she would change her mind and move back home and act like the daughter they had planned on having...the one who would go to college right after graduating from high school and then start a career and then, when they were good and ready for a grandchild, would marry and get pregnant.

She looked at the posters on the wall, wondering how Melanie chose her idols. Did these celebrities have anything to say that really mattered to Melanie, or did she just like their posters? What posters would she choose now that she was married and expecting a baby? Did it really matter what her values were or her hopes and dreams, for that matter? Her thoughts turned ruefully to the unpredictability of life. *Nothing turns out the way we plan. Life just happens and surprises us. Sometimes it's good, sometimes it's bad and sometimes it just doesn't make any sense at all. Like now. No frigging sense at all.*

Gloria felt sadness and fatigue overtake her.

CHAPTER 10

I knew that they wanted me to take my baby before it was born. They said I was too young and would not survive giving birth. There were already too many war orphans to be cared for. They didn't have milk and food for all the babies and children whose parents had died. I wondered if they were right. I didn't want to be a mother and I hated the man who raped me. I even hated myself for being raped. I wondered if I would end up hating the baby too. Would she be as evil as her father? The worst thing was that I wanted to tell my mother. I wanted her to comfort me, but she was dead, and now that I was safe, I could not get the image of her murder out of my mind.

There were other women in this hospital who had been raped too. Some of them had been beaten and even mutilated. At first I thought I was the only one in this situation, but after I got stronger they had me go to meetings with the other women. We sat in a circle and talked about what had happened to us. Some of us were pregnant. Some weren't. I don't know what happened to their babies. I kept thinking of my mother and what she had told me about war and how men used rape as a weapon. It still didn't make any sense to me. How could God let this happen? How could He let the way a woman gets pregnant be the same way a man could hurt her?

I was beginning to believe that God was cruel. When I talked about this in the circle, some of the women told me that I should never say that, but others nodded their heads. One woman said, "We will never understand God's ways until we are in heaven." I was not sure I ever wanted to go to heaven to be with a God who could let this happen.

The closer it got to my due date, the more scared I was. I remembered how much it hurt to be raped and I could not imagine how much it must hurt to have a baby go through that same place. The older women told me that it hurts really badly, but that you get through it and then you forget it. The nurses told me that they might be able to give me medication so that it wouldn't hurt. It would depend on what supplies they received by then. That made me more nervous because I had noticed that we were getting smaller meals. When I first arrived, it seemed that we had plenty to eat and drink but after the last bomb blast, our meals were much smaller. The doctors and nurses never talked directly about the war and we never talked about it in the group. I was very confused.

Whenever I tried to figure out the war, I thought about my brother. I wondered if he was alive. I hoped he was dead if being alive meant he had to rape someone. I didn't want my sweet little brother to become an evil man. I wanted him to be like our father...good and kind and loving. One day when I told another pregnant girl about my brother and my father, she told me that most of the men in the war were good and kind in their family lives, but that in war they became cruel and heartless. She told me her own father had bragged about cutting off a man's fingers when he found out that the man had thrown a grenade that killed his friend. She had heard him and some other men talking about the things they had done when they took over a village. Another man said he raped every girl in one family because they had hidden the enemy in their house.

I didn't want to believe her. I didn't want to believe that good people could do such awful things because of war. I wanted to believe that the men who tortured and raped and killed were bad to begin with, but she said they weren't. She said that fighting in a war made them act like that, and that some of them would never be the same again. The more I talked to her, the more scared I got.

I wondered if my brother was going to be like that. I kept thinking about how I left our mother's ring for him to find and how I hoped he would grow up and fall in love and never be part of war, but I knew that probably wouldn't happen. I knew that younger and younger boys were being recruited because the battles had gone on so long. Talking in the circle was supposed to help us feel better. The nurses told me that it would help me get over what had happened to me. But I must have been different from the others because it wasn't helping. Each day I felt so sad.

All I wanted to do was to go outside and feel the sun shine on my *face. I wanted to feel a breeze and to see green grass and trees and blue skies like I had seen in the pictures in the old books they had in the hospital library. The books we had at our school didn't have any pictures. It had been a long time since my brother and I even went to school. My parents couldn't afford to send us. My father once told me that they stopped putting pictures in books when he was a boy. It got too expensive to print books with pictures he said. Once, I heard him tell my mother that he thought they kept the pictures out of books because they didn't want the next generations to know how beautiful everything had been before the first great drought.*

Sometimes, I thought of leaving the hospital, but I knew I would starve – and besides I was afraid about when the baby would be born. I didn't want to be alone for that. The nurses told me that it wasn't safe to go outside. We had to wait until the fighting was done in our area. When the militias and bombs went to another area, then we could go outside again.

One of the nurses found a book with pictures of the ocean and of jungles and mountains. She gave it to me look at. I had never seen oceans or jungles before. I had seen mountains, but they weren't beautiful like the ones in the pictures. I wanted to see everything in this book. When I felt sad or scared I would look at the pictures and they made me feel at home, like I wasn't alone. They made me feel connected. When I looked at the pictures I felt like there was someone out there in one of those beautiful places who would help me and my baby.

Chapter 11

Gloria woke up with a start, like she always did after an Earth Girl dream. This was a new dream. What did it mean? When had Earth Girl lived? Where? What war was it? For the first time, she really wanted to know more details about her. She seemed so young in this dream. Was she really just 11 or 12 years old, and pregnant? Most of all, Gloria wanted to know if she was carrying Earth Girl's baby? It made no sense to her but she felt very strongly that it was true. She remembered that in the dream Earth Girl said when she looked at the pictures she felt connected to someone who would help her.

Am I that person? How could I be?

Jared and Melanie were the only two people who knew about her dreams and neither one of them believed her. She could tell Sheila, but what if Sheila, too, found it impossible to believe her? She held Sheila in her mind as the one person she could go to when she really needed someone to believe her. She wasn't ready to find out that her ace in the hole doubted her too. Besides, she was a little worried about Sheila lately. The last time they were together, Sheila seemed sort of different. She couldn't really put her finger on it but there was something going on with Sheila. She acted strange when they were at lunch together a few weeks ago. Sort of vague and indifferent but in a way that Gloria could not quite put in words.

They had been at Sheila's favorite restaurant with another friend, Darlene. The three of them always celebrated birthdays with a festive lunch. No matter what they chose to eat, laughter – sometimes a bit too loud – was the hallmark of the occasion. This time it was Sheila's birthday, but she wasn't enjoying herself and she seemed a bit confused by the familiar menu. The Sheila that Gloria knew would never let someone else order for her. But this day she flipped through the menu with an intent look on her face and then handed it to Darlene, "You choose for me. I just can't make up my mind," she said.

Darlene's large dark eyes darted quickly to Gloria's gaze and for a just a second they shared a quizzical look. At the time it made Gloria giggle because the three friends had a habit of analyzing each other. Ordinarily Sheila would have noticed their look, rolled her eyes and made a wisecrack. This time she didn't notice it at all. Gloria had not given this much thought, but now that she was feeling the need to confide in Sheila, she found herself wondering if everything was okay with her. She knew she should give her a call. She also knew that she had no space left in her handbag for the emotions to deal with another problem.

Years ago Gloria had begun to conceive of her life as a handbag divided into sections that held, each in its own zippered compartment, worries, rational thought and things that had to be done whether she wanted to or not. Her goal was to make sure that none of the sections got too full. When she would be upset about something, she would check to see if there was any more room in the worries section. If not, she possessed an amazing ability to let go of the worry and put it in the trash. If a new concern was going into the handbag, a worry that was already neatly tucked into the worry section would have to come out and be thrown away. It amazed her friends that she could do this in such a systematic and analytical way.

She treated the compartments for rational thought and things she was required to do the very same way. She did not want to let her bag to get out of balance by loading it down with too much rational thinking. This made no sense to Jared, but Gloria knew that she always needed some extra room in the bag for free-flowing irrational ideas. If she found herself getting too analytical or not having mental space to daydream, she made a conscious effort to clean out the thinking section. She knew intuitively that she needed mental and emotional room for plain-old daydreaming.

She never allowed herself to have a long list of "to dos." If she had to do income taxes she cleared all the other "to dos" out of the handbag because she really, really hated doing her taxes. If she had to clean the kitchen cabinets she left a few other "to dos" in the handbag because she didn't really mind cleaning the cabinets all that much. The fact that she could remove things from any section and mentally throw them away had, she believed, saved her from depression, exhaustion and maybe even a nervous breakdown. Now, with Earth Girl visiting her dreams and a real living baby in her womb Gloria had very little room in her handbag for anything else. So finding out what was going on with Sheila would have to wait.

* * *

Jared sat on a bench overlooking the beach. It was calming to look at the water. Maybe talking to Joe wouldn't be so bad. He could apologize for the way he reacted when his mother died. He could acknowledge that Joe had gotten Gloria a great job, and he could tell him that she was pregnant. He could tell Joe that she was upset by the pregnancy and had gone into a depression and that she really needed the job to hang on to her sanity. He could ask Joe for help. Joe liked to be in the position of helping. It made him feel superior and that was, after all, his favorite feeling. But what the fuck? He needed help; so if Joe felt like a big man by getting Gloria's job back, so what? Jared knew he had more serious problems than whether or not he was giving Joe a reason to feel superior to him. He had a wife who was either a cheater, or a lunatic. Neither option was comforting.

Joe responded to Jared's call with concern, sympathy and advice. He would do everything he could to get Gloria's job back. He asked if Jared wanted to go out for a beer and he suggested that Gloria seek therapy to help her deal with the pregnancy. He hinted that she might have to participate in therapy through the Employee Assistance Program in order to get her job back. Jared agreed that therapy might be a good idea for Gloria. It might help her deal with her guilt about cheating and then, hopefully, she would give up the crazy story about past lives and carrying some baby that was conceived in her dreams. Whether they would end up staying together would probably depend on how successful the therapist was at getting to the root of Gloria's issues.

How could she cheat on him? They had a good relationship. Maybe he was gone a lot for work but he stayed in close touch and when he was home they had plenty of sex to make up for the absences. It really didn't make sense that she would seek out another man's affections. But it made even less sense that she was pregnant without having sex. Jared took out his cell phone and opened the calendar app. He was meticulous about keeping track of his schedule. He looked back over the last few months, comparing when he was out of town with when Gloria must have conceived. There was no way the baby could be his, unless...

Jared hurried home. He couldn't wait to talk to Gloria. The doctor had surely made a mistake. He had confused Melanie's ultrasound with Gloria's. Melanie had kept her maiden name. They went to the same doctor. This was the answer. Gloria's baby was not really conceived while he was gone. They could go to the doctor and get this straightened out. Jared's excitement was mixed with guilt. Poor Gloria! What she must be going through. No wonder she believes that crazy story. How could I have been so mean to her? How could I call her a whore? I'm going to make this up to her.

Jared arrived home with a bouquet of flowers in one hand and a Starbucks coffee in the other. He found her sitting on the couch with her laptop. She was on a website that listed all the wars during the last 500 years. Jared sat down beside her, placed the Starbucks on the coffee table, thrust the flowers towards her and kissed her. Gloria kissed him back even though she didn't know what to make of this obvious apology. When she began to pull back from the kiss Jared took her face in his hands and said, "God I have missed you. You don't know how much I missed my little glow worm."

"Little glow worm? You haven't called me that in years."

"I know. But you are my little glow worm. Always have been. I'm so sorry I didn't believe you."

"I am too," she said. "What made you change your mind all of a sudden? Did you have a dream about Earth Girl too?"

"That's not the part I believe," he replied. "But I do believe that you didn't have sex with another man. The baby is mine. I think the doctor got you so confused with his wrong dates that your mind started playing tricks on you and your subconscious came up with the crazy story."

There was a hint of desperation in Jared's voice and it made Gloria apprehensive. She was glad he wasn't mad anymore but she didn't know what he was talking about and she didn't like the way he sounded.

"What are you talking about? Did you talk to the doctor? Did he say he made a mistake?"

"No, I didn't need to talk to him. I figured it out myself," Jared said. "He switched Melanie's results with yours. You're not really that far along. You have one of those 'change of life' pregnancies. That's all, Glo. Just a baby we weren't planning on."

Gloria sat silently.

"We're okay again, right?" Jared said. "We're good now. We didn't want a baby but we'll work it out. It will be good, really good. "

He sounded like the motivational speakers Gloria had heard at sales meetings. She didn't know what to say. What in the world is he talking about?

"Jare, honey, I don't think I understand what you mean."

"I mean I love you, Glo, and I know we can work this whole mess out with a few sessions of counseling."

Gloria was now convinced that Jared was truly desperate. He didn't even believe in counseling. He had actually made fun of friends of theirs who had gone to therapy. His eagerness for counseling pointed to how worried he was. Of course Gloria didn't know that Joe had said it might be a condition of getting her job back. To Gloria it seemed that Jared was counting on counseling to work everything out and, although she didn't believe it could, she decided to go along with it. Let the therapist handle it. *The best thing is to get an appointment soon while he is still in this frame of mind.* She caressed Jared's hand while sipping her caramel macchiato.

The first therapy session would have been a disaster except that Jared had called the therapist before the appointment and explained the entire situation, including his theory about the doctor's mistake and Gloria's fantasy about a past life. The therapist was uncomfortable about having a private conversation with one member of the couple without the knowledge of the other. She called Gloria and told her that she had spoken briefly to Jared about his concerns and wondered if she had anything she wanted to share prior to their first session together. Gloria told her that she thought it was important for the therapist to be prepared when Jared realized that the baby had been conceived by Earth Girl and could not possibly be his.

Both Gloria and Jared left the first therapy session, and every one thereafter, feeling things would be okay. Jared believed that the therapist knew that Gloria had experienced a psychotic break and that whatever she said in the sessions was based on her expertise in handling such breaks. Gloria believed that the therapist knew Jared was grasping at straws because he couldn't bear that the child wasn't his. Whenever the therapist tried to encourage Gloria to examine her dreams about Earth Girl, Gloria was sure that she was doing so to help Jared deal with the situation. Neither of them discussed the therapy sessions with each other, treating them as something totally apart from the rest of their life together. Slowly things returned to normal between them. Gloria knew this couldn't last but she had considered all the options and decided that getting through as much of the pregnancy as possible without more drama would be best for everyone, including Melanie. Earlier that week Melanie told her she had developed gestational diabetes and hypertension.

It was only after Gloria had a new dream...one in which Earth Girl died during childbirth...that Gloria abandoned the façade that everything was okay. She was terrified by this dream. She was pretty sure it meant she was going to die too. She shared this with Jared and the therapist at the same time. Jared hugged her and told her it was all part of the breakdown she had undergone. The therapist told her that Earth Girl's death might be a good sign. It might be her subconscious way of letting go of the fantasy. When they left the therapist that night, Jared felt good. He agreed with the therapist's interpretation and felt that Gloria's illness would soon be cured. Gloria, on the other hand, felt that her life would soon be over. She now approached each nap and night hoping to dream about Earth Girl. She needed a clue to help her understand this whole crazy situation and she really needed to find out that she was not going to die giving birth to Earth Girl's baby. Unfortunately for Gloria's state of mind the dreams of Earth Girl stopped.

During the last few weeks of her pregnancy, Jared was supportive and tender. He was still convinced that the baby was his and that the doctor was wrong about the dates. Gloria told the doctor that they did not want to know the sex of the baby and that they did not want any tests. "We will deal with whatever God gives us," was her mantra every time the obstetrician tried to convince her to have another ultrasound. It became clear during their therapy sessions that the less Jared knew the better. As for herself, if she really needed to know anything else Earth Girl would tell her in a dream.

Melanie's baby was born 6 weeks before Gloria's due date.

This came as a bit of a shock to Jared, but he didn't let it change his theory. *Babies come whenever they come and this one came early.* Thank God, he was healthy. That was all that mattered. Melanie and Roger decided to name him Roger Jared.

Gloria and Jared "ooohed" and "aaahed" over little RJ. Gloria did her best not to draw any attention to her own pregnancy. Melanie and her baby deserved to have the spotlight. Melanie seemed so happy. Gloria wanted nothing more than to be a loving grandmother. Gloria noticed, but never mentioned, that whenever she held RJ her own baby would begin to kick. Some things were better left unsaid.

As Gloria's due date drew near, she became more and more afraid. What if she died in childbirth? What if Jared finally looked at a calendar and counted backwards. She wasn't sure which would be worse. Her ankles were swollen all the time now and her blood pressure became dangerously high. She was restricted to bed for the last two weeks of her pregnancy.

Melanie found this annoying. She had hoped that Gloria and Jared would be able to babysit a few times before their baby was born. Instead, Melanie was cooking extra-large meals and delivering half to her parents each afternoon. Seeing her father massage her mother's feet while she was propped up in bed with her legs elevated and her stomach bulging upset Melanie. She didn't know how to identify what she was feeling but it was something akin to jealousy. Wasn't she the one who should be getting special treatment? She had just given birth a month ago, and already the attention was on her mother and her poorly timed pregnancy.

Before going to sleep each night Gloria said to Jared, "In case I don't make it, remember what your mother said, love lives on."

Jared repeatedly told her to stop being maudlin and to forget about her crazy Earth Girl dying dream. "You're not going to die. That was just your subconscious way of getting rid of Earth Girl so you could get well. It's a good thing you had that dream. Stop worrying. Modern medicine doesn't let mothers die in child-birth."

Three days before her due date, Gloria woke up with a terrible pain in her abdomen. Maybe it was the beginning of labor, but it didn't seem like a contraction. She got up to go to the toilet. Her feet were severely swollen and her back ached more than usual. Her head began to pound and her abdomen seemed to harden. As she noticed the blood dribbling down her leg, she called out for Jared.

The paramedic who arrived with the ambulance was sure that Gloria had preeclampsia and he suspected placenta abruption. Jared didn't know what any of this meant, but he knew that Gloria was losing blood fast. His face turned pale as he remembered that Gloria was sure she was going to die during the birth. "Damn you, Earth Girl, leave my wife alone," he muttered to himself. He speed-dialed Melanie as the EMTs put Gloria in the ambulance.

By the time Jared arrived at the hospital, Gloria had already been rushed to an operating room. Her blood pressure had gone dangerously high. An immediate caesarean section was the only way to save her life. When he asked to see her before the surgery, the nurse told him that she was already unconscious. Jared was a complete wreck. He called Melanie and Joe. Melanie and Roger arrived in a matter of minutes. Joe and Sheila were close behind them with baby RJ. Melanie had broken down in the parking lot and Sheila had taken the baby while Roger and Joe tried to comfort her. The five adults and little RJ began a vigil in the waiting room. The first report from the operating room was grim. Gloria had lost a dangerous amount of blood very rapidly and they had begun transfusing her, even before delivering the baby.

Jared took the news very poorly. He said to no one in particular, "I don't even care if the baby lives." He grabbed Joe, and asked him to find a nurse who could get a message to the doctor.

"Tell the doctor to do whatever they have to save Gloria, regardless of what that does to the baby. I can't lose Glo. I just can't."

The next report from the operating room was that the baby had been safely delivered. The nurse told Jared that it was a girl and that it was being brought to the neonatal intensive care unit as a precaution.

"I don't care about that. How is Gloria? How is my wife?" Jared demanded.

"We're not sure yet exactly how much blood she lost. We're still working on her."

Jared's knees went weak and he slumped down into a chair. Melanie stood behind him with her arms around his shoulders. "Don't let her die. Don't let her die," Jared repeated as he wept. Melanie said nothing, but her cheeks were covered with tears. Roger, Sheila and Joe tried their best to stay optimistic. In a few minutes, Jared stood up and headed for the exit.

"I can't stay here right now. I'll be back after I get my head together."

In the operating room, Gloria was barely clinging to life. She had lost more than half her body's supply of blood. She was completely unconscious.

Gloria, don't be afraid. It's me. You remember me, don't you, Gloria? Don't be afraid. You don't have to die. You gave life to my baby. That's what I needed you to do. You don't have to die just because I did. Gloria, my baby needs you to take care of her. She needs you to love her because I couldn't. Don't die, Gloria. Don't give up. I need you to stay alive for her. I want her to see the ocean and the trees and the earth before it starts to die. You must take care of her and listen to her. Gloria, please, please listen to her. I am sending her with a message for you.

Gloria opened her eyes for an instant. She saw a bright light aimed down on her. She wasn't sure where she was. She closed her eyes and fell back to sleep, but her pulse returned to normal. A nurse left the OR to tell the family that Gloria had stabilized.

Joe rushed to find Jared.

"Jared, they stopped the bleeding. A nurse just came out and told us that she is going to make it. She opened her eyes for a minute and she was responsive. They're pretty sure she is going to be okay."

"Thank God. Thank God," Jared sobbed as he fell into Joe's arms.

"It's okay, bro, it's going to be okay now," Joe whispered.

"I love you, man. You know that, right?" asked Jared. Somehow, in the midst of all this fear and then relief, it was important to Jared that Joe knew he loved him.

"Never doubted it, bro. Never."

CHAPTER 12

The news from the neonatal intensive care unit was not good. Jared was told that the baby appeared healthy and strong but she had a scar that resembled a puncture wound on her skull. She had not yet opened her eyes on her own. When the doctors opened them to examine her, the eyes appeared to lack pupils. The pediatric ophthalmologist had been called in for a consultation. She would contact Gloria and Jared as soon as she completed the examination.

Jared hoped that this news would not set back Gloria's recovery. She was still extremely weak and in pain from the caesarean. The last thing she needed was bad news, especially news that would be even worse to her because she was sure to blame it on her attempt to abort. Jared knew Gloria well enough to know that she would surely blame herself for anything that was wrong with this baby.

When the ophthalmologist met with Gloria and Jared she said that she was somewhat baffled by their daughter's condition. She had never encountered a baby born without pupils but she had read about them in research. The more puzzling thing about their daughter's eyes was their golden color and ball-like appearance. She took out a note pad and drew a quick sketch that contrasted the appearance of a normal eye with their baby's eyes.

"A normal eye," she explained as she drew, "has three main parts that you can see when you look at it without instruments. There is the sclera which a lot of people call the white of the eye. It surrounds the colored part which is called the iris. The iris surrounds the pupil. It appears that you daughter's sclera is deep blue in color, and her iris is golden. Her iris actually looks somewhat like a golden ball floating in the sclera. Very unusual. I have never seen or read about eyes with this appearance. Most importantly, however, it seems that she has no pupils. Most likely, she is blind."

"You said 'most likely.' Does that mean she might be able to see?" asked Jared, while squeezing Gloria's hand.

"It means I have only done a preliminary examination. This is highly unusual and, perhaps, unheard of. It seems hard to believe that she could be born with a condition that has never occurred before but it is not out of the realm of possibility. It is also possible that the golden dome is not actually her iris. It might be some sort of tissue that has grown over the eye and is covering both the iris and the pupil. Determining if this is the case is the next step."

"What would cause something like that?" asked Gloria

"I am not prepared to even hazard a guess about that. Our first task is to determine if the gold dome is integral to her eye. I have consulted two other pediatric ophthalmologists and we think the best approach is to wait four to six weeks and see if the eye sheds this gold covering naturally. We may even see a pupil come to the surface and push its way out. We really don't know. Our approach is to wait and watch. My best advice to you is to prepare to raise a blind child. Find out all you can about early intervention for blind children. They really can live perfectly normal lives with the appropriate intervention at a young age."

Gloria and Jared looked at each with dazed expressions. Although they had each privately worried about the health of this baby during the pregnancy, they had not spoken openly with each other. Jared did not really think the attempted abortion could cause a deformity, but he was fearful that Gloria's age could. Although it was more common now for women to conceive in their 40s, he knew that being pregnant at 46 increased the risks for both mother and baby.

Gloria had worried throughout the pregnancy both about her age and the impact of her attempts to abort. She was sure the scar on the baby's skull was from the knitting needle, but she secretly thought the eyes were some sort of a sign from Earth Girl. She knew that if she mentioned this to Jared, he would think she was relapsing into mental illness. So she kept quiet about it. Jared interpreted her silence as grief.

Neither Gloria, nor Jared, even saw the baby's eyes until she was nine days old. She never opened them on her own, and the doctors had decided it was best to let her keep them closed since they did not know if they had any protection from the bright lights in the nursery. During those nine days, Jared and Gloria spent hours worrying about their new little girl. Although most of their private thoughts were focused on the condition of her eyes most of their conversations were focused on her name.

They had a backlog of names left over from Gloria's pregnancy with Melanie. Because they each had favorite names that the other disliked, they had ended up with Melanie. It was not a favorite of either, but a name they both liked. When Melanie was born they both thought the name suited her perfectly.

During the nine days of this baby's life, Jared had been slow to bond with her. It was not until her one week "birthday" when she tightened her tiny fist around his baby finger and pulled it toward her mouth to suck on it that Jared felt a surge of love for her. At that moment he knew he wanted to name her Ella or Emma. They were his favorite names from 20 years ago.

Gloria had been looking at baby names on the internet trying to find a name that would suit the unique circumstances of this baby's conception. She had hoped to find a name that held some sort of significance, feeling that Earth Girl somehow expected this of her. She looked up names that meant "earth" and added Iris, Maia, and Tierra to her list. Of these, Maia was her favorite. She thought perhaps dream or vision should be the meaning of her name so she added Aislyn to her list. Then there was Nadia for hope and, of course, Grace. When they talked about names Gloria did not tell Jared the significance of the new names she had added to her list. She just suggested them as names she had heard of and liked.

Keeping the focus on her name, rather than her condition, had been calming to both Jared and Gloria. Without admitting it to each other they were stalling. Neither one wanted to talk about this little baby's health and future. So the list of names grew longer and longer as each day passed. Shiloh, Amanda, Hannah, Angelina, Jacqueline, Michelle and Opal were just a few names to be thoroughly studied and deemed acceptable. The discussion of each name included the derivation of the name and how it had been used in literature, including positive and negative connotations each name had developed over the years. Had any other couple been choosing a name this way both Jared and Gloria would have thought they were hopelessly compulsive. But this obsession with finding the right name provided a respite from thinking about things that were so much harder to think about...blindness, mental capacity and always, lurking deeply in the closed-off recesses of Jared's psyche, paternity.

While Jared had initially found it hard to love her, Gloria was already madly in love with – albeit bewildered by – this little girl. She was much more successful nursing her than she had been with Melanie. Each time Gloria brought the infant's tiny mouth to her breast she felt a surge of protectiveness towards her. Still she did not really feel as if this baby was truly her biological daughter. She believed that Earth Girl had conceived this child and somehow chose Gloria to raise her. Gloria rejected her therapist's warning that spending mental and emotional energy on these dreams, no matter how real they seemed, would endanger her connection to reality. She should not try to figure out when and where Earth Girl had lived and, certainly she should not indulge in the fantasy that Earth Girl was Gloria in a past life.

Ever since their therapy Jared seemed to accept the baby and treated Gloria with love and tenderness. She knew how upset he had been when she almost died and she did not want to cause him any more pain or worry. So she did not tell him that she continued to believe with all her heart that this baby was really Earth Girl's child. There was no reason to mention Earth Girl at all until Gloria saw the baby open her eyes. It happened while Gloria was nursing her. The baby opened her eyes wide and appeared to stare right into Gloria's eyes, or at least, that was how it *felt* to Gloria. What she actually saw as she looked into her baby's eyes were two golden orbs that looked as if they were floating in blue water. There was no way to tell if these eyes could see or not but Gloria felt they were looking directly into her eyes.

Gloria had screamed slightly when she first saw the baby's eyes. Jared was dozing in a chair next to her and he woke with a startle. "What's wrong?" he asked as he rose from the chair and went over to Gloria's bed.

"Look at her eyes. They're open!"

"Ohmigod! They're so...well, they're scary, or disconcerting, or something. They don't look like eyes really."

"I know. I thought they were sort of scary when she first opened her eyes, but look at them. I think she can see. I think she is looking at me."

"Oh, babe, I don't know. I don't think those eyes can see anything. How could they? They are more like gold balls than eyes. Poor little thing," Jared said, as he stifled the urge to cry. "I feel so sorry for her."

"Her eyes remind me of something, Jared, but I don't know if I should tell you."

"Why not? If this is some condition you have ever heard of, it would be good to know what it is."

In the back of his mind, Jared wondered if this could be the consequence of some sort of sexually transmitted disease, but he pushed the thought down and said nothing. Gloria continued to look straight into the baby's unblinking eyes. She wanted to tell Jared that they reminded her of something from her Earth Girl dreams but she was afraid of his reaction. She needed to think about it before she said anything. If only he could see what she had seen in her dream...two golden orbs of light dropping into the blue water...then he would have to believe her. Instead she told him that the eyes didn't remind her of a medical condition. She said they reminded her of a painting.

"Oh, that's nice. But it won't help her see," he said somewhat bitterly. "I wish she would close her eyes again. It's creeping me out to look at them, but I can't take my eyes off them."

"I know what you mean, Jare, except that the more I look at them, the more I think they are beautiful."

"That's not happening for me yet. We better call the ophthalmologist and tell her that she opened her eyes on her own."

"You call her, Jare, I don't feel like talking to her. I just want to sleep. I guess I'm still pretty weak."

Jared went to the nurses' station to make the call. Gloria felt as if she was being dragged into unconsciousness. She couldn't keep her eyes open any longer. She was asleep before Jared even dialed the phone. She awoke only when the doctor arrived. She didn't know if she had been dreaming, but she remembered that Earth Girl had spoken of a girl with golden eyes. Gloria felt more confused than ever. She wanted to go back to sleep and to wake up at home realizing that the last nine months had been nothing more than a crazy dream.

"Frankly, I have no idea what has happened to your daughter's eyes. I have been contacting doctors and doing research and no one has ever heard of a condition such as this. It is not described in any of the medical literature," the ophthalmologist said while shaking her head. "It is a total mystery to me and everyone with whom I have consulted."

The hospital's two resident newborn pediatricians stood looking at the baby and then at each other.

"What is the next step," Jared asked

"I'm not sure. I think watching and waiting is still the best bet.

But it is encouraging that she opens her eyes and that she does not show signs of pain from being exposed to light. As far as the three of us are concerned," she said as she nodded towards the other two doctors, "she can be released from the hospital as soon as her mother is able to go home."

"That's great news," Jared said unconvincingly. "It will be good to get home and back to a normal family life."

He gently touched the baby's head. Gloria took his hand and smiled.

"We'll take good care of her no matter what is wrong with her eyes. I know she'll be just fine."

"Good, good. That is certainly the best attitude to have in a situation like this," said the younger of the two pediatricians. "Sometimes nature just takes care of things. Let's give it time to do its magic."

The use of the word magic annoyed Jared, but he said nothing. *Our lives are about to change drastically and there is nothing magical about it.*

"I do have a piece of advice for you. Name that poor little thing today. She's been too long without a name. Give her a name, take her home and get used to her," said the older pediatrician with a tone that could be interpreted as condescension or pity.

The three doctors then walked out of the room and, as it turned out, out of the baby's life for good. As soon as the door shut, Jared blew up.

"Who does that asshole think he is? Telling us we need to name her. And that other one, spouting off about letting nature work its magic. I wanted to work some magic on her. I can't wait to get out of this frigging place! They don't have a clue."

"No," replied Gloria, "they don't seem to have a clue. But he was right. It's time to give her a name."

And so Ella Amanda was given her name when she was nine days old. She went home when she was ten days old.

CHAPTER 13

By the time she was a year old Gloria and Jared had stopped waiting for the Ella's eyes to change. They had gotten used to their daughter's appearance and actually had come to regard her eyes as beautiful. They were not sure how well she could see, but they were sure she was not totally blind. She seemed to be developing normally and they eagerly awaited each of her milestones...first steps, first words, even feeding herself and potty training. If her vision was less than perfect, there was no indication that it was hindering her in any way. Despite the mysterious circumstances of her conception both Gloria and Jared had grown to love her every bit as much as they had loved Melanie.

It was not until her fifth birthday that they began to think she might be quite different from other children. They had celebrated RJ's birthday with a big party, just a month before. Ella had been excited by the festivities and eager for her own birthday party. This was to be expected but her response whenever her parents asked her what she wanted for her birthday struck them as unusual. Ella wanted nothing more than for them to plant a garden.

"But Ella, sweetie, your birthday is in autumn. Spring is six months away. That's a long time for a little girl to wait for a birthday present," Jared said as he sat Ella on his lap to comb her hair.

"I want a garden with flowers that I can smell and touch and with food for eating. I want a garden. A garden, a garden. I want a garden."

Gloria and Jared decided to buy Ella a toy garden for her birthday. On the day of her party, Ella opened each gift carefully. She watched the faces of the children at the party and if she noticed that someone looked like they wanted to play with her new toy she walked over to that child and said, "You can have it."

Finally she came to her parents' gift. It was in a big box. RJ couldn't wait to see what it was. He knew that he would probably get to play with it a lot because Gloria babysat for him frequently. As Ella pulled the paper off, she kept saying, "Please be a garden, please be a garden." When she saw that it was a garden made of plastic she threw herself on the floor, buried her head under her hands and began to wail.

"Sweetheart, what's wrong?" Gloria asked. "You said you wanted a garden and you know we can't plant a real one until the spring, so we got you a pretend one to play with."

"It doesn't feel like a garden. It doesn't smell like a garden. I can't sip tea made from the leaves or plant seeds. I only want a real garden. How can we feed hungry people with a pretend garden?"

"This is your fault, Glo, letting her watch those TV shows about Saving the Children or whatever they are called. She's so worried about starving children that she thinks she has to grow food for them. You gotta stop letting her watch that stuff."

Jared picked up Ella and gave her a hug.

"It's all right, my little sweetpea, we won't let any children starve. Now let's have some birthday cake because I'm starving right now."

That night after Ella was in bed, Jared and Gloria discussed Ella's reaction to her gifts. They were troubled by her reaction to the toy garden. They wondered how Ella had developed so much compassion for starving people at such a young age. They were truly baffled by the way she spoke about the garden.

"She didn't sound like herself," Jared noted, "more like an adult with a little kid voice. Where did she get the idea about tea leaves? What was that all about?"

"I don't know. It surprised me too," answered Gloria. "Maybe she got it from television. Sometimes the things she comes up with sound a lot older than she really is. We worried about her so much when she was an infant, but she is actually precocious."

"I'm not sure about that," Jared mused. "There's something else I noticed that has me worried. She didn't recognize her own reflection in a mirror today. She should definitely be able to do that by now."

He had already observed that she didn't seem to recognize herself in pictures. Even though she seemed to be able to see well, she did not have any idea what she, herself, looked like. Wasn't this odd for a child her age?

Gloria agreed that it was very unusual. When she thought back to Melanie at the same age, she remembered how she liked to stand in front of the mirror dancing or making faces. Gloria hadn't noticed it until Jared brought it up, but Ella seemed to have no interest in seeing herself.

"Could it be that she was self-conscious about her strange eyes and doesn't want to look at her own face," wondered Gloria.

"That would be so sad," Jared said, with just the tiniest hint of anger in his voice.

As Gloria fell asleep that night, she found herself unable to stop thinking about Earth Girl and the woman with the golden eyes. *How old will Ella be when I can finally tell her about her real mother? Jared will be furious if I tell his beloved Ella Amanda about Earth Girl.*

For the next two weeks, she was unable to get a good night's sleep. She tossed and turned for hours and when she managed to fall asleep it was a fitful, restless sleep. She didn't dream, or at least, she didn't remember dreaming. Finally after too many nights without sleep she took a sleeping pill and fell into a deep sleep.

CHAPTER 14

I know you are worried about Orelia. That's what I told them to name her just before I died...because her eyes are made of golden light. Don't fear her difference. It is why she had to survive. It is why you had to give birth to her. She will begin to know who she is when the time is right. She will begin to have dreams about the golden eyes.

In your dreams I only told you part of my story. You think all of me died when I was trying to bring life to Orelia. But it was only Earth Girl, the little girl who was the vessel, who died. I am so much more than that little girl. My life began before hers and it continues beyond it. It is hard for you to understand because you live in the illusion of chronological time. I live in the reality of eternity.

When I was in my celestial life I wanted to come back to earth, to live on the earth that I had grown to love in a different lifetime. But I wasn't careful about when I came back and I ended up in a terrible time, a time of famine caused by unending wars and waste. I was born as a girl and I lived in the body of Earth Girl until she died giving birth. She was not ready to die. She wanted to live to take care of her daughter. She wanted to live to see oceans and beautiful gardens and majestic mountains. She wanted to live to see peace among people. She wanted more than the life she was born into could give her. She saw suffering and brutality and, at the end, kindness too.

But she could not survive. Her body was not strong enough. That is why you had to bear her baby. You have wondered if you are Earth Girl because you had her baby. I can only tell you that you chose to have her baby in this place and time. Earth Girl knew that her baby had to live; that earthly life can be good if only people understand. You will know this too someday.

I know you don't understand any of this right now. I just want to tell you not to worry. I first appeared to you as Earth Girl and you began to wonder if Earth Girl is you from another life. Now you wonder if Orelia is the girl with the golden eyes that Earth Girl dreamed about. You cannot understand the answers. Not yet. You are not ready.

I will be back to help you. I may come in different bodies with different voices but I am always who I am. You will know when I come as Earth Girl because you will hear her voice telling the story of her life. When I come as who I am in eternity I will explain things to you but only as you are ready.

Today, right now, my lesson for you is that the life on earth can never be fully understood. Life and all it holds is too big for humans to understand. There is the possibility for more joy than they can ever comprehend and there is the same possibility of pain and suffering. Humans have embraced pain and sorrow much more fully than they have embraced joy. This is why the world suffers. The earth was a beautiful place to live when I first took a body. Remember the joy. Seek the light. Orelia will be your guide, just as you are her mother.

Chapter 15

When Gloria awoke she was covered with sweat. Her heart beat rapidly. She wanted to tell Jared about her dream, but she was afraid that he would be angry. She had the lonely feeling that something important, even precious, was being shared with her and she couldn't share it with anyone else. *Is this what if feels like to be crazy?* Was craziness really just understanding and experiencing the world in a different way from those around you? She wanted to give this idea more thought but Jared was standing over the bed looking at her sweat-soaked sheets.

"Wow, you're really having a hot flash this time."

"You're not kidding. I feel like I'm sitting in a sauna," Gloria lied. She knew it was her mind, not her body, that was making her sweat.

"I'm going to get these sheets in the laundry and get Ella ready for kindergarten. They're having mandatory vision screenings at her school today. I'm really nervous about it. We've been avoiding doctors for years. But, I don't know why I'm so nervous. I know she can see," she said.

"Me too. But we're with her all the time. Maybe we're missing something. No time to talk about it now. I have an important early meeting. I'll call you on my way home."

As Jared grabbed his wallet and keys and headed out the door, Gloria stripped the sheets off the bed and got Ella's breakfast, but her mind was on her dream. She looked at Ella as she dawdled with her breakfast. *Orelia. I wonder why that name never made it on our list. It's pretty.*

When Gloria picked Ella up from school, she found her sitting by herself crying. Her first thought was that some children had teased Ella about her eyes. This had happened before so Gloria was prepared to comfort her. She was surprised when Ella ran to her saying, "Mommy, Mommy, that man over there said I am blind. Why did he say that? I don't want to be blind."

"You're not blind, honey. He made a mistake, that's all," Gloria said as she picked Ella up and gave her a hug. "You can see everything you need to see, sweetpea."

"But why did he say I'm blind?"

Ella's teacher approached Gloria with a look of concern on her face.

"I tried to call you. She's been crying ever since her vision screening. I know she can see. She does just fine with everything here, but the screener said she is legally blind. He recommends that she see an eye doctor immediately."

"Of course he recommends an eye doctor. I would too if I saw a child with eyes like Ella's but Jared and I crossed this bridge a long time ago. They had no answers. So we stopped going. I assure you I will check this out. Meanwhile, please don't mention any of this to Ella or me again," said Gloria curtly.

"Of course, whatever you want. We are required by law to have the screenings and share the result with the parents. We aren't trying to cause any pain for you or Ella. Like I said, she does fine here. Her vision deficit doesn't seem to affect her in any way as a kindergartener. But a time will come..."

"Yes," replied Gloria hastily, "a time will come and we will be prepared. Ella, say goodbye to Ms. Merton. Let's go have some lunch!"

Ella kept her eyes closed in the car on the ride home. Gloria didn't ask her why, hoping that she would soon forget about her vision screening. But Gloria would not be able to forget it. Just the night before she had dreamt that Earth Girl told her that Orelia's eyes were made of golden light. The memory of that dream left Gloria feeling scared and confused. *What did Earth Girl mean when she said that Ella would be her guide someday?*

She wanted to talk to Ella about her dreams but she felt that Ella was way too young to understand anything about past lives and she knew that Jared would be furious if she told Ella anything about her dreams.

"Mom, how could I be blind? I don't even have to open my eyes to see. All the other kids have to have their eyes open to color. But I don't have to."

"Oh, Ella, of course you have to open your eyes to see. Everyone does. Don't be silly."

"No I don't."

Ella closed her eyes and walked into the kitchen. She took off her backpack and hung it on the peg next to the kitchen door. Then she took off her purple hoody and hung it on the peg too. She started to walk away from the door, but then turned around and said, "I forgot to show you what I did in school today. I made a mask out of paper all by myself." Ella reached into her backpack and took out a piece of orange construction paper. A cat's face was drawn on it with a little black nose, whiskers, cartoon-type cat lips and two eyes with very long eyelashes. A piece of elastic string was stapled clumsily to each side. Ella slipped the mask over her face, catching some of her curly hair in the string.

"Ouch! Mommy, my hair is tangling. It pulls."

"We'll have to cut holes in the eyes so you can see," Gloria said as she adjusted the mask.

She wondered to herself if this was true. Ella turned her face up towards Gloria's as if to look at her. Then she got down on all fours and started crawling.

"Meow, meow. Kitty wants some milk. Meow."

Gloria wondered if Ella's eyes were opened or closed behind the mask. After putting Ella down for her nap Gloria called Jared to recount the incident at kindergarten and Ella's belief that she could see without opening her eyes. They decided to watch her closely to see if they ever saw her doing things with her eyes closed. They also decided it might be time to find out more about Ella's condition, that is, if they could even find anyone who could diagnose it.

A visit to an ophthalmologic specialist resulted in a visit to a neurologist, a neuropsychologist and, eventually, an invitation to appear on *Oprah*. Ella was considered medically blind by everyone who examined her. Yet they all had to admit that she could see. Numerous examinations of her eyes failed to detect a pupil, a developed retina or a normal iris. Two of the many eye exams detected light projecting from her eyes but other repeat exams failed to produce this effect. The neurological exams showed that vision processing centers of her brain were fully developed.

Functional MRIs showed that Ella was able to activate these areas of the brain with her eyes opened or closed. When the centers were not activated she could not see, thus causing her to fail many of the traditional vision tests. Since she had no interest in letters on a chart or bouncing mechanical dogs she failed the tests. Because she had none of the eye structures necessary to produce vision she was considered blind. Yet, it became alarmingly clear to all who examined her that Ella could see when she wanted to see.

Ella's case became the cause celebre of the medical world. Here was a child who was born with eyes that could not see and yet she had vision. She even had the choice of when to use vision. If she wasn't interested or didn't feel like cooperating, the vision centers of the brain shut down completely. The most intriguing finding was that the gold domelike tissue that Ella had in the place of a normal eye could project light. Gloria and Jared were unaware of this ability until one of the tests triggered the response. Ella seemed oblivious to this ability. Her neurologist suspected that she could not activate this response at will. Since Ella seldom chose to cooperate with the researchers' testing, very few people actually witnessed this effect in person, but word of it spread quickly among the doctors studying her case.

Within a month, Ella was examined by leading ophthalmologic and neurological doctors from around the world. None of them had ever encountered a case even remotely similar to hers.

Articles about Ella's condition appeared in numerous medical journals, and despite her parents' request for anonymity, her name was becoming well known in the medical world. One of Oprah's producers read about Ella in a medical journal. She felt certain this would be a story that would captivate Oprah's audience and perhaps even bring about a cure for blindness. At first Gloria and Jared were reluctant to have Ella appear on the show. But after a tabloid published a story calling her "half human, half alien" her parents decided appearing on *Oprah* would be a way to squelch any more tabloid speculations about their child.

CHAPTER 16

The *Oprah Show* was having them flown to Chicago from Providence. As they drove to the TF Greene Airport an amber sun was just beginning to rise. Ella was sound asleep in the back seat. To Jared she looked angelic and, he had to admit to himself, so normal. It was true, Jared thought, that Ella never really looked normal when she was awake. Due to all the recent scrutiny he had come to realize that over the years he had gotten used to Ella's appearance but that she was truly unusual-looking if you had never seen her before. He hated to think about it, but her behavior was becoming rather odd also. He considered the possibility that her behavior was being affected by all the visits to specialists and attention from the media, but when he thought about it he traced it back to her fifth birthday. Ever since that day she had been acting rather strange.

Gloria was lost in her own private world of contemplation. Should she tell Jared about Orelia and the woman with the golden eyes before they go on *Oprah*? What if Oprah started asking probing questions about the pregnancy and Ella's birth? She had been asked the same questions by numerous doctors. She never revealed her dreams of Earth Girl or the fact that she was sure she had never actually conceived Ella but she did tell them about the attempted abortion and all the complications at the time of the birth. She worried that Oprah would be able to get answers from her that the she had kept from the doctors.

Her greatest fear was that Oprah had found another child like Ella and was going to arrange a surprise meeting of the two families. In some ways finding out there was another child like Ella would be a relief, but if that child had also been conceived in a dream and the parents spoke about it, Gloria would feel trapped into telling Ella's true story. She wanted to discuss this with Jared in order to prepare him. Plus, after years of waiting and wondering what would happen next she really wanted Jared to know the truth. If only he could be open to it.

By the time they reached the airport, Gloria had worked herself into a major migraine. This had happened to her before and she knew she was too sick to fly. Jared was hesitant to leave her at the airport but he was desperately hoping that the appearance on *Oprah* might lead to some answers from the medical community. During the last few weeks he had gradually abandoned the idea that Ella could be raised just like any other child. Now that he had turned that corner he was eager to have scientific answers about her condition and how to cure it.

After searching the airport shops for pain medication Jared returned to Gloria with a small packet of aspirin and a bottle of water. She emptied the packet into her mouth, gulped down the water and closed her eyes. After a few minutes she kissed Ella and Jared goodbye and headed for the airport parking lot. Before she even reached the car she knew she would not be able drive all the way home.

After they boarded the plane, Ella looked at Gloria's empty seat beside her and said, "Daddy, are you taking me to see my real mommy?"

Jared was flabbergasted.

"Your real mommy?? What are you talking about? You only have one mommy. She doesn't feel good so she isn't coming on the trip. You know that."

"I know, Daddy, but I mean the other mommy. The one who looks like me."

Jared felt a mixture of relief and dread. Relief because Ella had probably made up the idea of a mommy who looked like her so that she felt better about herself, and dread because he had never forgotten that Gloria had insisted Ella was conceived by someone else from a past life. He felt a shiver go up his spine.

"Ella Amanda, I have to tell you something. I want you to listen carefully to Daddy. When we are on the television show I do not want you to tell people you think you have another mother. That would hurt Mommy's feelings. You don't want to do that, do you.?"

"No, Daddy. I love Mommy. When are we going to go up in the air?"

"Very soon, sweetpea. In just a minute or two."

Ella looked out the window with great interest as the plane rose.

"It looks pretty down there, Daddy."

"Yes, it does, sweetie."

In a matter of minutes the plane had stopped ascending and had leveled off. Jared looked at Ella as she peered at the window. He leaned closer to see what was creating the light glare on the window. To his great surprise he saw that Ella's eyes were radiating a bright light. A moment later, she began to convulse and he realized she was having a seizure.

"Help, get me help, my daughter's having convulsions. Help, please, help!"

* * *

Afraid to set out onto the highway, Gloria rented a room in the airport hotel. She knew that she needed a dark room, total quiet and probably a toilet in which to vomit. That's the way her migraines usually went. As soon as she got to her room she plodded down the hall to the ice machine and filled the ice bucket. Back in her room she fashioned a makeshift ice pack from the towels in the bathroom. Then she covered her head and the ice pack with her pillow and found the blessed relief of sleep.

It is beginning. The time is coming for Orelia to find the message. When she understands it she will bring it to you. You must be willing to let her hear the message. Remember to let her guide you. You are the mother and must provide for her needs but she is the guide and you must listen to her.

When Gloria woke up she didn't know where she was or why

her head was wet. When she reached up and felt a few pieces of still melting ice she remembered the migraine, the flight she had been unable to take and the *Oprah Show*. She wondered if she had missed the show. Luckily it was being recorded on the home television. She wondered briefly why the room didn't have a clock and then she remembered that she had unplugged it because she couldn't stand the light from the digital numbers. Still groggy, she sat up and reached for her cell phone.

* * *

Jared's plane had just made an emergency landing at Bradley Airport in Connecticut. Ella was taken by ambulance to Johnson Memorial Hospital. Her seizure had ended before the plane was able to land but Jared was relieved to be met by an ambulance. Jared noted with some dismay that the emergency-room doctors seemed to recognize Ella. They were almost agog with excitement because her eyes were still radiating a bright golden light.

Ella was pale but her vital signs were good. She was sleepy and she didn't speak. The staff neurologist suggested that she stay overnight for observation. Jared suspected they wanted to see how long her eyes continued to project light. He was pretty sure that within a few hours every neurologist and ophthalmologist affiliated with the hospital would have examined her. He was right. They suggested that she have a battery of tests but Jared declined, saying that he wanted to wait until they returned home the next day.

Ella was admitted to a private room in the pediatric ward. While a nurse settled Ella into her bed Jared fished for his cell phone so that he could call Gloria. She was alarmed by Jared's news. Ella had never had any health problems before. What could make her have a convulsion? Overcome with panic, she wanted to know every detail immediately, but Jared wanted to wait until they were together to discuss it. He decided he wouldn't even mention Ella's eyes to Gloria until he could tell her in person. He told Gloria he could not stay on the phone because he had to call Oprah's producer to explain that they would not be arriving in Chicago.

The producer was concerned about Ella's condition and also worried about its impact on the show. Within minutes he called Jared back and said that they had arranged for a network affiliate to send a crew with a camera and a monitor so that Ella and Oprah could see and talk to each other. It would be broadcast through a live feed to the TV audience. It wasn't as good as being there in person, but it would satisfy the audience's desire to see Ella. After Jared informed him that the convulsions had activated her light projection the producer hoped that her eyes would still be glowing when they got Ella on camera

When Jared called Gloria back she didn't answer so he left her and Melanie a text. *Watch Oprah. Broadcasting from hospital.*

Gloria decided to drive home so that she could watch with Melanie. She needed some company after the terrible migraine and the disturbing news about Ella. Plus, she wanted to be distracted from her latest dream. *It is time now.* What does that mean? After five years of a relatively normal life with Ella and Jared, Gloria was not ready to be pulled into some past-life cosmic drama, and she wasn't willing to let that happen to her little girl either. Deep inside, however, she knew that Ella was not hers alone. She began to fight that knowledge with every ounce of determination she possessed.

When Gloria arrived at the house, Melanie had mulled cider and plain biscotti for dipping. RJ was playing with his Legos on the floor near the sofa.

"Okay, here it comes. It's about to start."

"Is Ella really gonna be on television, Grandma?"

"Yes, she and Granddad. Isn't it exciting!"

"I want to be on television too, Mommy."

"I know you do RJ," Melanie tried to placate him, "but Ella's on television because of her eyes and you're luckier than she is. You don't have anything wrong with your eyes. Right, Mom? RJ is just as special as Ella without having those eyes."

"Yes, RJ is special and perfect. He's my perfect little grandbaby. Come give me some sugar, my little man."

RJ gave Gloria a quick kiss and then moved close to the television. Oprah appeared on the screen. She was explaining that Ella was in the hospital and they were going to broadcast from her room. Within seconds Jared's face appeared on the big screen behind Oprah. He looked nervous. Oprah greeted him and Ella warmly.

"Look at Ella. She looks funny!" exclaimed RJ.

"Hush RJ! That's not a nice thing to say."

"But he's right, Melanie. Look at her eyes. They look kind of weird, like they are sort of shining. It must be the lighting in the hospital room."

"Or maybe, Mom, they're doing *that thing* you told me about," Melanie said in a tone that meant *you know what I mean, but don't say it out loud.*

Melanie did not want RJ to know what she was talking about. She felt the less he knew about Ella's condition, the better. He was in the same class as Ella at school. She was his first and closest friend. To him she was normal except for her eyes. On the playground he was often her defender, more often than Gloria and Melanie even knew.

Oprah's face appeared again.

"Ella, I'm so sorry you weren't feeling well today. Promise me, you will come visit me on my show when you feel better."

"I promise," Ella smiled at Oprah. "I want to be on television."

"You're on television right now, darling. Just look up at your television screen. You'll see yourself."

Ella and the television audience saw Ella's upturned face

staring at the TV screen mounted above her

"Oh, is that me?" she said excitedly.

"Of course, that's you. That's what you look like on television," said Jared

Suddenly he felt very embarrassed by Ella's inability to recognize her own face. He had not even considered that she would see herself on the television screen during the interview. Oprah's face appeared again.

"Jared, can you tell us what happened today on the airplane?"

"Ella had a seizure. She has never had one before. We are still trying to figure out why. The doctors think it might have been a reaction to the altitude."

"I notice that Ella's eyes seem to be glowing. It has been reported in the media that she can make her eyes project light. Is that what I am seeing now?"

"Yes that's what you are seeing. We don't think it is voluntary," answered Jared in an uncomfortable voice.

Although he hoped this appearance would make people see that Ella was basically a normal little girl with an unusual medical condition he was beginning to worry that it was having the opposite effect. Ella's face was still projected on the large screen behind Oprah. As Oprah began to speak the large screen projected a split-screen image. Oprah on one side and Ella on the other. Ella started to pick her nose. Jared's hand appeared on the screen moving Ella's hand away from her face.

"Give her a Kleenex, Dad!" Melanie said into the television.

RJ was overcome with giggles and Gloria merely sighed.

"She's only five years old. Little kids do that all the time."

Her tone was more defensive than embarrassed. The split-screen view became a single screen showing Oprah.

"That's okay, baby. We all get a tickle in our noses sometimes. Ella, can you tell me how you feel right now? Do your eyes hurt or feel funny."

Back to Ella's face on the screen.

"My eyes feel like they are going to see so many sad things. My eyes are sad."

Back to split screen. Oprah looked visibly surprised. Ella closed her eyes. Oprah hesitated before speaking.

"Did you close your eyes just now so that you don't have to see sad things?"

"I can still see. I already told my mommy I don't have to open my eyes to see."

"That's something most of us can't do," said Oprah looking out to the audience. "This little girl may have something to teach us all about sight."

Cut to commercial. Jared seemed visibly relieved that there was a break in the show.

"Is that it?" he asked.

"No, we'll be back on in about 90 seconds."

"Oprah, I want to bring this to a close as soon as possible. I think Ella is getting tired."

Oprah told Jared she had an ophthalmologist and a neurologist from Johns Hopkins who were going to comment on Ella's case, and ask her some questions. Jared agreed, but he insisted that it not last more than five more minutes. When the station returned from the commercial break the two doctors were sitting on either side of Oprah. The large screen behind Oprah then projected Ella's image. She was twirling a piece of hair that hung over her left ear. Her eyes were still closed.

"Ella, can you open your eyes again for us?"

"Okay, Oprah."

"Thank you, honey. There are some doctors here who would like to ask you some questions. Is that okay?"

"Yes. I'm used to it."

"I'm sure you are, baby," Oprah said sympathetically.

"Ella, you said you could see with your eyes closed. Do things look any different than with your eyes open?" asked the ophthalmologist.

"Sometimes."

"When do things look different?" he prodded.

"When I'm really sad or really happy."

"Oh my. That's interesting. How do they look different."

"Just different. Like they look happy or sad."

The neurologist jumped in.

"I think many of us see things in a different way when we are depressed. Maybe that's what she means. Is that what you mean, Ella?"

"I don't know. What's depressed?"

"Depressed is when you feel very sad for a long time. Have you ever felt that way?"

"Yes."

"When?"

"Today."

"You are depressed today? How long have you felt this way?"

"I have been sad since I had to come to the hospital. It was scary."

"Oh, yes, of course. But that's not real depression."

"All of us feel scared when we have to go in an ambulance," Oprah added. "That's okay, baby. I understand that feeling."

"So, do things look sad to you right now?" asked the ophthalmologist.

"Yes."

"Describe what you see."

"I see sad people who don't have anything to eat and there aren't any flowers and there aren't any trees and everything is brown and grey and babies don't have mommies. I see the end of the world."

Ella began to cry and Jared said it was time for the interview to stop. Oprah was clearly shocked by Ella's answer. She looked directly at Ella.

"It's going to be all right, little angel. Everything is going to be all right. Thank you for talking to us."

"You're welcome."

"And thank you, Jared, for allowing us to spend time with your beautiful little girl. We'll be back in a moment and the studio audience will have a chance to ask the doctors questions."

Jared shut the television off quickly. He thanked the television crew for coming, then he pulled the curtain around Ella's bed. The television crew didn't waste any time packing up their gear. It was obvious that Jared wanted them to leave The way they looked at Ella was making him both angry and embarrassed. He needed to talk to Gloria.

Chapter 17

As Jared dialed Gloria's cell, reporters for numerous news magazines and tabloids were furiously dialing up their editors to tell them to save space for the story of little Ella the five-year-old who claimed to see the End of The World. Immediately after Jared shut off the television, both the ophthalmologist and the neurologist declared that Ella seemed to be suffering from some type of mental illness that was manifesting itself in the form of visions.

When Oprah asked them if they had any explanation for how Ella could see, the ophthalmologist said that he doubted that she could see. His hunch, based on what he had read about her and his brief interaction with her, was that she could not actually see at all. He hypothesized that she was highly intelligent and was able to function as a sighted person because she was so gifted at picking up other clues from her environment. He said he was eager to talk to her parents in detail about her infancy and early development.

The neurologist agreed that she was highly intelligent. Based on the fact that she had suffered a seizure he guessed that she might have been suffering from akinetic seizures throughout her childhood, and these seizures might be responsible for electrical impulses in her brain that caused her to see things such as the vision she described. These same impulses could account for her happy and sad feelings. He wished aloud that they had asked her what things looked like when she was happy. Both doctors were eager to spend more time with Ella and her parents.

A member of the studio audience challenged the doctors by asking them how they would prove she was not really seeing into the future. "Who were they," she asked, "to assume that science could solve all mysteries? Wasn't it possible that this little girl was really a prophet?" A few people in the audience began to clap after she spoke. A few others guffawed at the idea that Ella was a young prophet. Oprah ended the show by saying, "Surely, there is much more to learn about this beautiful little girl and maybe as we learn about her, we will discover there is much to learn from her."

Gloria and Melanie stared speechlessly at each other. RJ had stopped watching as soon as Ella's appearance was over. Melanie set him up in his room with favorite DVD and told him it was quiet time. When she came back to the living room Gloria was on the phone with Jared.

"How is she? Did she see all that?" she asked.

"All what? I turned off the television. I didn't think it was a good idea for her to hear the doctors," he said.

"Good thinking. The doctors do think she is blind but they also think she is mentally ill and some lady in the audience thinks she is a prophet."

"Terrific. Now every wacko on the planet will want to get to know her," said Jared. "I've got to get her out of this hospital before the media descends on us. I'm going to call Joe to see if he can meet us on the highway somewhere."

Ever since Ella's birth, Joe and Jared had been close. It felt good to both of them to have a close bond. Jared felt that he could count on Joe to help him out.

"Joe, did you see the show?" asked Jared.

"Yeah, I did. What was all that bullshit about mental illness?" Joe asked.

"I didn't see it. Gloria told me about it. I can't believe some idiot thinks she's a prophet. I think this was a huge mistake. Hey, do you think you could pick us up near here so I don't have to rent a car. I don't really want anyone to know where we are right now. I just want to get home."

"Sure, bro, it will take me a few hours but I'll be there."

An orderly wheeled Ella out to the taxi area of the hospital. Jared quickly put her in the cab and jumped in beside her.

"Take me to the first rest stop on the Interstate."

"Sure, mister."

Jared called Joe and described where the rest stop was. He said he would be waiting in the food court. He got himself a cup of coffee and a newspaper. Ella slept in the booth beside him. When she woke up he carried her to the Cinnabon counter. Ella loved the gooey cinnamon treats and Gloria never allowed her to have them.

A few minutes later, Gloria called. She sounded a little frantic. She had just received a call from the producers of the *Ellen Show*. She turned them down and asked for privacy. Both Jared and Gloria feared that the appearance on *Oprah* had been a mistake. They worried that things were about to spin out of control. While Gloria was talking to Jared, Melanie was mindlessly flipping through the channels with the remote.

"Oh my God, Mom, come quick! Oh no, no!"

Gloria ran back into the living room to ask what was wrong. Jared waited on the phone expecting to hear something else about Ella.

"Mom, look at this. There was a nuclear explosion somewhere in the Indian Ocean!"

Gloria felt her stomach do a flip. Had a nuclear war just begun? Concerns about Ella's fame disappeared from her mind. Gloria told Jared to get to a radio or TV as soon as possible. She told him the little bit that she knew and tearfully told him she loved him.

"Please, get home as soon as you can. I need you here!"

Jared hung up and looked around the food court. Everything looked so normal. *No one knows yet.* He began to dial Joe on his cell phone as he headed toward the TV that was suspended over the sitting area in a far corner of the rest stop. As he approached, a small crowd was gathering in front of the television. The president was speaking. He was apologizing to the international community. Now the image on the screen was divided between the president and the explosion in the ocean.

"We deeply regret the accidental explosion of a nuclear warhead in the Indian Ocean, near Comoros at 2:32 p.m., Eastern Standard Time. My office was notified of this accident at 2:36. Immediately we dispatched a team to assure that all possible remedies are being taken to prevent the spread of radioactive materials. A tsunami alert has been sent to Comoros and we assure you that those affected by the tsunami will have the full assistance of the United States government in the days and weeks following this tragic accident. The State Department is, as I speak to you, contacting the leaders of the Trilateral Nuclear Power Alliance to make recommendations about the most prudent course of action. As you know along with the security provided by a nuclear arsenal for our defense comes the risk of a nuclear accident. Be assured that we took every precaution to prevent such a tragic accident. I will be updating the news media and Congress on an hourly basis. May God Bless the United States of America and the residents of Comoros."

Ella stood beside Jared, looking at the TV screen. When the image of a large fireball burning in the ocean appeared on the TV screen Ella looked at the screen intently and then she began to cry.

"All the fish will die. Lots of animals too. The gardens won't grow and the people will starve."

Jared and the people around him looked at her in amazement. Ella's eyes were glowing intensely. They illuminated her tears before they fell from her eyes onto her cheeks. Jared picked Ella up and hugged her tightly.

"Ella, sweetie, don't cry. It's going to be all right. Everyone is going to be okay. Promise."

Ella leaned back so that she could see Jared's face. Her eyes were open wide.

"Daddy, don't you know? It's going to get worse before it gets better."

Jared thought the light in Ella's eyes flashed red for an instant.

Later he was sure he imagined it. As he tried to comfort his little girl Jared noticed a couple staring at them. "That's the little girl that was on *Oprah* this morning," he heard one of them say. "Remember, she said she saw the end of the world. Ohmigod! Do you think she saw this before it happened?"

Jared wanted to disappear. He wanted to get Ella away from everyone. He wanted to protect her. Most of all, he wanted to convince himself that Ella could not possibly have seen the end of the world. This was all just crazy coincidence and an overactive imagination. Sweat was pouring from Jared's face and his shirt was soaked. He had never felt this way before. His heart was beating rapidly and he kept repeating to himself, "Where is Joe? Why isn't he here yet?"

Gloria and Melanie were glued to the television. Most of the networks were devoting hours of coverage to the nuclear explosion and the subsequent tsunami. Images of destroyed villages and people fleeing the tidal wave were coming in from Comoros. The Red Cross and the US military had arrived. Anderson Cooper was being dispatched to the tent city already being set up by the Red Cross. CNN was already advertising the special coverage. In other cities on the coast that had not been directly hit by the tsunami, protests against the United States had already begun. Wolf Blitzer was calling it a public-relations nightmare for the current administration and the Trilateral Nuclear Alliance. It was an unfortunate twist of fate, he pointed out, that the tsunami had struck a predominately Muslim area. This would do nothing to diffuse the escalating tensions between Muslim countries and the U.S.

Gloria had almost forgotten about Ella's appearance on *Oprah*, but when Roger arrived home he took out his cell phone and showed Gloria a picture he had just taken on his way back. It was a picture of a man standing on the sidewalk in front of Touro Park holding a sloppily hand-lettered sign: 'The end of the world began today in the Indian Ocean. ELLA IS A PROPHET.'

"Oh, my lord! I know who that man is. He's that homeless guy. He hangs out near the tower in Touro Park. He always says hi to us."

"Do you think he knows that the girl he saw on *Oprah* is our Ella? Do you think he recognized her?" asked Melanie.

"Proabably. Sometimes when we go for walks we bring him coffee or soup. He is one of the only people who never looked at her oddly when he first saw her. I don't think he even noticed her eyes. Ella likes him. "

Gloria's thoughts turned to the conversation she had with him the day the gynecologist confirmed that she was pregnant. They had never spoken at any length since that day. She remembered that the first time he saw Ella in her stroller he had winked and said, "I got your back, Curly." Gloria did not share this story with Mel and Roger.

"He seems harmless, but I don't really want him drawing attention to Ella that way."

"I'm sure Dad doesn't either," said Melanie. "Roger, do you think you could ask him to stop holding the sign...tell him it's scaring Ella, or something like that."

"I'll tell him to take it down or I'll kick his butt. I doubt he is the type to reason with," Roger responded heatedly.

He slammed the door as he left the house. A few minutes later Jared and Joe arrived. They all exchanged hurried hugs. Joe wanted to get home to Sheila to watch the developing news with her. Melanie was secretly relieved that Gloria and Jared decided it was best to get Ella home to her own bed. She wanted to concentrate on the nuclear explosion, not Ella. Plus, she didn't really want her parents to hear Roger's ranting when he got home.

She was pretty sure he was going to say that Gloria could never babysit for RJ again. She had to agree that it was pretty foolhardy to let Ella make friends with a homeless man, even if he wasn't dangerous. She knew that Roger blamed Gloria's attempted abortion for everything that was wrong with Ella. He could not think of her eyes as anything but a deformity and he felt extra protective of her because of them. Melanie was pretty sure Roger wouldn't think twice about punching a homeless guy if he thought that he was endangering Ella in any way. She turned the news back on and waited nervously for Roger to return.

Jared and Gloria were nervous too. They could not wait to get safely inside their own home. Jared jumped out of the car and grabbed Ella in his arms. She was sleeping soundly. He carried her into her bedroom and placed her gently on the bed. Gloria, following closely behind him, kissed Ella's forehead, took off her shoes and sox and her favorite sweater. Ella rolled over and began to suck her thumb.

"I haven't seen her do that in awhile," Jared remarked.

"You haven't watched her sleep in awhile."

Gloria turned on the television to watch the coverage of the explosion and the rest of the world's reaction to it. Jared tried to concentrate on the news but he could not take him mind off of Ella. No matter how hard he tried to convince himself that it was nothing more than a coincidence, he was shaken by the fact that Ella's vision of the end of the world preceded an explosion of a nuclear warhead by less than an hour. He went back to Ella's room and looked in on her sleeping peacefully just like any other young child. Jared wanted to feel relief. Instead he felt as if his life would never be the same.

CHAPTER 18

Gloria sat staring at the television. Her mind was flitting back and forth between the explosion and Ella's appearance on *Oprah*. She wondered if Ella's vision about the end of the world was the message that the voice in her dream told her Ella would bring. *If only I could talk to Jared about this.*

As Jared sat down next to her, CNN was showing a protest in Pakistan. An angry mom was burning their president in effigy. They carried signs calling for the downfall of the U.S.

"Not more of this crap! Why don't they get it? We didn't do it on purpose. They know we're already sending help. What more do they want?" Jared asked angrily.

He switched the TV to the DVR setting and turned on the recording of *Oprah*. After seeing the whole show, he took Gloria's hand and said, "What is going on with her? Really, Glo, I didn't think I would ever ask you this again but I can't help it. Who is her father?"

Gloria looked as if she had been punched in the stomach. She felt like it too. She tried not to cry as she responded to his question.

"Jared, I don't know. I can't tell you anything different than I told you when I was pregnant. I don't know how I got pregnant. I don't know anything. I don't even think she is my daughter. I feel like she was just put inside me against my will. But now I love her, love her more than anything."

"Me too," Jared said sadly. "I'm sorry I asked. She's just so weird, so…"

Gloria looked at him directly.

"Jared, I love her, but to tell you the honest truth, I wish she had never been born. Ever since I got pregnant, I have been scared that something bad is going to happen."

Jared listened quietly. He didn't know what to say. Ever since the *Oprah Show*, he had been having the same feelings.

"I still believe she is from a past life and I know that no one else will ever believe that. I stopped talking about it because I know you wanted me to and I wanted things to be okay between us. So I went along with everything the therapist said, but I never stopped believing. And I..." she paused, "I still have dreams and messages..."

Jared interrupted before she could say more.

"I don't want to hear about dreams and messages. Please, Gloria, let's not go there again."

"But I want to tell you about them because you're my best friend in the whole world. It hurts so much that I can't talk to you about it because it makes you mad and it makes you think I cheated on you and I...I guess I wish I had died in childbirth."

Jared took Gloria in his arms and hugged her. He pushed her hair back from her face and kissed her wet cheek. Then he handed her a Kleenex and waited while she wiped her eyes and nose.

"Glo, don't cry. I'm sorry I said that. I don't know what I believe about Ella anymore. But I do believe that you have those dreams and I don't think you cheated on me anymore. I think you might have been raped and your subconscious created this whole dream thing as a defense mechanism. That actually makes sense to me but it doesn't explain her eyes and the weird things she has been saying lately."

Gloria looked at him with sorrowful, pleading eyes.

"Doesn't that prove it to you? She's not from us. She came from those dreams. It gives me chills and scares me when I think about it but I know it is true. My dreams are telling me that she has a message for us. Just think about it. Maybe her message is that the end of the world is coming."

Jared leaned over with his elbows firmly planted on his knees. He held his head in his hands. He sat silently rocking back and forth.

"No. This can't be real. It can't be. Our little girl was not born to be a prophet of doom. I know that for sure. I ended the interview on *Oprah* when she said that thing about the end of the world. She was literally creeping me out and I'm her father."

"I know. Me too. And Melanie too. I think she is afraid to let RJ play with her anymore."

Gloria began to sob. She stood up and walked toward the family portrait hanging on the wall. Jared and Gloria were seated on the sofa with Ella on Gloria's lap and RJ on Jared's lap. Roger and Melanie were standing behind them with their hands on Gloria's and Jared's shoulders. Everyone was smiling, even Ella. She looked perfectly normal except her eyes were closed. Gloria examined the picture. She could see RJ's resemblance to both Roger and Melanie. But Ella didn't look like any of them. There was no resemblance at all.

"Poor little Orelia," she whispered.

* * *

During the days immediately following the explosion of the nuclear warhead, diplomatic relations between the United States and the rest of the world were strained. Even the U.S' staunchest allies found it hard to accept an accidental explosion of a nuclear weapon. If it was an accident, they reasoned, that made the U.S. a real threat to the rest of the world. After all, the world's largest nuclear power should have foolproof safeguards on its weapons systems. If it was not an accident...that spoke for itself and even the U.S.' avowed enemies did not want to contemplate what that really meant. Either way, the U.S. was in the position of being seen as a dangerous country by most of the rest of the world.

The president and the State Department were doing everything in their power to modify world opinion. The president made numerous speeches that were meant to strike a balance between apologizing for an accident and reassuring that no such accident could even happen again. Beyond that, the U.S. sent immediate aid in the form of money, food, medical supplies and personnel. A month passed without any credible threats of retaliation, and with promises of continuing U.S. aid for as long as it was needed. The international community began to reduce its focus on this tragedy. So did the U.S. media. The unexpected death of a popular starlet became the focus of the daily news shows.

Gloria and Jared had been deeply affected by the international situation because, despite their desire not to feel this way, they both wondered if Ella really had a special insight into the end of the world. As tensions were reduced it became easier for them to dismiss these feelings. Their new focus was how to make life for Ella as normal as possible.

Despite their interest in knowing what the specialists would find if they were allowed to examine Ella thoroughly they refused to take calls from doctors wanting to scrutinize their little girl. They also refused all media calls and letters. They hoped that resuming their everyday routine would help them deal with their bewildering predicament. Secretly they each hoped that the other would forget the past events and that life with Ella would return to what it was before she appeared with Oprah.

Gloria decided that one way to change the focus was to spend some time with Sheila and Joe. Gloria and Sheila had been able to maintain their close relationship no matter what was going on between their husbands, but as couples they had spent very little time together. Gloria had confided with Sheila about how much of a strain Ella's birth put on her relationship with Melanie but she had never told Sheila the whole story. Although Sheila was her closest friend, she did not have to courage to tell her about the dreams and her belief that Earth Girl had been conceived in a past life.

Gloria decided to invite Joe and Sheila for dinner as a thank-you for Joe's driving to Connecticut to pick up Ella and Jared. Melanie agreed to babysit at their house. She wanted to be able to leave RJ home with Roger. Gloria was hurt on Ella's behalf but she understood. As they walked to a restaurant overlooking the water, Gloria hoped that tonight would be the beginning of a new normal.

The two couples thoroughly enjoyed their meal together. Joe and Jared seemed to be closer than they had ever been and the four of them laughed, joked and drank. After her second glass of wine Gloria broke down and told Joe and Sheila all about her dreams. They both listened quietly without interrupting. When she finished Jared, who was clearly annoyed that Gloria had told them about the Earth Girl dreams, ordered another round of drinks.

"You probably need a few more after that crazy story," he joked feebly.

"Sometimes I have dreams that are so real that when I wake up I am not sure whether it was a dream or real life," said Sheila diplomatically.

"Yeah, me too," Joe offered.

On the way home Jared berated Gloria for telling them.

"It's one thing for me to know that you have lost touch with reality. It's another thing for the whole world to know. Sheila is probably on the phone right now. Probably didn't even wait to get home to start calling people. All this time and Melanie never told anyone and now you go and tell them. What were you thinking? I thought we agreed not to talk to ANYONE about this."

"I was thinking that I can't pretend any longer. Have me committed if you want but I am not keeping this a secret anymore."

"I don't want to have you committed. I just want you to keep your dreams to yourself, dammit."

His voice was loud and high-pitched. Gloria knew he was really mad at her.

"You know," Jared said somewhat desperately, "you never

should have started reading all that new-age crap. You know how susceptible you are. Someone comes along with a new idea and you jump right on the bandwagon. That's all this dream stuff is. You're letting yourself be influenced."

"Maybe so. But that doesn't explain her eyes and the stuff she says. You heard her this morning, almost wailing in pain about all the people who were going to starve because of the radioactivity. Five-year-old children don't think like that. Admit it."

As soon as Gloria said this she regretted it. When she had heard Ella that morning she had decided not to mention it. Jared had made the same decision, convincing himself that if he ignored it, it didn't exist. He knew it was magical thinking and he was completely against such an illogical way of thinking, but he desperately wanted Ella to be just like any other almost six-year-old child.

"She gets it from television. She parrots what she hears. I told you to stop letting her watch so much TV, dammit!"

"I don't think it is from television," Gloria retorted. "She says a lot of stuff that ordinary five-year-olds don't talk about. Haven't you noticed that?"

"To tell you the truth I have been trying not to listen to her when she talks like that."

"Jared, that's because it scares you to think it's true. But, honestly, how can you be so sure that she wasn't sent to us from a past life? I can't figure out how it could happen, but I do know that millions of people in the world believe in reincarnation."

"Good for them. Do they also believe that babies who were conceived in one life show up in the womb of the wife of some poor unsuspecting shmuck in another lifetime? I doubt they believe that. It is just too far-fetched to be true."

Gloria and Jared walked the rest of the way home in silence. When they entered the house, Melanie was glued to the television. It had just been reported that three Red Cross workers and 14 U.S. soldiers had been killed in the tent city set up for refugees from Cormoros. The president had made a brief speech and hinted at retaliation. Melanie was a pacifist by nature. She had protested against each of the wars that the U.S. had started since she was a teenager. The prospect of retaliations sounded like the path to war as far as she was concerned.

"How can we retaliate against them when none of this would be happening if we didn't let off a nuclear explosion?" she asked angrily.

Jared was listening intently to the news. He had a sick feeling in the pit of his stomach. He wondered if there was actually going to be an all-out war after all. The four of them continued to watch the news for the next hour. Other countries were weighing in on the killing of the soldiers and Red Cross workers. Some were also commenting negatively on the president's newly belligerent tone. Most of the commentators were saying that war seemed like more of a possibility now than it had at any time since the initial explosion.

When Melanie realized how late it was, she decided to head home. As she stepped out the front door she was shocked to find a small group of people gathered in front of the house holding signs and candles. The signs said: 'WE BELIEVE ELLA' and 'NO MORE WAR.'

Melanie closed the door and told Gloria to look out the window. Gloria gasped when she saw them. She quickly closed the curtain, hoping that Jared would not realize what was going on.

"I don't want your father to see this. It will just upset him," Gloria warned.

"I think it's kind of nice. They don't think she is a freak," said Melanie.

Earlier that day Melanie had seen a story Ella on the cover of a tabloid when she was in line at the grocery store. The headline was 'Golden-Eyed Blind Girl Predicted Cormoros Debacle.' She hadn't told her parents. They were upset enough already. Now she reconsidered. After she told them she brought Jared to the window. Jared frowned his disapproval. His reaction was pretty much what Gloria expected.

"This has got to stop. I will not have this in my yard. I'm calling the police."

A few minutes later a reporter from the local newspaper called asking for an interview. Jared refused and hung up just in time to hear Ella crying. Jared and Gloria both went to her room. Ella sat up in bed.

"Mommy, you have to listen to me. Don't let any more bombs explode. The world is going to die"

"You had a dream. Go back to sleep, sweetpea," said Jared

Ella put her head on her pillow and fell right back to sleep. Gloria was visibly shaken. Melanie asked what happened. She surprised her parents by chuckling when they told her.

"That kid is my sister, for sure. She's just a whole lot smarter than I was at five."

Neither Gloria nor Jared found any humor in Ella's request. In truth Melanie was pretty freaked out by it too but she felt so sorry for her parents that she was trying to act like it was normal. When she got home she went into RJ's room and knelt beside his bed. She thanked God that RJ was ordinary in every way. She hoped that being ordinary and unnoticed would save him from whatever their family was about to undergo.

When she told Roger about the vigil and what Ella had said to Gloria, he replied sardonically, "I always told you it was a mistake to live so close to your parents." Melanie rolled her eyes, but she thought that maybe he was right.

CHAPTER 19

Joe called Jared first thing the next morning. He wanted to meet him for coffee. When Jared arrived at Gary's Handy Lunch, Joe had already ordered a stack of pancakes and a cup of coffee. He was eating rapidly and Jared noticed that he looked really agitated.

"Whoa, slow down, big guy, you're going choke on that."

"I wanted to finish this before you got here because once I start talking I'm not going to feel like eating."

Jared wasn't sure what was wrong, but he braced himself for the tirade. Joe had an explosive temper once he got started, and it looked like he was going to start.

"Why didn't you tell me about Gloria's hallucinations?" he demanded.

"They aren't hallucinations. They're dreams."

"Big fucking difference. I got her job back for her. You owed it to me to tell me."

"I thought she was okay. She stopped talking about them. When we went to therapy, she stopped. I thought she was better."

"I can't believe you wouldn't tell me. I'm your brother. You came to me for help and then you didn't even tell me the truth. Here's the money for my breakfast. I'm outta here. Don't call me."

Joe stormed out of the diner. It bothered Jared more than he cared to admit. With everything that was going on, he needed his brother more than ever. He was even looking forward to talking to him about Gloria. Now he would finally have someone to confide in. *Well, so much for that,* thought Jared, bitterly, *so much for brotherly love.*

Jared sat staring at the table. He didn't know whether he was more hurt or angry, but he knew that he felt very alone. His brother wasn't speaking to him and his wife spoke mostly nonsense. His oldest child was married with a life of her own now and his youngest was some sort of freak of nature.

Jared's love for Ella was a given. He adored this little girl and wanted to protect her. But he had to admit it. Lately he couldn't shake the feeling that she was really weird. He had gotten used to the appearance of her eyes almost as soon as they brought her home as a newborn. But that was before he knew she could "see" without opening them and it was before her behavior had become so unusual. Most of all it was before the media had taken an interest in her and strangers had declared that she was a prophet.

Jared had never been much for religion. He didn't read the Bible and he didn't go to church and he was sure that he did not want his daughter to end up standing on a street corner preaching about the end of the world. Jared, without ever proclaiming it, was an agnostic. He considered all the big questions about God, creation, afterlife, and eternity to be unknowable. He had reached that conclusion early in his life, and really had not given it much thought since. There was something very disconcerting about having a child who was considered even by one person to be a prophet.

Nevertheless Jared headed to the nearest church he could find. As he entered the doors the first thing he noticed was the light streaming through the stained-glass windows. The pictures portrayed in the stained glass seemed to be glowing. It reminded him of something but what was it? The more he thought about it the more uncomfortable he was. Then it hit him. The glow through the windows reminded him of Ella's eyes when they had projected light. Her eyes had the same luminosity as the bright colors in the windows. Upon realizing this Jared turned around and left the church. His visit to the house of God had not been comforting.

On the way home he kept thinking of what his father had told him when he was a teenager. "There are some things you can't ever really understand. It is a waste of energy to keep trying to figure them out. Some parts of life just aren't meant to be understood." He had found that comment annoying as a teenager and he still did now. He needed to understand what was going on with Ella and Gloria.

Gloria was looking for answers too. Now that she had shared her dreams with Joe and Sheila she felt she could finally talk to Sheila about it. She knew that Joe and Jared were having breakfast. It seemed like the perfect time to call Sheila. She told Sheila about the argument she and Jared had on the way home, and about the vigil in front of the house and how angry it had made Jared. Sheila sympathized and told Gloria that Joe had been really upset about her dreams. Gloria wanted to know what she thought about them. Although she was afraid of Sheila's answer, she needed to know. Did Sheila believe her or not?

Sheila didn't know what to say. She found the whole story unbelievable and confusing. She wanted to believe Gloria and if she couldn't believe her she, at least, wanted to stand by her. But the story was so confusing to her. It was hard to grasp it really. She couldn't quite figure out why but thinking about it was overwhelming to her. Maybe she should just let Gloria talk and ask a question now and then.

"I...I want to believe you, but I guess I don't really understand it," she offered.

"Sheila, I know exactly what you mean. I don't understand it either. I'm still trying to figure it all out. Lately, I've been racking my brain for details from the dreams that would help me understand it all. Maybe if I go over it with you in detail, you can help me figure it out."

"Yeah, maybe..."

Gloria told Shelia that she had started to have her original dream about Earth Girl again. This morning Gloria was focused on the very beginning of the dream.

"I keep wondering what Earth Girl meant about her 'celestial life' and coming back to earth? Do you think there is a clue there, Sheila?"

"I don't know. Maybe."

"Well, do you think Ella is a celestial being who chose to come back at this particular time in history?" pressed Gloria.

"I guess she could be."

"Do you think that Ella is Earth Girl's child? I mean...I'm pretty sure she is. But what do you think?" asked Gloria.

"I am having trouble remembering who Earth Girl is. Is she the one in the dream?"

Gloria felt slightly exasperated. How could she not remember who Earth Girl is? *Earth Girl is the link to everything.*

"Earth Girl is the one who talks to me in the dream. She is the one the whole dream is about."

"Oh, right, right. I knew that."

"Okay, so do you think I might be a reincarnation of Earth Girl?"

"I guess you could be."

"Yes, that's what I think too. You know, I'm pretty sure that I was meant to give birth to her baby. I don't know if that means I am her reincarnation or not but it could. Either I had to be born to have *her* baby or I am actually Earth Girl having come back now to have *my* baby."

None of this made any sense to Sheila. When there was no answer from Sheila, Gloria said, "Well, I guess all I really know is that life and death are very different from what I used to think."

"That makes sense to me," said Sheila, "I don't think we really understand it all. I mean that's what religion tries to answer, right?"

"Yeah, religion is about things we can't really know for sure, I guess. But I don't think I can go through my whole life not understanding what the relationship between me and Earth Girl is. It sort of makes me feel panicky to think that I may die without ever understanding this."

"That probably won't happen. Someday this will all make sense to you," suggested Sheila without much conviction.

"I hope you're right. The voice in my dream tells me that when I am ready to understand it, all it will be revealed. I guess I just have to believe that."

"Right."

"Wait a minute, that thing you said about religion just made me think of something. Earth Girl says that she had lost her connection with her celestial life. Now I think I know what that means. That's why I can't understand this all! I've lost my connection to my celestial life."

"Maybe," Sheila replied. She wasn't sure what Gloria was talking about anymore but she tried to cover her confusion.

"That's what is wrong with the world. We have lost touch with our celestial lives," Gloria said excitedly.

Her mind started racing now. She felt that she understood for the first time why there were so many religions in the world and so much suffering.

"The reason there are so many religions is because people have such a strong desire to connect with their celestial lives and no one knows how. Over the history of the world people have come up with so many ideas about God and heaven and eternity. We suffer when we don't feel the connection. We long for it and we can't feel the joy that is always available to us because we don't know how to connect to it. But we do know how to connect to pain and suffering. I bet that is what original sin is or maybe that is hell."

Sheila wasn't sure what she thought of any of this. Gloria sounded like a preacher. She was talking way too fast for her to follow it. She didn't always talk this fast, did she? Sheila was pretty sure that she didn't always find Gloria's conversation so hard to follow.

"I think I am beginning to understand why some people are so rigid about what they believe...why they have to believe that their religion is the only true one, the only way. It's because they desperately want to make that connection to their celestial life!"

Sheila was having trouble sharing Gloria's enthusiasm. She was searching for something to say that would sound like she even understood what Gloria was talking about.

"I guess. I'm not very religious so I don't have much of an opinion on this," said Sheila.

Gloria was undeterred.

"I really get it now! That's why people need religion. It's the need to have answers, to be sure. It helps them feel connected to their celestial life. That's probably why people have waged wars about religion. I never understood that before but now I do."

"Right," said Sheila, without really meaning it.

"It is the need to know something that can never really be known or proven. But if they win the war they feel like they have proof that their religion is the right one."

Sheila listened quietly. She was having trouble paying attention to Gloria's long explanation.

"That is what is wrong with the world," Gloria said triumphantly. "I get it now. We humans have lost our connection to our celestial lives. I totally get it. People are trying to know the wholly unknowable, or is that the holy unknowable? Wholly with a W or holy with an H, get it?" she chuckled.

Sheila was silent.

"Get it? The wholly unknown is also the holy unknown. It is what religions are built on; trying to know the Holy Unknowable who is wholly unknowable."

Sheila didn't get it but she didn't want to admit it. She had no idea what any of this had to do with Ella but it seemed to be making Gloria feel better and that was good. Sheila, on the other hand, was developing a headache and feeling sleepy.

"Gloria, it's beginning to feel like nap time for me."

"Nap time? Since when do you take a nap in the morning?"

"Lately, whenever I can. Guess I'm getting old. I feel like I want to nap a lot."

"Probably a good thing. Some people nap everyday. I take one whenever I can."

After Sheila hung up, Gloria held the phone in her hand for a moment. She was trying to shake the feeling that something about Sheila was different. She hoped that it was not Sheila's reaction to her dream that made her sound so...so unlike the witty, fast-talking woman she had grown to love. Gloria had noticed this at dinner too, but had attributed it to the copious amount of wine Sheila had consumed.

After a minute, Gloria's thoughts returned to the holy, wholly unknown. *If I ever started a religion, I would call it The Church of the Holy, Wholly Unknowable. There would be no dogma. I would preach that there is so much more than we can ever comprehend in this earthly life. That it is all just about love. There would be more peace and less war if people weren't so obsessed with convincing others that they have to believe certain things and worship in certain ways. That's a religion I could believe in.*

CHAPTER 20

Although Jared was hurt and angered by Joe's reaction to finding out about Gloria's dream, both he and Gloria were determined to find some peace of mind. As the weeks passed this became easier and easier. This was partly because the public's interest in Ella began to die down as soon as the crises in the Indian Ocean ended. For a few tense weeks it seemed that the retaliatory killing of the U.S. soldiers would result in all-out war. However, when China, the most influential member of the Trilateral Nuclear Power Alliance, took on the role of peacemaker war was averted. The American public took a collective sigh of relief and promptly forgot about the devastation caused by the blast. Those few individuals who had thought that Ella was a prophet sent to foretell the end of the world lost interest in her when the threat of all-out nuclear war waned.

The doctors who were fascinated by her condition did not lose interest but Gloria and Jared decided not to allow any further examinations or public appearances. Ella's brief moment of fame had frightened them. They wanted nothing more than to return to anonymity even if it meant never fully understanding Ella's condition. They knew now that she could see with her eyes closed when she wanted to. They also knew that sometimes what she saw with her eyes closed had nothing to do with what was in her visual field. They discussed this over and over again during the first few weeks after Ella's appearance on *Oprah*. Finally they concluded that her visions were no different than daydreams. Being able to actually see with her eyes closed, they agreed, was unusual and due to the golden dome.

They decided not to make an issue of this with Ella. From here on in, their goal was to treat her as much as possible as a totally normal little girl. They also agreed to prohibit her from watching or listening to the news until she was older. They felt that she was highly intelligent, extremely sensitive and overly impressionable.

It was their job to protect her. So they set out to do just that.

The other reason for their peace of mind was that Jared was no longer mad at Gloria. The anger he felt after Gloria told Joe and Sheila about her dreams had gradually dissipated. It was true that he would have to mend his relationship with Joe again, but he decided to let some time pass before even making an attempt at reconciliation. In the meantime he and Gloria had agreed on how to handle Ella's differences and how to protect her. This felt good to Jared and he was relieved to be able to let go of his anger. Despite everything that had happened he loved Gloria deeply and he wanted their life together to return to what it used to be.

So did Gloria. She did not totally agree that the best way to deal with Ella was to ignore her obvious ability to see both what was visible to others and also what was not visible to the human eye. She could not let go of the feeling that Ella really was Orelia and that she was here to bring a message to the world. However, her desire for her life to return to normal and for Jared to love and trust her motivated her to go along with the plan to protect Ella by treating her exactly like any other young child.

Their day-to-day life took on a predictable pattern Gloria and Jared were more than content with the simplicity of it. For a few years life seemed both simple and sweet. They had grown to accept Ella's uniqueness. As long as they kept her in a protected environment she seemed almost like any little girl. Much to her relief Gloria stopped having dreams about Earth Girl. Occasionally she would feel an unsettling desire to know if Ella really was Earth Girl's child but mostly she denied those feelings. Ella's behavior made it easy for Gloria to convince herself that Ella was an ordinary child with a birth defect that affected her eyes. She was quiet and preferred to spend time alone. She did well in school and had become a voracious reader. Indeed, she was turning out to be an easier child than RJ.

RJ was having a lot of trouble in school. He seemed interested in doing well, but he got in trouble often for disruptive behavior. He was curious and wanted to learn, but it seemed that something was preventing him from being able to apply himself. Melanie blamed it on his relationship with Ella. RJ had been her only real friend at school and Melanie thought that this was too much of a burden on a young child. She began to limit the amount of time RJ spent with Ella and requested that he be transferred to another class. Gloria was hurt by this, but Jared vehemently defended Melanie's decision. Gloria eventually decided that it was probably for the best.

She began to realize that her role as a mother had prevented her from spending much time with RJ. Now that he was exhibiting some problems, she vowed to spend more time alone with him. She wanted to treat him to some special Grandma time. During one of her special outings with RJ he cried when she asked about school. Gloria was so surprised that she pulled the car over to the side of the road and turned off the engine. She felt a momentary fluttering in her stomach, a sure sign that she was upset. Gloria had long ago learned to control her outward reactions to things that upset her, but her stomach had not learned the same lesson. When she was worried or upset her stomach would begin to flip around inside her, making her feel nauseous as well as worried.

She took a deep breath as she got out of the car and opened the back door. She unhooked RJ's seatbelt and lifted him out of the car. She realized she had not held him in her arms in years. He was almost too heavy for her, much bigger than Ella although they were so close in age. Gloria opened the passenger door to the front seat and sat sideways with her feet on the ground and RJ on her lap. She rubbed his back gently and told him that it was okay to cry but that sometimes talking about something makes it feel better.

"Sweetie, tell me what's wrong."

"I miss Ella, but Mommy and Daddy don't want me to play

with her. She's not in my class anymore and I never get to see her."

Before Gloria could think of the right thing to say, RJ added, "And Daddy's mad at me because I don't like to go to school anymore."

RJ started to cry again.

"Daddy says it's Mommy's fault. He's always mad at me and Mommy."

"Oh, sweet boy, I am sure your daddy is not always mad at you. He loves you so much. He's probably just tired from working when he comes home at the end of the day. When people are tired, it makes them cranky and they get mad when they don't even mean it."

RJ climbed off Gloria's lap and looked up at his grandmother. When Gloria returned his gaze she saw a little boy with big blue eyes, long wet eyelashes and a stream of clear mucous dripping from his reddened nose. She grabbed a tissue from her pocket and wiped his nose. As she started to hug him he pulled away and looked directly in her eyes.

"Does being tired make people cry a lot too, Grammy? I think Mommy must be very tired."

"Yes, RJ, being tired can make someone cry a lot too. Mommy is probably tired. I don't think she is really sad."

RJ continued to look directly at Gloria.

"Are you tired too?" he asked.

Gloria quickly rubbed her finger along her bottom eyelids.

"Yes, sweetheart, I am a little bit tired too," she lied.

Until this conversation Gloria had been feeling almost serene. But now she felt a heavy weight descend upon her. The flip-flopping of her stomach continued. She knew her tears were not from being overtired. They were caused by sadness.

Gloria thought about going home to get Ella. Maybe all RJ needed was a chance to play with her. But she knew Melanie and Roger would disapprove. They had been pretty clear about not wanting RJ to spend time with Ella except during family get-togethers. So be it. This was supposed to be RJ's special time with Grammy. She was determined to make it fun for him.

"RJ, tell you what! You get to decide where we go today. We can go to Playday or bowling or the movies or mini golf or wherever you want to go."

"I don't care. You pick," he said.

The lack of enthusiasm in his voice sent a little surge of pain through Gloria's back. She barely noted that she must be really upset to be feeling it as a cramp in her back. She didn't want RJ to know that she was upset

"I have a great idea. Let's go to the beach. We can make a picnic and look at the waves roll in while we eat. The ocean always cheers me up when I am sad. I bet it will make you feel better too."

"Ok, Grammy."

When they got to the market to buy their picnic fare Gloria allowed RJ to make all the food choices. He was surprised and even smiled when he was allowed to add chips, cookies and soda to the cart. As Gloria watched his mood brighten, she thought how odd it is that food that is bad for us can make us feel so good. Although she was usually dedicated to healthy eating for children, at this moment she gave a silent thank-you for junk food and its restorative powers. She knew that RJ would not be the only one enjoying this usually forbidden menu.

When they arrived at the beach Gloria took a blanket out of her car's trunk. She spread it out and weighted the corners down with 4 cans of soda. She sent RJ to search for a few large stones with which to replace the cans as they drank their sodas. While he was looking along the water's edge he saw a teenage boy playing with a dog. The boy threw the ball into the water and the dog ran in to retrieve it. Every time the dog came out of the water he would shake water all over his owner. RJ found this extremely entertaining. He was laughing out loud when Gloria walked over to join him. Gloria felt relieved when she saw him laughing happily. He didn't want to eat until the dog left. The dog's master was very friendly and let RJ throw the ball a few times. When they finally sat down to eat their cookies and chips RJ's cheeks were red with excitement.

"That was so much fun, Grammy. I love playing with dogs."

"I could tell."

Gloria smiled at RJ and handed him another soda.

"You have to promise you will go to bed at bedtime tonight even though I let you have all this sugar."

RJ and Gloria watched the sunset as they stuffed themselves with chips and cookies. Gloria was tempted to feel guilty about this, but instead she felt good and the pain in her back had gone away. While they packed up their leftovers and shook the sand off the blanket Gloria decided to stop at the local souvenir store to see if there was a stuffed animal there that RJ would like. She thought it would be good for him to have a cuddle toy that he associated with a happy day.

Lying in bed that night, she couldn't get RJ out of her mind. She kept thinking about how ironic it was that he, a normal child, was so unhappy while Ella, who was certainly not normal, seemed like a pretty content little girl. Once they had stopped allowing her to hear the world news she had become more cheerful. She never asked about her eyes and seemed to accept her differences without too much concern. Even though she wished that RJ was happier a little part of her was glad that he missed Ella. It was good to know he loved her.

Gloria tossed and turned while trying to find a comfortable position for her back. She was amazed at how sensitive it was to stress. Her stomach had long since stopped flip-flopping, but her back pain had returned as soon as she lay down. *Better start exercising every day again.* She could not fall asleep. She kept thinking about RJ and suddenly she was worried about Ella too. They both seemed so vulnerable to her, and she literally ached to be able to protect them. She recognized that she had lost her cherished peace of mind when she found out about the problems Melanie and her family were having. Now her worries seemed to be cascading back. She recognized a familiar pattern. *If I let myself worry about one thing, soon I am worrying about everything.* When Gloria finally fell asleep the sun was beginning to rise.

Try not to worry. I am watching over you and Orelia. You are doing the right thing by letting her be a little girl and protecting her from the pain and suffering in the world. When she is ready you will not be able to protect her anymore. She will seek the message and she will become your guide. You will be tempted to shelter her, but she will not let you. Be open to the signs.

Gloria was troubled when she woke up. This was the first dream with a message about Ella in more than a year. She did not welcome it. What did it mean that she was dreaming about her again? She had long ago accepted in her mind that Ella was Earth Girl's child. This belief had wreaked havoc with her life, but she had never really changed her mind about it. What she had done was push it back somewhere out of her daily consciousness. At least for a while.

Ever since their life had returned to normal after Ella's brief notoriety, she had been able to live her life as if Ella was just Ella. Not Earth Girl's child, not a cosmic being with a message, just her precious little Ella who she and Jared loved so dearly. Having time without the dreams had given Gloria the hope and even the belief that her life would return to normal. They would protect Ella and life would be normal. This was the bargain she had made with herself: *If Ella really is Orelia and if she is really here with a message it won't happen while she is a little girl.* Was this dream telling her that Ella would deliver her message sooner than Gloria could bear? The more Gloria thought about the dream the more her back ached. Gloria knew that she would continue fretting all day if she didn't find something to distract her. The gym, shopping, calling Sheila, renting a movie. She wasn't really in the mood for any of that. Maybe the beach.

Gloria spread a blanket and laid down on it with her feet planted in the sand and her knees bent. The sun on her face felt good. Soon she was drowsy. But her active mind was keeping her from falling soundly asleep. She would feel as if she were dreaming and then immediately wake up. Finally she fell into a deep sleep. When she woke up she remembered that she had dreamt of herself kneeling in church and praying, "Glory be to the Father, the Son and the Holy Spirit." *That's odd. I haven't said that prayer in years.* As she lay there letting her thoughts wander, she thought that if she was a priest she would change it to "Glory be to the creator, the child and the holy spirit." Then she laughed at herself, still reacting against sexism after all these years. The Holy Unknown might be a woman. No wonder she remains wholly unknown. She smiled at her little joke.

While bending over to gather up her blanket she felt a dull ache in her back. Before she knew it her car was heading toward Melanie's house. She knew Melanie would be home making the most of her house-cleaning time before RJ got home from school. Gloria had to admit that Melanie was a far better housekeeper than she had ever been. She managed to accomplish more in a morning than Gloria could accomplish in two or three days. She wondered how Melanie had developed such focus. She probably was not going to welcome this interruption, but Gloria could not help herself. If she did not talk to Melanie she would never get rid of her backache.

"I saw your car pull in. What's up?" asked Melanie as she met Gloria at the door. "Is something wrong? Dad okay?"

"Yes, Dad is fine and so is Ella. But there is something on my mind. I'm quite worried about RJ. Can I come in?"

"Sure, alright, for a few minutes. I don't have a lot of time before RJ gets home and I don't want to talk about this while he's home."

"Mel, I knew he was having some problems at school because

you told me about it, but yesterday when I asked him how school was he started crying. He told me he doesn't like school anymore because he misses Ella."

Melanie's expression hardened.

"I'm sure he does miss her, Mom, but he will get over it. It's not healthy for him to feel so responsible for her. He was her only friend. It's not good for either of them."

"But maybe if he could just see her at our house – or yours – once or twice a week, he might, you know, he might not be so sad. Maybe he would do better in school too."

"Look, Mom, Rog and I have talked this over. We just don't think it is good for RJ to spend time with Ella. I'm sorry. But that's the way it is…at least for now."

"Mel, RJ says that Roger is always mad at him…and at you too."

"Mom that's a little kid's interpretation of things. Roger isn't mad at RJ. He's impatient with him because he's sure he can do better in school. You know how Roger is, sort of driven. That's why he's successful. He wants RJ to be the same way."

"I think RJ is rather young to be worried about success," chided Gloria.

"You don't have to convince me, Mom. I agree with you on this one. So Roger and I are at an impasse. But I'm sure we'll figure it out."

"But what about RJ being so unhappy?"

"Things will even out for RJ when he starts making new friends. He's really having trouble letting go of Ella. That's our fault for letting them get so close in the first place."

"What does that mean? They're cousins. Of course they're close. I wish I had grown up near my cousins. It's a blessing!" said Gloria heatedly.

"Do you also wish you had to fight to defend your cousin? Do you wish you had no friends because everyone thinks your cousin is so weird?" replied Melanie angrily.

"Has it really been that bad for him, Mel?" asked Gloria.

"Yes, Mom, it has. It's time for it to end. They can see each other at family occasions. Just like thousands of other cousins."

"Well if that is what you think is best, Mel. I'll go along with it, but I'm not comfortable with it."

"Look, Mom, Roger thinks it is best and I'm willing to try it. To tell you the real truth Roger blames me because he thinks you're half crazy and I let you have too much influence in our lives."

"Oh, Mel, I'm sorry I caused so much distress in your family," said Gloria in a sarcastic tone.

"Until you can let go of your fantasy about Ella's conception I don't think it will change," retorted Melanie. "You really don't get how hard it is for me to always have to defend you to Roger. It's not just you and Dad that are affected. It affects all of us more than you know."

Gloria noticed tears beginning to well up in Melanie's eyes.

"Look, Mom, RJ's going to be home soon. I've got to finish what I was doing."

To Gloria this sounded like an invitation to leave. So she obliged.

"I've got to get home anyway. I'll call you in a few days."

Gloria's cheeks were flushed and she had tears in her eyes as she turned to leave. She reached for the doorknob and then turned to face Melanie.

"I am so sorry I've caused you so much pain. I love you so much, Mel. I just wanted to help, but I...well, I guess I can't help. You know you can come to me anytime, right? You're still going to let me see, RJ, aren't you?

"Yes, Mom, you can still see RJ. He's too young to be affected by your craziness."

Gloria opened the door and walked to her car in a daze. She sat behind the steering wheel for a moment before starting the car. *That wasn't what I expected. I guess she will never forgive me. Not that I really blame her.*

Melanie waited at the door for RJ and gave him a big hug when he got there. She helped him take off his backpack and carefully took out the papers he had stuffed into it. They were crumpled and filled with erasures. It looked to Melanie as if he had purposely crumpled them up. She started to ask him about them but changed her mind. Instead she hugged him again and told him she had made his favorite cookie. RJ showed little interest in this treat.

"I hate school," he said. "Can I quit?"

"No, sweetie, you can't quit. You know everyone has to go to school. Why do you want to quit?"

RJ couldn't bring himself to tell his mother how hard it was to be Ella's cousin. Even though he was no longer in the same class, he still heard the things other kids said about her and he could see that she really didn't have any friends except for him. It made him sad and mad at the same time. He loved Ella and he wanted to be allowed to play with her, but he didn't want to be her only friend. It felt like too much of a burden to him. These were confusing emotions for a young boy.

CHAPTER 21

When Gloria left Melanie's house her heart was heavy with grief. It was clear to her that Melanie was unhappy. Knowing that both Melanie and RJ were suffering was heartbreaking for Gloria. She had always thought that she would be the kind of mother that Melanie could turn to with any problem. It was clear now that she had failed miserably. Even though she and Jared had mended their relationship successfully, Gloria could not feel joy if her daughter was suffering…and RJ being so sad…that was the worst part of all. Her back began to throb again. It hurt enough to make her feel a little weak.

She could not wait to soak in a hot tub. She hoped to get some relief from the pain in her back and the pain in her heart. As she filled the tub, she realized that this was the first time since she tried to give herself an abortion in this very tub, that she was more worried about Melanie than she was about herself. The guilt of that realization engulfed her.

As she climbed into the tub, she remembered her mother telling her that she was doomed to feel guilty about almost everything. "After all, my dear daughter, your mother is Catholic and your father is Jewish. You are the product of the two most guilt-ridden religions in the world." Gloria had actively striven to avoid guilt in her life, and until becoming a mother, she had pretty much succeeded. But motherhood had brought out in her that long submerged tendency towards guilt and when it surfaced it had the same power as water rushing through a broken dam.

She had felt it when she was too exhausted to sing Melanie another lullaby when the toddler could not sleep. She had felt it if she skipped a few pages in the storybook because she was anxious for the bedtime ritual to be over so that she could have some time for herself before she exhaustedly dragged herself to bed. She had felt it when she brought Melanie to daycare because she wanted to go back to work. She had felt it when she quit her job to spend more time with Melanie because Melanie was not doing well in school. She was rent with guilt most of the time she was raising Melanie, even though she knew she was doing the best job that she could. Somehow, when it came to motherhood, she could just never be good enough.

Ever since Ella's birth she had been trying to push down the onslaught of new guilt; guilt for not wanting her in the first place; guilt for the pain all of this had caused Melanie and Jared; guilt for not being a better grandmother to RJ; and most exasperatingly, guilt for believing the Earth Girl dreams, and guilt for doubting the dreams. Now, here she was, engulfed in guilt, not about Ella, but about Melanie. The old saying is true, she thought, "Once a mother, never free again." Loving so completely denies the possibility of real freedom, and although this thought disturbed her, she embraced it. It made her, somehow, feel like she must be a good mother.

Ironically, the guiltier she felt about Melanie, the less she felt like she had been a bad mother. A bad mother wouldn't feel so bad about her weaknesses as a parent, right? After a half hour of wallowing in the accumulated guilt of 28 years of motherhood, Gloria felt her back muscles ease a bit.

She spent the next few days trying to figure out what she could say or do to mend things with Melanie. She called Sheila to ask for advice. Although Sheila sounded sympathetic, she didn't offer any advice. Gloria wondered again what was going on with Sheila; she just didn't seem at all like herself lately. Having not gotten what she needed from Sheila, she decided to ask Jared for advice about Melanie. He told her to give it some time.

"You know Melanie," he said, "when she flies off the handle like that, she can be pretty stubborn about making up. I wouldn't push it yet."

"But what about RJ? He was so sad. I want to help him if I can."

"Well, take him out now and then, but keep the conversation with Melanie to a minimum. You know you have a way of setting her off."

"You're right, Jared. I need to give her some space. If I had it to do over again, I wouldn't have had Ella when I did. That was supposed to be Melanie's time."

"If I remember, you tried pretty hard not to have Ella."

It was one of the very few times that Jared had mentioned Gloria's attempt to abort Ella. As soon as he said it, he wished he could take it back.

"Not my finest hour," Gloria said quickly. "Let's leave it at that."

Jared was more than willing to leave it at that. Things between him and Gloria had been so good for the last two years. He had no desire to dredge up the past. Even Ella, unique a child as she was, appeared to be thriving in their happy home. *Life really is good*, Jared dared to think. He hoped that it was not the calm before the storm.

"Let's rent that new Disney movie and have a movie and popcorn night with Ella," Gloria suggested.

Jared was on it immediately, heading out the door to get both the popcorn and the movie. While he was gone, Gloria's thoughts went back to Melanie, but only briefly. The ringtone on her cell phone told her that Sheila was calling.

"Hey, Sheila, what's up?"

"Nothing really, just felt like saying hi. We haven't seen each other in awhile. If we wait for the Js to set it up, it may never happen. So I thought you and I could set a date for dinner. "

"Sounds good. I'll look at the calendar, pick a few dates and get back to you with them. I'll check to see if I can get a sitter. You know we usually only use Mel, and she's a little annoyed with me now. So I don't want to ask her."

"Seems like she is annoyed with you a lot lately. What did you do this time, oh evil one?"

Gloria was both annoyed and surprised that Sheila didn't remember that she had called her to discuss this very issue.

"Nothing really. Just being myself, but she feels like I am interfering in her life. What can I say? Just typical mother daughter stuff I guess. Same thing I called you about," she said pointedly.

"Oh, that…I thought maybe it was something new," Sheila said, trying to cover the fact that she didn't remember their previous conversation at all.

"Well, check out some dates and get back to me. I think Joe could use a night out with other people. He's kinda down lately."

Gloria doubted that Joe and Jared would choose to spend time with each other if it was up to them, but maybe being forced into it would be good for both of them.

"Sounds like maybe you and I need a girls' night out too. Lots to talk about…husbands, daughters, maybe even world affairs. Gotta go now because we're getting ready to have a movie night with Ella. I'll get back to you tomorrow."

"Okay. Bye now."

"Bye."

Two days later when Gloria texted some dates to Sheila, she was surprised by the response she got: *Confused. what r these dates 4?*

Gloria decided they needed to talk, rather than text.

"Hi Sheila. I got your text. Now I'm confused," said Gloria.

"You don't know why you sent them either?" laughed Sheila.

"Of course I do, but why don't you? When we talked the other night, I said I would come up with dates for us to get together. Don't tell me you forgot."

Sheila hesitated, but very briefly, before answering. "I guess I forgot because I have so much on my mind. You know, things to get done around here, work, getting ready for my cousin from Nebraska to visit. The list of things to do never gets shorter. Anyway, now, I remember. I called you to set a date. I'll check these dates with Joe and get back to you. Take care. Bye now."

It seemed that Sheila was trying to rush her off the phone. Gloria tried to make sense of Sheila's recent behavior. She and Joe were probably driving each other nuts the other night and the next day things were fine so she forgot. She was slightly annoyed, but she let it go. *Don't sweat the small stuff.*

Besides, Gloria had begun to fall behind on her work ever since her outing with RJ. Between the backaches and the worries, she had not been very productive. Nor very motivated. She really felt like taking a nap, but forced herself to stay up. She had napped yesterday and the day before and she really needed to get caught up or she would lose her job again. Heading for her computer with a cup of coffee and two aspirin, she thought how great it would be to be, as her mother had often said, "independently wealthy." *No need to work. Loads of time to do whatever I want. Now that is living the dream!*

Gloria had barely begun working when Ella popped in. She was carrying an old history book that she had found in Jared's bookshelf in the spare room. She brought it to Gloria excitedly and showed her a picture of a farmhouse burning. It was taken during the Civil War. Ella was a good reader for her age, but she was having trouble sounding out Manassas.

"Mommy, what is that word?

"Ma naas ses"

"Is that a place?"

"Yes, it's in Virginia, I think."

Ella took the book back and studied the picture.

"Mommy, what's this word?"

"Marauder."

"What is a marauder?"

"That's a bad person who goes around looking for places where he can steal stuff."

"They burn things too, Mommy. The book says that marauders burned down the farm house after a battle with a running bull."

"What? That doesn't sound right. Show me."

Gloria skimmed the page and chuckled.

"Not with a running bull. The Battle of Bull Run. Bull Run must be a place."

Gloria didn't really know much about Civil War battles and she wasn't sure if Bull Run was actually a place. But she didn't care if her answer was accurate. She was preoccupied with trying to figure out how to end this conversation. She and Jared had done a good job of keeping Ella away from the news and stories about war, strife and other upsetting topics. Consequently, Ella seemed to be happier and, though she hated to put it this way, more normal. They had not had a conversation about war, bombs, or starving children during the last two years, and Gloria did not want to have one now. She was trying to think of how to change the subject when she noticed that Ella was staring at the book with her eyes closed.

"Mommy, that was a really sad time. So many people died. It was horrible. There were lots of battles and people were starving. Women and children were scared and crying. It was awful. Why did it happen?"

"Ella, it is hard to explain why. It was a very complicated war...much too complicated for a little girl to understand. Why don't we talk about something else, and when you are older we can talk about this."

Ella did not open her eyes, but she closed the book and carried it to her room. Gloria waited a few minutes and then went to Ella's room to check on her. Ella was lying in bed, crying so hard that she was shaking.

"Ella, baby, what is wrong?"

"I can see the war. It was awful. Mommy, is that ever going to happen to us?'

"Of course not, Ella. We don't let things like that happen here anymore. You don't have to worry. We will always be safe and you will always have Mommy and Daddy to take care of you, no matter what."

Gloria hoped with all her heart that everything she had said to Ella was absolute truth. She knew for sure that she and Jared would always protect Ella, but the rest, well who could really know for sure?

When Gloria went to bed that night, she tossed and turned, too restless to come close to sleep. She had told Jared about Ella and the Civil War picture. His reaction was even stronger than hers had been. He said that it was a good indication that Ella was still too young and impressionable to see the news, or to watch movies or read books, even children's books, about war and disasters. Some kids could handle that sort of stuff, but not Ella. She was just way too sensitive.

Jared's perception of Ella's extreme sensitivity was one of the things that made him so protective of her. When she was first born, he had thought that he would be protecting her from other kids who would make fun of her appearance, but now he realized he was really protecting Ella from herself, from her extreme impressionability and compassion. She was so vulnerable because she was so sensitive to the suffering in the world. And the more vulnerable she was, the more needed he felt. Jared realized that he loved her in a very different way from the way he loved Melanie. In his eyes, Ella was a delicate flower that had to be nurtured and protected from life's inevitable harsh realities in her own little hot house created by Jared's love for her.

Gloria's thoughts about Ella took a different turn. She loved her dearly too, but there was a little part of Gloria that almost feared Ella. *Who is this child? Where did she come from and why? Most of all, why? Why to me? Why now? Why in this day and time? None of the dreams have given me the answers I need to understand who she is.*

Was she born during the Civil War? Is that when Earth Girl lived?

Why can she see with her eyes closed? Why do they look like gold balls instead of real eyes? What was she seeing when she looked at the book through closed eyes? Was she really seeing back into the Civil War? Why won't the voice in those dreams answer these questions?

It was all so unsettling. For the first time in a very long time, she actually wanted to have an Earth Girl dream. She literally begged for one before she finally fell asleep that night. Her plea was answered.

Chapter 22

Before I was born, my father got some goats, a few rabbits and a rooster and a hen. My brother and I thought of them as pets. We liked to collect the eggs each day, and we loved it when the goats and rabbits had babies. My father used to sell the babies to other people who wanted pets for their children. I'll never forget the day I heard him talking to my mother. She was crying and saying things like, "I didn't think it would come to this" and "Don't talk about it in front of the children." She told him she didn't want us to lose our childhood because of worrying. But I was already worried. I had overheard many of their conversations when they thought I was sleeping. I knew that my father was worried because many people were saying that there was going to be a second great drought. He said that if it happened again so soon, millions of people would starve to death. He said it was pretty clear that the drought had begun. He said that people didn't pay attention to the first great drought until it was too late.

Most of what they talked about was so confusing to me. They talked about how people should have known this would happen; that there was plenty of warning, but no one had really paid attention. I remember my father saying, "When I look at the pictures in my great-grandfather's albums, I can't believe how rich they were, and how blue the sky was. It was like a paradise on earth, back then."

Once I heard him tell my mother about going to the ocean with his parents and grandparents when he was very young. He said that was the only time he ever saw the ocean and that he would never forget how beautiful it was. When I heard him talk about it, I decided that someday I would see the ocean, even if I had to travel very far to see it.

They said that all the people who had argued for years about what to do, had caused this problem and that once the leaders failed us, there was nothing everyone else could do. I didn't really understand what that meant. My father used to say that waiting for God to fix every-thing was a big mistake and my mother would say that he should keep that idea quiet in public. "*Blasphemy is not tolerated, you know,*" she would say adamantly, like she was scared he was going to make someone mad. I didn't see why anyone would be mad at us. We were churchgoers and said prayers before we went to bed at night. Sometimes my mother would kneel down and pray during the daytime too.

The other thing they talked about a lot was what that it was harder and harder to buy food. They talked about how everywhere in the world farmers were having terrible trouble growing the crops they used to grow. They said the changes in the weather were having a drastic impact on the growing season and that food was getting so expensive. That's why my father stopped selling the babies. He said we needed them for meat, but my mother hated the idea. She didn't want to eat animals that were our pets. Sometimes they would argue about this. My father would yell at her and say, "*If we are going to survive, you are going to have to toughen up. Do you want your children to starve because of your soft heart towards animals?*"

She would cry and say, "*We could grow beans and rice and become vegetarians if we have to.*"

Then he would say, "*If the farmers can't grow food, what makes you think we can? At least we get protein from animals, and when the food in the stores gets so expensive that only the rich can buy it, at least we will have protein.*"

My mother would always say, "*It's not going to get that bad in our lifetime.*"

After awhile, it seemed like every night when I was in bed pretending to sleep, I heard them arguing about food, or talking about how awful it was that the world was changing so much and so quickly and that there would probably be another war. My father said that people used to think that prosperity would spread all over the world, but that it turned out just the opposite. Once the economy got so bad, people started getting angry and scared and making stupid decisions and not thinking about long-term consequences.

He said that the worse the economy got, the worse everything else would be. He said people would turn against each other because they were losing their way of life. He said that they would make up reasons to hate each other because they wanted a way to justify wiping each other out so that there would be more resources for the people left. My mother would always say that they just needed to have faith and that God would take care of us because we were good people.

I heard these arguments so many times that I asked my teacher at school about it all. She told me not to worry. She said that our country always found a way to stay strong and we would now too. She said the people who were worried didn't have faith in their government or their God. She made me feel guilty for asking. That night when I said my prayers, I prayed to God to forgive me for doubting Him and my leaders. I never mentioned it in school again.

But I think I got her thinking because one day she did a lesson on hurricanes and tornadoes. She said that part of the reason there might be a food shortage was because of extreme weather. She said that natural disasters have a bad impact on the world's economy. I remember her saying how important it was for us to remember that it "is no one's fault." She said that anyone who tried to find reasons for these disasters should look to God for their answers.

I wanted to tell my parents this, but I never did because I knew they didn't want me to worry. I didn't want to let them know that I was worried, and I especially didn't want my little brother to worry. I knew that something must be wrong since my parents were worried, but to me our life still seemed the same as always.

That's why I was so surprised the night my father came home and told my mother that he had joined the militia. She was surprised too. She started to cry. He hugged her and told her it was just a precaution. He said that it was just a show of strength so that they couldn't get any more power. I wondered who he meant.

My mother said that if every town had a militia, soon the militias would turn against each other. Then the ones with the most arms would have the most power.

"Then we need to make sure we have the most arms," said my

father.

"God help us! Where will it all end? If you don't want another war, it doesn't make sense to join a group of armed men," said my mother.

My father got really mad and shouted at her. "This is to prevent war! Don't you understand that the only way to prevent war is to show that you have greater strength than they do?"

He was in the militia for a long time before the really bad times started. He went to meetings every week. Sometimes when my father told my mother what they talked about at the meetings, she would cry. She said that things were worse than she thought. My father said things were going to get even worse. It was the first time I was ever really afraid for our family. I had no idea how bad it would get.

CHAPTER 23

When Gloria awoke, she struggled to remember every detail of the dream. Was Earth Girl talking about the time before the Civil War? She wrote down as much as she could remember. She chided herself for not knowing more about history. She was going to have to do some reading quickly. Maybe she should start with the book Ella had been reading. She hoped that she would read about what Ella had seen and cried over. Gloria felt it would be reassuring if she could find the scenes that made Ella cry in the history book. She was anxious to peruse the chapter on the Civil War. How good it would be to discover Ella had read these things instead of remembering them from experience.

But first, she would have to get Ella off to school. Jared would leave for work within the hour and Ella's bus would come shortly after that. Then she had to get a report finished for work. She should be able to get to the book before Ella got home in the afternoon. Her face was flush with anticipation. She believed that she might finally get some answers.

She grabbed two aspirin before fixing Ella's breakfast. It seemed that no matter what she did lately there was always that nagging pain in her back. *I really need to get back to Pilates.* Then she cut up some fruit to add to Ella's oatmeal. Despite her concerns, this day was beginning as any other day. Gloria thought about how odd it was, that even when something really important is on your mind the daily routines of life still take precedence...meals, work, laundry, caring for family.

She considered that having to take care of the routines of life might be a very good thing when one was worried or traumatized. Maybe these routines provide an anchor; a way to tie down your sanity, when you feel like it might be carried away by worry, fear, mourning, dread, depression, or any of the other debilitating emotions that humans experience. So she finished preparing Ella's breakfast while mentally going over what she needed to do to finish her report for work. The sooner she got that out of the way, the better.

Just as Gloria was closing down her computer she heard Sheila's ringtone. She thought about letting it go to voicemail, but changed her mind. Most likely it would only be a short conversation confirming the date for their dinner. When she answered, Sheila did not respond.

"I think we have a bad connection. Can you hear me, Sheila? Sometimes my phone doesn't work well in this part of the house."

Sheila's response was incoherent, but Gloria was pretty sure she was crying as she spoke.

"Sheila, what's wrong? Did something happen? An accident? Is Joe okay?"

"He's okay, but he's really mad at me."

Sheila sniffled, while trying to regain her composure.

"Why? Did you guys have a fight about something?"

"No. Not a fight really, but I lost the check book and he had to order new checks and then I found it in my lingerie drawer this morning. I thought it was funny, and that made him furious. He called me stupid and careless."

"And that made you cry, hon? That doesn't sound like you, Sheila. Maybe your hormones are going crazy."

"God, not you too! Why does everyone have to attribute a woman's reactions to hormones? You know I finished having periods."

"Okay, sorry, sorry, I just know that I'm going through menopause and I get crazy hormone fluctuations. Just doesn't seem like you to cry over his saying that stuff. The Sheila I know would give it back to him."

"Usually I would, but I just didn't have it in me this morning. I don't know, maybe I'm under too much stress at work or something. I seem to keep falling apart and I don't know why. Anyway I'm sorry I bothered you. I know you're probably busy."

"No problem. I totally hear you. I'm stressed out too. Maybe going out to dinner together will give us all a needed break. Did you and Joe come up with a date?"

"Uh, no...not yet. I'll talk to him about it tonight. Can you text them again? I might have erased the text by mistake."

"Sure, I'll resend the old one. I'm gonna sign off. Got lots to do before Ella gets home. You okay now?"

"Yeah, I'm fine. Just a silly over-reaction. I'll talk to you later."

"Ok, bye now."

The line went silent. *She didn't even say goodbye. She really is out of it lately.* That thought was rapidly forgotten as she headed to find the history book Ella had been reading. Gloria found the reading slow going. She realized she didn't really know much at all about the war, just the basics: North vs. South, slavery, Abe Lincoln. That was about the extent of her knowledge. As she read the chapter on the Civil War, she had to keep turning back to previous chapters to figure out the references to things she knew nothing about. This was going to be harder than she thought, but so far, she noted with dismay, there were no graphic depictions of women and children crying. Before she could consider the implications of that realization Ella was bouncing in the door. She looked as happy and carefree as a child of seven should be.

"Hi, sweetpea!"

"Hi, Mommy. What's for snack? I'm hungry."

"How about an apple and some carrot slices?"

"Okay, but can I have a cookie too?"

"Sure, you can, after you finish your fruit and veggie."

While she was eating, Ella asked if she could look at the history book. Gloria changed the subject by suggesting they go for a walk and buy a special cookie at the People's Café instead of having an Oreo. Then, they could walk down Thames and look in the shops. Gloria was trying to find a substitute for Touro Park, Ella's favorite destination. She loved the mystery tower, but most of all, she loved the trees on the grounds of the Athenaeum.

Gloria had once told her that they must be very old because they were so big. Ella loved the idea that the trees had been alive longer than any people on earth. Gloria had tried to keep her away from the park ever since the homeless man had held the sign about Ella being a prophet.

Ella eagerly agreed to go to People's Cafe. She knew that it had once been a bank and she loved the enormous vault in the dining room. She ran to her room to get her hat and mittens. There was often a coolish breeze on that part of Thames. While Ella was looking for her mittens Gloria took the history book and tucked it away on the top shelf of the cluttered closet that she and Jared shared. Gloria thought about calling Melanie and inviting her and RJ to join them for cookies and hot chocolate. She changed her mind when she remembered the look on Melanie's face when she had left her house that last time. Melanie did not appear to want to spend any time with her. *Too soon, just too soon. Gotta give her time to get over it.*

Thinking about Melanie had a deflating effect on Gloria's mood. It didn't bother her as much that Melanie was angry with her as it did that Melanie seemed so unhappy. Gloria wondered if all mothers shared her inability to be happy if her child was unhappy. It had plagued Gloria from the time Melanie had learned to talk. If Melanie seemed unhappy, not just annoyed or disappointed, but generally unhappy for more than a day or two, Gloria would feel her own mood plummet.

After a few years of this she had come to the conclusion that motherhood forever tied the mother's happiness to the child's happiness. That thought had even provided a slight bit of comfort after her miscarriage when Melanie was four. Anyone with more than one child had less chance of being happy unless all of the children somehow managed to be happy or sad at the same time. *My Lord*, she had thought, *imagine mothers who have big families. Are they ever really at peace or always worried about one of their kids? Or maybe it is just me, and that's why I shouldn't have more than one child. Maybe I just got saved from constant worry.* But that was years ago, and now she had two children and was worried about both of them.

She tried to brush all thoughts of Melanie, the Civil War, and the myriad other things that worried her, completely out of her mind as she and Ella headed down Thames. This was a chance to enjoy an afternoon with Ella and she was going to make the most of it. She really didn't want Ella to pick up on what she was feeling. Ella sometimes seemed like a mind reader to Jared and Gloria. She seemed to be able to sense their moods and even the reasons for them. Hopefully today Gloria could fool her.

At dinner that evening Ella caught both Gloria and Jared off guard by bringing up a topic she had never discussed before. She wanted to know where babies came from. Jared looked at Gloria as if to say, "This one is all yours." Gloria looked at Ella, as if to say, "Do you really want to know that already?" Ella looked back and forth at them with an expectant look on her face. Then she said, "I think I might know already."

"Oh, sweetpea, maybe you do," replied Gloria. "Tell us what you think."

"I think there is a place in the sky with all the babies in the world and they take turns coming down here. They fly around looking for the parents they want, but no one can see them because they are invisible. When they find the parents they want, they go inside the mommy's tummy and when they get big she goes to the hospital and the doctor takes them out. But the part I don't get is how they get inside the mommy's tummy."

Before Gloria could say anything, Jared jumped in.

"You are such a smart little girl. I think you are right about where babies come from."

"But how do they get in the mommy's tummy, Daddy."

"Well, that's the tricky part, sweetpea."

Gloria wondered if he was really going to go there. Ella seemed too young for penises, vaginas, uterus, sperm, eggs, all of it. Yet she didn't think lying to her was a good idea. She looked at Jared quizzically, wondering just how he would explain the tricky part.

"Well, you see, Ella, the babies are so very tiny when they come down here, that the daddy can just put them in the mommy's tummy."

"But how? Does he have to cut a hole in the mommy's tummy?

"No," Jared said slowly, "uh, the mommy...help me out here, Gloria."

"Well, okay, you see the mommies already have a hole," offered Gloria.

Ella was enthralled.

"They do?? Where is it?"

"Well, it is in their private part," Gloria said while trying to figure out the answer to the inevitable next question.

"Ooooh, I know where you mean," said Ella knowingly. "You mean where the pee comes out."

"Well, not..."

Jared cut Gloria off before she could finish.

"Yes, there."

Ella contemplated this information for a moment. Then she said she had to go to the bathroom. In a minute she was back with another question.

"Why doesn't the baby fall out when the mommy pees."

Gloria took over.

"Well, it is not exactly that hole. It is another one that mommies have and it is near it."

"Oh," said Ella. "Well how does the daddy put the baby in it?"

Jared looked proud of himself, as if he had figured out a somewhat truthful way to avoid the truth.

"Well," he said. "Every daddy has his own special way."

"How did you do it, Daddy, when you put me in Mommy?"

Gloria's heart started to race. This was the worst question Ella could ever ask. She hoped, beyond hope, that Jared would not begin to doubt her again.

"I did it very carefully because I love Mommy so much."

Jared reached for Gloria's hand across the table. When she took it she had tears streaming down her cheeks.

"What's the matter, Mommy? Did it hurt when Daddy put me in your tummy?"

"No, my dear one. I'm crying because I love you and Daddy so much. I am so lucky to have you both. Sometimes people cry when they are happy. Those are very special times."

When Gloria and Jared were out to dinner with Sheila and Joe, Jared told them about Ella wanting to know where babies come from. He repeated with obvious delight Ella's theory about all the babies waiting up in the sky and taking turns to come to earth.

"Did she want to know the details, you know the birds and the bees stuff?" asked Joe.

"She did but Jared avoided it rather masterfully, I'd say," answered Gloria.

"I hope she didn't ask where she came from. That would be quite a story, wouldn't it?" said Sheila.

Before she got the last word out, Joe kicked her shin.

"Ouch! What did you do that for?"

"Inappropriate, Sheila" mumbled Joe.

"Hey, no worries. We're past all that now. It's all good," said Jared.

Gloria put her hand on his thigh and gave it a little pat. Jared knew that she was trying to show her appreciation that he didn't allow the conversation to go to Ella's conception.

The rest of the evening was uneventful; pleasant chit-chat about sports, work, movies the usual conversations that people have when they want to avoid other, more difficult topics. Gloria noticed that Joe seemed a little short with Sheila now and then. She wondered if she would have noticed if she and Sheila had not talked about it before. Probably nothing, she concluded. But when they were getting ready for bed, Jared said that he thought Joe had seemed awfully tense and kind of snippy with Sheila.

Gloria recounted the conversation they had when Sheila called her in tears. Jared was surprised by all of it. It seemed out of character for Sheila. Privately he marveled and thanked his lucky stars that he and Gloria were in a better place than Joe and Sheila. *Who would have thought it? After everything we have been through?* It wouldn't be too long before Jared was truly counting his blessings as he compared their situation to Joe and Sheila's.

The next morning, Jared decided to stop by Melanie's just to check in. He didn't want Melanie's difficulties with Gloria to sour his relationship with her. Roger answered the door after Jared rang the bell twice.

"I didn't know you were coming over this morning. Did Mel call you?"

"No, I just was out and thought I'd drop by to say hi. I probably should have called. I haven't seen you guys in awhile. That's all."

"You might as well come in now that you are here," offered Roger, sounding only slightly more cordial than he had a moment ago.

"Well, if it's not a bother. If I'm interrupting something I can always come back another time."

"No c'mon in. I'll get Mel. She was sleeping in this morning, but it's high time she got up anyway. RJ's been driving me crazy. Maybe he'll straighten out because you're here."

Jared sat down on the living room sofa. He could hear Roger telling Mel to get up because her father was here. He sounded sort of annoyed. *Must have caught him at a bad time. Maybe I should have called. But heck, she is my daughter. I ought to be able to drop in without an engraved invitation.*

Mel came downstairs looking as if she had literally just rolled out of bed. Her hair was pulled back in a low ponytail, but half of it had fallen out of the elastic and was hanging on one side of her face. She was wearing sweat pants and a tee-shirt with a faded peace symbol on it. Jared was fighting the thought that his young daughter had become rather frumpy since RJ was born.

"Hey, Mel, got a hug for your old man?"

"Sure, Dad. Sorry I'm such a mess. Just couldn't drag myself out of bed this morning."

Melanie looked around the room and asked where RJ was.

"He's in the yard. I made him go outside to play. He wouldn't settle down and he was driving me crazy so I told him to blow off some steam outside," replied Roger.

Melanie plodded into the kitchen shuffling her fuzzy slippers along the floor.

"Dad, Rog, do you guys want coffee?

"I've already had mine for the day," answered Jared.

"Dad, let's go outside with RJ for awhile. He'll be glad to see you."

RJ raced up to Jared as he stepped out of the back door into the back yard. He jumped onto him with so much enthusiasm that he almost knocked Jared over.

"Whooaa, buddy! You gotta give me warning before you tackle me like that. You almost knocked me over."

"Oh great. You're mad at me too. Everyone is always mad at me no matter what I do."

"I'm not mad at you, RJ. I was just surprised when you jumped up on me that way. It's ok. No one is mad at you."

"That's just a lie!" RJ said angrily. "Grown-ups are always mad at me and they always want to tell me what to do. Do this, do that. Don't make noise. Don't make a mess. Don't talk back. I'm sick of it!"

RJ ran over to a punching bag hanging from a tree limb. He started hitting it wildly.

"Wow, Mel, what got in to him? He seems furious!"

"He IS furious, Dad. He's always sort of angry and then when Roger yells at him it just gets worse. That's why I didn't get up this morning. I just couldn't take it anymore."

"Oh, Mel. I don't know what to say," stammered Jared. "I hope I didn't make things worse."

"No, Daddy, you didn't. This is just the way it is for us. RJ is always upset. He hates being told what to do. I try to give him choices so that he doesn't feel so bossed around, but Roger thinks I am spoiling him. About the only thing we could agree on was getting that punching bag. It's a way for him to let out his anger."

"What's he so angry about?"

"I wish I knew, Dad, I wish I knew. It started when he was in kindergarten with Ella, like once in awhile and then it got more frequent and now it has really escalated since we had him transferred to a different class. Seems like I have to walk on eggshells around him and Roger."

"Why Roger?"

"Because Roger thinks it's all my fault."

Melanie's face began to crumple in the very same way it did right before she would cry when she was a little girl. Then the first tears showed up in the corner of her eyes. Soon they were streaming down her cheeks.

"He thinks I'm a bad mother, Dad."

"Oh, baby, you're not a bad mother. Most of the things that are hard about kids are born in them. It's not your fault. I know you're a great mother, but I guess you got a really hard kid."

Melanie hid her face in her father's chest to muffle her sobs. Jared knew these were the miserable sobs of someone who was tired and overwhelmed. He didn't know what to say so he just patted her back.

"Sorry, Dad, it just hurts so much to have my precious son be so unhappy and so alone. I don't think he has friends at school."

"Have you thought of counseling for him or maybe family counseling?"

Jared could not believe he was suggesting counseling. Until he and Gloria had gone to a therapist, he had thought of counseling as little more than paying someone to listen to your problems. But when he and Gloria were going through the worst time in their marriage, counseling had saved it.

"I have suggested it but Roger won't have anything to do with counseling. He says it is how rich, self-absorbed people get someone to pay attention to them. It's so weird! He has all these ideas that are so different from mine and I didn't even know it until we had RJ."

"Yeah, people learn a lot about each other when they start raising kids together," offered Jared.

To himself, he thought ruefully how it could make or break a marriage. He wanted to suggest that Melanie talk to Gloria, but he didn't know if that would just upset Melanie more. So, he left it unsaid.

"I'm going to say goodbye to RJ. I don't want him to think I am mad at him," he said.

Jared went back outside and sat down next to RJ who was digging a small hole in the yard.

"Whatcha doing? Digging for worms?"

"No. Just digging. I found this."

RJ was holding a tarnished ring.

"Can I see, it? Looks like you might have found buried treasure!"

"Naw, it's just an old ring. It was wrapped in this beat-up rag."

Jared was fascinated by RJ's find. He had never seen one like it. He suggested that RJ go inside to show his parents.

"I don't want to. I want it to be my secret. Besides, my dad said I have to stay outside until he tells me I can come back in. I drive him crazy. He can't relax when I'm around."

"Oh, buddy, dads say stuff like that sometimes, but they don't really mean them. Your dad is just tired from a long week at work."

"You and Grammy keep telling me how tired everyone is.

Why don't grown-ups just go to bed earlier if they are always tired and cranky?"

"That's a good question, my man. I'm going to go home and try to figure that one out."

Jared felt like it was a feeble response, but couldn't come up with anything better.

CHAPTER 24

On the drive home Jared kept changing his mind about whether to share what Melanie told him with Gloria. He really wanted to, but he feared that Gloria would not be able to resist the urge to call Melanie. He knew Gloria well enough to be sure that if she knew how much Melanie was hurting she would be there whether Melanie wanted it or not. And he knew Melanie well enough to know that Gloria's concern would really piss her off. He didn't have to make the choice, however, because Gloria greeted him at the door saying she was glad he was home. She had gotten a call from Sheila and she felt like she better get over there. Sheila was crying again.

When Gloria arrived, Sheila thanked her for coming.

"There's some stuff I have to tell you. I wasn't going to say anything yet, but I need for someone to know. Just one person, Gloria! I don't want Jared to know. Promise, Gloria, you won't tell anyone."

"Wow, Sheila, that's a heavy-duty promise when I don't even know what we are talking about."

"Okay, I understand. It's probably not fair. Never mind."

"Wait, Sheila, if you need to talk, you should and I won't say anything right away, but depending on what it is, I might have to sometime. Like, if you have cancer or something. You can't keep that a secret for long, you know."

"I don't have cancer. But I think I might have Alzheimer's. There I said it."

"What do you mean, Sheila?" gasped Gloria. "Why do you think that? I hope it's not because you forget a few things now and then. We all do that."

"I know, but I think my forgetting is worse. I can't find the words I want sometimes, and lately some simple things have really confused me. Things I usually understand."

"Like what?"

"Like the other day, I wanted to open the padlock on the shed door. I've been opening that thing for years, and I just couldn't do it. I even looked for the old instructions with the...you know...the set of numbers...what's it called...the, the..."

"Combination. Do you mean the combination?"

"Yes that's it. See what I mean. I know that word but I couldn't think of it."

"That happens to me too, sometimes, Sheila. I get a word on the tip of my tongue but I just can't remember it, and then later I will. I don't think that is Alzheimer's. I think that is being tired or stressed or just plain getting older."

"But Gloria, even after I read the instructions and the combination, I couldn't make it work. I was embarrassed to ask Joe for help. So I just didn't open the shed. I piled all the weeds in a trash bag instead of the basket we usually use."

"Why would you be embarrassed to ask Joe? He's your husband."

"That's just it. Lately he thinks I'm careless and stupid, and I don't want to give him any more ammunition. I don't want him to know all the trouble I'm having."

Sheila tried to explain to Gloria that if she really had Alzheimer's she wasn't ready for Joe to see her that way yet. She didn't want him to see her as a sick person or someone to pity or, worst of all, someone he would be stuck taking care of when she was drooling and incontinent. As Sheila talked she began to feel extremely vulnerable. Sheila's grandmother had died from Alzheimer's and she knew what the disease could do.

"I just needed to be able to tell one person, so that I am not carrying this alone. Maybe it's not Alzheimer's. I'm not ready to know for sure yet. I don't think I could handle it if I was sure. But I really don't want Joe to know that I even suspect it. I don't want him to start looking for signs and getting all upset when I forget something. He has enough to worry about with work and all."

Although Gloria didn't know what specifically Joe might be

worried about at work, she could believe that he was worried. She was too. They were laying people off left and right.

"Gloria, please don't tell anyone."

"I won't tell anyone, for now, but if you're right – and I doubt that you are – I will have to tell someone eventually. But not until you're sure," Gloria said softly.

"Not until I am ready," Sheila said firmly. "Not until I am ready. It should be my decision. Okay?"

"Okay."

Sheila hugged Gloria and suggested that she should leave because Joe would be back soon and he would wonder why Gloria was there. Gloria realized that she was going to have to come up with a story for Jared; some way to explain why Sheila had been crying that didn't involve Joe. Gloria wracked her brain all the way home. Finally, she thought she would say that Sheila was in menopause and she was crying like that because she had gained a few pounds. Gloria knew that most men feared the weird behavior their wives might engage in during the hormone-depleting, raging storm taking place in their wives' helpless bodies. They had all heard stories. Jared would believe this one.

A few days later, Sheila called Gloria and dissolved in tears before she could even tell her what was wrong. Gloria dropped everything and went to their house. She found Joe in his sweat pants and a robe. Sheila was still in her nightgown. Her eyes were swollen from crying and her face was mottled. Gloria figured that Sheila must have been crying for a long time. She hugged her briefly and asked her what was going on.

"My boss called me in for a meeting yesterday and he told me that he wanted me to apply for disability. He said that I should get a complete physical and discuss neurological issues with my doctor. He said that they were looking to hire someone to replace me, and that I could take paid leave until I have the physical."

"Oh, Sheila, no wonder you are upset. Is that why Joe stayed home from work today?"

"No," Sheila whispered, "he got laid off two weeks ago. He didn't want you to know, especially since you work there too. I'm not supposed to tell anyone. He didn't even tell me for the first week. He left the house every morning, like he was going to work."

"Omigod, this really sucks. No wonder he's been on edge," Gloria said, while thinking to herself that she sure hoped Sheila qualified for 100% disability.

"Sheila, how can I help?"

"Gloria, I don't think you can help. Maybe Jared can find work for Joe and that would help, but he can't really do anything until Joe decides to tell him what is going on."

"I could tell Jared what is going on and he could start looking so that something is lined up when Joe tells him. He has lots of contacts, but with the economy the way it is, it will probably take awhile for him to find someone who wants to hire."

"I know that and I also know that he is so worried about me that he probably hasn't even been able to concentrate on work. I hate myself for putting him through this. At first I was really resentful when he kept pointing out the things I was forgetting. It would make me so mad when he would yell at me. But now I know he must have been so worried about everything."

"He shouldn't yell and get mad at you. That just makes it worse."

"It's really not his fault, Gloria. Look, you can't imagine what it is like to live with someone who keeps forgetting and getting lost and confused. I know what my grandfather and my mother went through with my grandmother. It was awful for all of them."

"I remember you talking about that in high school, about how upset your mom was because of it."

"Yeah, it was really hard on the whole family especially in the beginning because so much of the time she was still normal. No one knew what was going on with her. Out of the blue she would do some weird thing or get lost right in their neighborhood."

Sheila took a deep breath and continued.

"That's the way I'm going to be soon..."

"Aw, Sheila, I think you're over-reacting. You're not like that at all. Even if you do have Alzheimer's, you have years before you are like that."

"Probably not, Gloria. They say the younger you get it, the faster it progresses. I haven't gotten lost yet, but I am forgetting lots of things. Mostly, I can still usually figure out how to cover it or make a reasonable excuse. Eventually I won't even know I forgot."

"Sheila, don't say that. You don't know for sure that you have Alzheimer's. Have you seen a doctor?"

"No, I know I should. It's crazy not to because I am almost a hundred percent sure that I do have it, but I don't want a doctor to confirm it. Then I won't have even a little bit of hope."

Tears started streaming down Sheila's cheeks. Gloria grabbed her close and hugged her tight.

"We'll be here for you no matter what. Do you want me to try talking to Joe?"

"No way! He's already mad at me for getting fired. I know he didn't mean it, but he said, 'You sure have great timing...screwing up at work right after I get laid off.'"

"Geez, Sheila, that's pretty cold. He must be really worried. Do you need to borrow some money?"

"I don't know. I think I paid everything for this month, but I can't find the check book or the stubs. Maybe he paid them. I'm afraid to ask him. I don't want to set him off again."

Gloria sat in silence for a moment as she tried to figure out what to say. Just as she started to speak, Sheila put her finger to her lips and said, "Shhh! Don't say anything. There's no way to help me."

"That's not true, Sheila, there are medications and exercises and computer programs and they are making progress towards a cure every day."

"Not enough progress, Gloria, not soon enough. The best thing you can do for me is promise to help me if I decide to kill myself."

"Sheila, you don't mean that," shrieked Gloria

"Don't tell me what I mean unless you are in my situation. You don't know what it feels like to know that you will lose your mind, your memory, everything that makes you who you are and that the people who love you will suffer even more than you."

"Sheila, oh, sweetheart, that's not gonna happen. You're strong and smart and so full of life. You have lots of good years ahead of you. You're scared now, that's all."

"Glo, I wish you were right. But, I've seen this first hand and I know I don't want Joe to go through it and I sure as hell don't want Roger to have to go through what my grandfather went through. I've thought about it a lot, a whole lot and I really do think that suicide could be the best solution for everyone involved."

"Oh no, Sheila! That would be the worst thing you could do. If you care about the people who love you, you can't kill yourself. Promise me you'll give Joe and your sister and me the chance to help you. No matter what the doctor says."

"Okay, but only if you promise not to tell Joe yet, or even Jared."

Gloria nodded, but in her mind she was already making excuses for breaking Sheila's trust. Sooner or later, she was going to tell Jared and Joe. Right now the best she could do was to fix them some thing to eat and tidy up the house a little. She wondered to herself what the right balance was. Doing what was needed, yet not doing so much that it seemed as if she was really worried about her. As she walked toward the refrigerator Sheila noticed and got up. She reached for the coffee pot and filled it with water.

She tried to sound casual as she said, "Great hostess, I am! I ask you to come over; cry on your shoulder; and don't even offer you a cup of coffee." As she waited for the coffee to brew she paced around the kitchen, her slippers scuffing along the tile floor. She thought briefly of how happy she had been the day the work on the floor had been done.

She and Joe had taken great pride in renovating their dilapidated Victorian themselves. They had worked together well and felt a real sense of accomplishment when each task was complete. The kitchen had been the most difficult and most expensive. Sheila had spent months choosing tiles, cabinet handles and finishes for the cabinets. Joe had let her make all the decorative decisions and she had really enjoyed it watching it all come together. She felt that they had worked well as a team. Thinking back on those hours spent collaborating, with each of them bringing their own skills to the task, was frightening. She was sure that this collaboration would not be possible now. What she had been capable of a few years ago seemed to be so much more than she was capable of now. Her heart sank into the pit of her stomach. Trying to shake the thought, she reached for the coffee pot.

Gloria sat politely waiting for a cup of coffee and not having any idea what to say or do next. How could she keep this secret from Jared? More importantly, from Joe? Gloria hadn't felt this confused and unsure of what to do since she had discovered she was pregnant with Ella. She had taken comfort in thinking that she would never find herself in such a quandary again. But here she was not knowing what to do and wanting so very much to do the right thing

CHAPTER 25

The ride between their houses was less than five miles, but it took Gloria over an hour. Every time she got near her street she turned in another direction, not wanting to enter the house without resolving the dilemma of how much to share with Jared. She didn't want to break Sheila's trust, and she certainly did not want to create alarm about Sheila's health, but she also felt in her gut that if Sheila did have Alzheimer's her husband needed to know sooner, rather than later.

Her inability to decide kept her driving up and down local roads, buying time before going home. It reminded her of when she would take Melanie to the store with her when she was a toddler. If this active little girl fell asleep in the car Gloria knew she could get an hour or more of peace and quiet by just driving around. But if she tried to take her home and put her in bed the nap would surely end and she would end up with a tired, cranky child. So she drove up and down and all around just to keep little Mel asleep.

On this day she was retracing those old routes with a heavy heart and a racing mind. It seemed that the peace of the last year had all come crashing to a halt. She was finding it hard to quell her need to know who Ella really was and why she forced her way into Gloria's mundane, yet pleasant life. She was worried about RJ and even more worried about her own relationship with Melanie. And now this revelation from Sheila! It was starting to feel like too much. *What did Earth Girl say...I had lost my connection to my celestial life? Can all of life's struggles be explained by this? Is life really supposed to be this hard?* She didn't know what she believed. If only she could talk to Jared about it.

There was almost no way Gloria could have any peace of mind while carrying this secret, but she had promised to wait. So she couldn't talk to Jared about this, but she could talk to him about Melanie. As she drove she tried to convince herself that if she could concentrate on Mel she could stop worrying about Sheila for a little while. If so, then maybe she would get rid of her nagging backache. All this stress was making the backache an incessant nuisance.

When Gloria finally arrived home she was surprised to find Ella in the back yard digging a shallow hole with Jared's garden hoe. As she approached her Ella jumped up and said, "Mommy, I'm so glad you're home. We have to go buy seeds for my garden."

"Garden? I didn't know you were planting a garden. It's the wrong time of year for a garden. We have to wait until the weather gets warmer."

"But Daddy said I could," was Ella's emphatic response. "He gave me this little shovel and told me I could start digging the garden."

"Well, Ella, I guess Daddy doesn't know much about gardening because nothing will grow at this time of year," replied Gloria with a hint of exasperation.

Ella began to cry. She had never been the sort of child to have temper tantrums, but when she was truly disappointed she would usually dissolve into tears. Gloria reached down to hug her, but Ella pulled away.

"We have to do something soon, Mommy! If we don't, we'll starve to death."

Gloria picked up Ella, who in the short time that she had been home had morphed from a rosy-cheeked, cheerful child into a splotchy-faced, tearful, frightened one. She had never seen Ella's mood change so dramatically so quickly.

"Ella, sit on Mommy's lap, and tell me what this is all about. Why do you think we are going to starve? We have plenty of food, and there is plenty more in the grocery store. You know that."

"It's because of the famine."

Gloria held back a smile.

"Honey, we aren't in danger of a famine. Where did you ever get the idea we were going to have a famine?"

"I saw it in one of Daddy's magazines. There is a famine already and children are starving and they are really skinny and they look real sad and sick."

"Oh, sweetie, you are right. There is a famine in Africa but that is not here. We don't have famines here."

"But why not?"

"Well, I guess we don't have the weather conditions that lead to famine and we have fertile land here and big farms that make lots of food."

"Then why don't we share our food with those children?"

"We do share it with them. We have organizations that give them food."

Ella thought for a minute. Then she climbed off her mother's lap and said, "It doesn't look like we are giving them enough."

"No, Ella, it doesn't seem like enough. But these are very complicated questions and there are things we can't control, like droughts."

"Droughts? What is a drought?"

"It's when there is not enough rain, so the crops, you know, the food can't grow."

"Did we ever have a drought here?"

"No, honey, we never did and we never will. We know how to keep these things from happening."

"Why don't we tell Africa how to keep it from happening?"

"Oh, sweetie, it is much more complicated than that. I think you should stop reading Daddy's magazines until you are older and you can understand these things better."

If there was one thing Ella could not tolerate, it was being told that she was too young to understand something.

"You're wrong, Mommy. You don't understand. You don't even care about those starving children. But I do and I am going to send them food."

Gloria decided not to argue about it. Explaining the intricacies of the world food system, something she herself had never thought about and didn't really understand, to a seven-year-old seemed like a futile endeavor. Besides, Ella's concern about famine and drought gave her an uneasy feeling. Wasn't there something in her last Earth Girl dream about that? She was sure there was but she wanted to check the notes she had written when she woke up.

"Speaking of food, it's time for your lunch. How about mac and cheese?"

"Okay," Ella answered sullenly.

Gloria opened the refrigerator, took out some leftover organic whole-wheat macaroni and cheese and heated it in the microwave. While it was heating, she poured Ella a glass of organic apple juice. Lunch was on the table within minutes. Ella looked at her plate. Then she very carefully divided the serving of macaroni and cheese in half. She ate all of one half and left the other half untouched on her plate. She carried her plate to Gloria and asked her what kind of envelope they should use to send the mac and cheese to Africa. Gloria put it in a plastic container in the refrigerator and said that she thought they should accumulate more before they mail it. She sent Ella to the bathroom to brush her teeth.

Gloria hurried into their bedroom looking for the magazine that Ella had read. Wondering how Jared could be so careless after they had both been so careful to make sure Ella never saw the news, she searched the room without any luck. Heading next to Ella's room, she couldn't wait to confront Jared and tell him about the effect the article had on Ella. She spotted the magazine on Ella's bed. It was next to a doll, a raggedy old stuffed bunny and her favorite picture book. The magazine was open to a page that was devoted to pictures of Somalian children and families suffering through the ever-expanding famine. Gloria grabbed the magazine and tucked it under her sweater.

"Top shelf of the closet with the history book for you," she said to herself, while thinking that she was going to need to find a bigger hiding place if the trend continued. Ella seemed to be almost searching for sources of information that would upset her.

Gloria found Jared in the basement, tinkering with his old ham-radio set.

"What in the world were you thinking, letting Ella get hold of that magazine?" she demanded angrily.

"What magazine? Oh no! Did she find my Playboy stash?" Jared's face turned scarlet. "I'm really sorry. I didn't think she would..."

"Playboy stash?" she interrupted. "I didn't know you have a Playboy stash. What are you, a 12-year-old? No, not your precious Playboy stash. Newsweek! The one about the famine in Somalia. That's what magazine!"

Jared looked alarmed.

"She found that? Oh no, that's got some pretty graphic pictures."

"It sure does. I can't believe you would leave it around where she could find it! Why do you think she wanted to plant a garden and why in the world did you tell her she could?!?"

Gloria was surprised at the sound of her own voice. It was angry, desperate and almost hysterical.

"You should have seen what she did with her lunch. She would only eat half of it. She wants to mail the other half to Africa."

"Aww, that's not so bad, Gloria. It's sweet. It shows how kind she is. She's very compassionate for her age."

Gloria was not to be pacified.

"Too compassionate for her age and for her own good. You know that. You know how she is when she finds out about something like this. Isn't this why YOU said she should never see the news and then YOU leave this magazine lying around for her to find and YOU tell her, sure go ahead, plant a garden. Are you insane?"

"No, but I'm beginning to think you are. Don't you think you are over-reacting just a tiny bit?" responded Jared.

"No I don't and you won't either when she starts asking you about famines and droughts and starving to death. Just wait, you'll see."

Jared wondered if Gloria was hormonal. First Sheila's crying jags, now Gloria's anger. He and Joe were in for a rough ride. At the same time, Gloria realized that she was so angry because she was so scared. Scared that Ella was Earth Girl's baby. Scared that if she kept finding stuff about wars and famines and other things that Earth Girl talked about in her dream, she was going to be forced to do something. Hadn't the voice in the dreams told her that Ella was going to be her guide? Well if Earth Girl or whoever she was, thought that Ella could convince Gloria to join Red Cross or become another Mother Theresa, she was dead wrong.

"I am not changing my entire life because of this. No way!" she vowed silently.

"Gloria, what is wrong with you? You look like you are in a trance, or something. Do you feel okay?" asked Jared.

"I'm just tired and really worried about Ella. She's so overly impressionable. I need to lie down and clear my head for a few minutes. Maybe you should go talk to Ella and try to repair the damage."

Gloria turned around, feeling slightly dizzy and disoriented. She held one hand on her lower back as she slowly climbed the stairs. She passed the mirror in the hallway, but she did not look at herself. If she had, she would have seen how pale she was.

Gloria closed her eyes as soon as her head hit the pillow. She thought she would sleep but her back was now throbbing with pain. The best she could do was rest her eyes as her mind jumped from one idea to another. She called to Jared and asked him to take Ella out for a few hours. She told him she needed some time to herself. What she actually meant was she needed time to get back to reading about the Civil War and to checking the notes from her dream. She was pretty sure Earth Girl had talked about drought, famine and war. If that was the case it was probably more than a coincidence that Ella was worrying about famines.

When Gloria stood up, she noticed a small stain on the sheet. *Oh crap, don't tell me I am having a period. Really?? I thought I was finished with that! What a perfect fucking day this is turning out to be.* Gloria went to the bathroom and took out a half-empty box of tampons. *Guess it is good that I never throw anything away.*

Gloria fixed herself a cup of Be Calm herbal tea and started looking through the history book. As she thumbed through it she noticed a page with a picture of one of the large graves commemorating the deaths on the Western Front during WWI. She had never seen this picture before and she was struck by the seemingly endless rows of simple crosses. She realized that she didn't really know anything about WWI. Wasn't it "the big one" that Archie Bunker used to talk about? No, maybe that was WWII.

She was embarrassed to admit to herself that she sort of mentally put WWI and WWII into the same file cabinet in her brain. Big wars in Europe that the U.S. helped the good guys to win. She turned back a few pages to the beginning of the chapter on WWI. It was titled "The War to End All Wars." Gloria chuckled wryly. *Hmmm, they need to get a new title. How many wars have we had since WWI? Let's see. WWII, Vietnam, Iraq and Afghanistan. Are they even wars or just invasions? This book is too old. It doesn't even have anything about them.* She continued skipping around through the book, talking to herself as she looked for pictures from wars.

"Korean War? When was that? I don't think I ever heard of it. Well, whatever. WWI sure wasn't the one that ended all wars. Kinda sad really. I wonder how many wars the U.S. has been in since the Revolutionary War? Probably about 6 or 7, if you count the Civil War."

Gloria's curiosity was piqued. She went to Google and entered "all U.S. wars." She found a link to a site headed Wars with U.S. Involvement. She skipped the six wars listed before the Revolutionary War because those wars involved the colonists and the U.S. wasn't actually a country yet.

She was amazed to find that starting with the Revolutionary War the U.S. had been involved in twenty wars. She wondered if other countries were involved in that many wars and then she started wondering if anyone had ever counted all the wars since recorded history. She doubted it, but what the heck, back to Google. After a less-than-thorough search, she decided that probably no one really knew. But one source estimated that since 3500 BC more than 14,500 wars had taken place, leaving only 300 years of peace in approximately 5500 years. She was astounded.

This was eye-opening. She had never really thought about it much before. How could there be so much war? She assumed that some of the early wars were probably small-size battles, *but still, that's a lot of death and destruction, no matter what you call it.* She wondered if there ever would be a war to end all wars and if the way it ended all war would be by wiping out humanity altogether.

Using war as a way to solve problems seemed so futile. If war really was a solution, why did new wars keep breaking out? In all the years that humans had inhabited the earth, with all the progress that had been made, why was it that humans still thought attacking each other was the way to solve a conflict?

After contemplating this idea for a few seconds Gloria decided this was information she would never want Ella to have. It was hard enough for Gloria to think about. She was sure it would totally devastate Ella. So she decided to just concentrate on the Civil War, because that was the one Ella was so concerned about. It worried her to realize that Ella was so upset about the Civil War and she didn't even know the part about slavery yet.

Gloria turned back to the chapter on the Civil War. Although there was a lot of information about specific battles, Gloria did not find anything about drought and famine. Not that it meant much whether the book included that or not. She knew that history survey books only covered a small fraction of what actually happened so it was still possible that Earth Girl had lived during the Civil War and that was why Ella was drawn to that chapter. Gloria rubbed her forehead and closed her eyes. *I really need to understand all this. At the very least, I need to keep Ella away from everything that makes her think about this kind of stuff. Because I am beginning to realize that when she thinks about this stuff it hurts me as much as it hurts her. It makes me so anxious and worried.*

Gloria stood up and stretched her back. She didn't know where she was going with all this research. She felt the need to know if Ella saw something about the women and children being scared and crying in this book – and she definitely didn't. Ella's vision must have come from another source or right out of her own head. Could she really be remembering the war at Earth Girl's time? If she was really Earth Girl's baby, she died during her own birth. How could she remember any of that? Gloria flushed and her heart beat rapidly. She was more confused than she had when she began. It just didn't make sense.

Gloria closed the book and looked at the notes she had scribbled after her most recent Earth Girl dream. *Yes. It is right there. Drought and famine. Just like I remembered.* The hairs on her arms tingled. *Something is definitely happening. She is finding stuff that is like the stuff in my dreams.* Then she spoke aloud. Her words sounding like a prayer or, perhaps, a plea.

"I am not ready yet. She is still too young. Please, I'm not ready. Not yet. Not yet."

That night Gloria had the briefest of dreams. This one seemed as if it was a direct response to her plea.

"You have sensed that Ella is beginning to search for the message. You are right about this. And you have asked for more time, but I can not give you more time. You don't have that much time, and Ella will

need you to help her prepare."

Gloria woke up immediately. She remembered every word of the dream clearly. *What does she mean that I don't have much time?* Suddenly her back hurt more than ever. The following morning, Gloria was surprised and delighted to get a call from Melanie.

"Hi, Mom, it's Mel. I know things have been a little tense between us and I just wondered if you would want to go out to coffee with me. I've been sort of missing you."

"I would absolutely love to. Name the time and place I'll be there. What about RJ?"

"I know Dad's schedule is pretty flexible. I wondered if we could go sometime when he can watch RJ."

"I'm sure that would work. I'll ask him when."

And so the plans for rapprochement between mother and daughter began. Two days later, they sat at the People's Café drinking coffee and sharing a pastry. After a few minutes of pleasant chit-chat, Melanie took her mother's hand.

"Mom, I have to get something off my chest. I'm sorry about the other day. I couldn't help it. The whole thing about how you got pregnant still really bothers me. I won't deny it."

Gloria's jaw tightened *Here we go again.* She sighed and looked into her cup.

"But when I got mad at you that day at my house I saw the look on your face when you left and I've been feeling kind of bad ever since. I mean I, well, I just want you to know I love you and I love Ella too."

A flood of relief rushed through Gloria's veins. She could literally feel herself relax.

"I know you do, Mel, and I have missed you so much. I feel like it's my fault we're growing so far apart. I need to apologize for not being there for you when RJ was born. I should have apologized for that years ago and for not being a better grand-mother to him. I was so excited when you got pregnant. I really wanted to be a good grammy."

"You are a good grammy. He adores you."

"It's mutual.

Gloria's smile masked her feelings. "Okay Mel, maybe I shouldn't even say this. Maybe I should just learn to mind my own business. But I can't. I'm really worried about him. He's so sad."

"Yeah, Mom, he really is sad and it makes me feel like an awful mother. That's part of why I got mad when you came over. I feel like RJ's problems are my fault and Roger keeps me telling me it's my fault."

Gloria regretted that she had voiced her concerns about RJ. "Oh, Mel, I'm sure you're a great mother. Roger is wrong to blame you."

Melanie's eyes filled with tears. Gloria wished she could make her feel better the way she could when Mel was still her little girl.

"Mom, what did you do when Dad blamed stuff on you and criticized you?"

Gloria paused and reflected a moment before answering.

"I don't really remember Dad doing that. Well, except for when I was pregnant with Ella and then I didn't know if we would make it, you know, make it work, stay together."

These words brought back a flood of difficult memories for both of them. The two women sat facing each other and holding hands. Both had tearstained cheeks. Neither said a word. Each was lost in her own thoughts.

CHAPTER 26

When Gloria pulled up to their driveway she realized that she did not remember anything about the drive home. She had been on automatic pilot the whole way, distracted by thoughts of Melanie and how sad she was. It was not until entering the house that thoughts of Ella entered her mind. She couldn't wait to find a private time with Jared to tell him what was going in with Melanie. Of course, first he would have to return from babysitting at Mel's house and maybe she would have already told him herself by then. Gloria brewed herself another cup of Be Calm tea. It seemed that she felt the need for it more and more lately. Within the last few weeks, everything in her life had begun to change. Ella's interest in war and famine, Sheila's possible dementia and Melanie and RJ's sadness. So much bad news about people she loved. And this constant pain in her lower back.

She was beginning to feel like just giving up. Just letting whatever was going to happen, happen without her interference. She had never been capable of this and probably wasn't going to be. But at this very moment, she felt so sad and overwhelmed that she just did not have the energy to think about how to help Melanie and Sheila or how to figure out Ella. She just wanted it all to go away.

As she drank her tea, she wandered aimlessly around the house. In Ella's room she found Ella's art box open. Next to it was a piece of paper with nothing but rows of simple crosses on it. It reminded Gloria of the picture of the grave markers she had seen in the history book. She didn't want to think about what it meant.

By the time Jared returned home with Ella, Gloria had fallen asleep on the couch. Jared bent over to kiss her and noticed that she looked rather frail. Not really like herself. He considered the possibility that she was coming down with something. Maybe she ought to call work and tell them she needed to take a sick day or two.

Gloria woke up to the sound of Ella's voice asking her father for two snacks. One for herself and one for children in Africa. Jared obligingly made up two sandwich-size bags of crackers. He gave one to Ella and, because he didn't know what else to do with it, he put the other one in the refrigerator. Ella had collected quite a stockpile of food to share with African children and neither Gloria nor Jared had figured out how to tell her they weren't going to mail it to Africa.

"If you can take care of things around here, I think I might just go to bed for awhile."

"Sure, Glo, no problem. You look beat."

She got up from the couch gingerly, noting that standing up from a prone position was making her back hurt more. Jared followed her to the room.

"Hey, Glo, after Ella goes to bed tonight, we need to talk."

"About Mel?"

"No, about RJ, but yeah, Mel too. I want to hear how your visit with her went."

"Talking after Ella is asleep sounds good. I'm going to try to get a little nap in now. I'm just really tired for some reason."

"Sleep tight."

Jared closed the door. He hoped that Gloria would wake up feeling refreshed. When three hours had gone by and she still wasn't up, he went in to wake her.

"Glo, you won't be able to sleep tonight if you don't get up soon."

Gloria was so sound asleep that she did not hear Jared. He noticed that she didn't even stir. He decided to let her sleep longer.

I know you are overwhelmed now. So much is happening in your life and you don't think you have the energy to pay attention to what I am telling you. But you must listen and you must try to understand. You must not keep any secrets. You have to tell Jared everything that you are holding inside. Everything. Do not be afraid. He will stand by you no matter how hard the future is. Once you unburden yourself of these secrets, you will be ready to learn more about Ella and how you can help her.

Gloria did not remember the dream when she woke up, but she felt anxious to talk to Jared. She just didn't feel like she could deal with all of this by herself. She got out of bed hoping that Jared had started dinner. She wanted to get Ella to bed early, if possible. Jared hadn't started dinner, but he had brought home Chinese take-out. It was one of Gloria's favorite meals. She smiled when she saw a plate of crab ragoons and a large container of duck sauce.

"Mmmm, it looks so yummy. Thanks for getting this, Jare. How did you know I was craving comfort food?"

"Good guess on my part. You were so sound asleep I thought it would be best to get dinner on the table one way or the other. Glad I made the right choice. Could've been salad with grilled chicken."

Ella didn't really like Chinese food that much, but she loved reading the fortunes. She took each of the three cookies and placed it in front of their three place settings. She asked if she could open the cookies and read their fortunes to them.

"Sure," said Jared, "but you have to eat at least a little dinner first."

Ella obligingly ate a chicken finger and a spoonful of fried rice.

"I'm full now. Can I read the fortunes now?"

Jared looked at Gloria with an amused smile.

"I guess she doesn't have much of an appetite tonight. What do you say, Mommy, can she read the fortunes now?"

"Sure," replied Gloria, not caring very much one way or the other. She really just wanted to get dinner over with, Ella bathed, read to, and in bed. Ella opened Jared's fortune and started reading.

"Eat happy, be healthy."

"That doesn't make any sense, does it, Daddy?"

"Well, I guess it depends on how you think about it. If you eat food that makes you happy, maybe you digest it better."

"I still don't get it. Eating candy makes me happy, but you and Mommy say it isn't healthy to eat a lot of candy."

"Good point, sweetpea! Why don't you read Mommy's now."

"Okay. Here goes. Much will be revealed in due time."

"I don't get that one either. I hope I get a good fortune instead of these dumb ones."

"Well, why don't you find out? Read yours now."

Ella was grinning with anticipation as she opened hers.

"We each have in us all the wisdom in the world. What in the world does that mean? These aren't very good fortunes, are they?"

"I guess not, sweetie. Oh well, maybe you will like the cookie," Jared consoled.

Gloria didn't say anything, but she wondered if her fortune was actually prophetic. After dinner she rushed Ella through her bedtime rituals. Eager to share her worries with Jared, she began with Sheila and Joe's situation. She recounted Joe's being laid off and Sheila's being asked to apply for disability and told not to return to work.

Jared, as Gloria, was overwhelmed by the cornucopia of bad luck that was afflicting his brother and his wife. He felt great sympathy for them and also great relief that all of this was happening to them and not to Gloria and him. It occurred to him that Gloria could easily have ended up in a mental hospital due to her insistence that Ella was conceived in a past life. It was a thought he had not really allowed himself to have during the last few years.

Since Gloria had been sworn to secrecy on both issues, neither one of them knew how to approach Sheila and Joe. Finally they decided that Jared should invite Joe out for a beer, and see if Joe opened up to him about his job. He could, Jared suggested, bring up his sense that Gloria was having menopause problems and see if Joe brought up any concerns about Sheila. Although Gloria was relieved to have told Jared, she had a twinge of guilt about betraying Sheila's trust. She figured she would work that out later. Right now she wanted to move on to the topic of RJ and the effect it was having on Melanie's marriage.

Gloria and Jared shared stories about Melanie. Gloria was holding back tears as she sat silently rubbing her back with one hand and using the other to support her head as she leaned on the table.

"I wish I didn't feel quite so tired. Maybe, I could help her more with RJ."

"Glo, you've got enough on your plate. You look exhausted. I think you're worrying about everyone too much for your own good. Maybe..."

"Jared, there's something else. I need to talk to you about Ella."

"What about Ella?" Jared asked. "Is she having trouble with the kids at school?"

"No, nothing like that. Look, I might as well just say it. I'm too tired to beat around the bush. I started having my dreams again."

Jared's face fell. Maybe they had not dodged the mental-illness bullet after all. He had been sure for years that Gloria had been raped and the trauma of it had caused her subconscious to create this elaborate and unbelievable story about Ella. But since the dreams had stopped he assumed she was getting better. Now, here they were, back where they started.

"Look, Glo, I'll listen to you talk about your dreams if you want. But I don't believe they are anything more than dreams. Ella is a human child and there is only one way a human child can be conceived. I may never know who her biological father is or what sort of condition he passed on to her. But I know that from the day we brought her home from the hospital I have been her real father and that's the end of the story for me."

Gloria put her arms around Jared. She was deeply touched by his love for Ella.

"Please, please, just listen. Let me finish. Because something is going on with her lately and we need to understand it. We both want what is best for her. We have always been completely united on that. So, please hear me out."

Before telling about her recent dreams, Gloria reminded Jared about Ella's interest in the history book and her possible vision of women and children who had starved during the Civil War. When Jared heard Gloria use the word "vision" he cringed.

"Ella does not have visions," he insisted.

"Alright, maybe it's not a vision, but it's something she saw with her eyes closed and I couldn't find a mention of it anywhere in the book. Anyway, there's more."

Gloria reminded Jared about the magazine article on Somalia.

"Surely, I don't have to point out that she is trying to save food for starving children and that she was desperate to plant a garden because she was worried about a famine."

"No, you don't have to point it out. I am well aware of it and I apologized for leaving the magazine out."

"But, see, that's just it, Jare, I feel like she is looking for things about war and devastation. Like she is somehow being driven to seek these things out even though they upset her. And then at the same time she is doing this, I start having these dreams again."

"Don't you see, Gloria, that is WHY you are having these dreams. Ella's behavior is upsetting you and so the dreams have started again. Like..." he hesitated before continuing, "...like when you were raped."

"Okay, fine, if that's what you want to believe, fine, but I am just warning you that I know something is going to happen to me, and to Ella. That is what the dreams are telling me."

Jared didn't know whether to be concerned or amused. He

knew Gloria could be dramatic when she wanted to make a point. But he also wondered if she was, perhaps, beginning to develop paranoia.

"Alright, I'm sorry. I'll shut up and listen. What is going to happen to you?"

"I don't know. But I think maybe I am going to die soon," Gloria said softly.

"Holy cow, Gloria. That's what you're dreams are telling you? C'mon, you don't really believe that do you?"

"I don't know if that is what the dream actually means, but I believe something is going to happen."

Gloria told Jared that there were two different beings who spoke to her in the dreams. She had never told him this before because talking about the dreams had always upset him. She explained that one being was Earth Girl who told the story of her own life, the one who had been raped and died in childbirth and who somehow chose Gloria to give birth to her baby. She couldn't look at Jared as she spoke because she knew that he did not believe any of what she was saying.

"The other being is just a spirit I think. With her I only hear a voice. I don't see a story. But she tells me things to help me understand what is going on. She says that she came to earth for a while as Earth Girl, but it was the wrong time. She told me that Earth Girl wanted her baby's name to be Orelia. Do you know what Orelia means, Jared? It means golden!"

"So you have a good vocabulary in your dreams. That doesn't prove that any of this is real," replied Jared.

"No, listen, please. She said that Ella will be my guide, and that she has a message to bring and that we can't keep protecting her because she needs to discover the message. The first time I dreamt about the spirit voice was when Ella was going to be on *Oprah* and there was a nuclear explosion in the Indian Ocean. While I was in the hotel with a migraine, I had the dream and she said that this was the beginning and that Ella was almost ready."

Jared tried to remain calm. He didn't want them to argue about this again.

"And, then all that stuff happened with people saying she was a prophet. So we didn't let her see the news anymore, and now the voice is telling me that we can't protect her anymore; that she will need my help to find the message, and so we have to let her find out now because I don't have much time. That's why I think I might die soon."

Jared looked at her in disbelief. For all these years, they had been living a normal life, and yet Gloria clearly had continued to believe in the dreams.

"Don't you see, Jared, it's all happening already. Even though we're trying to protect her, she is finding stuff, magazines, history books, she KNOWS she needs to find the message. I found a picture she drew and it was nothing but rows of crosses filling the whole page...just like that famous grave from WWI. There is something going on with her, and I don't think we can stop it."

Jared said nothing. He had not told Gloria that the day they went to babysit for RJ, during the car ride Ella had asked him if he remembered the big explosion in the ocean that happened right after she was on television. He told her he did remember. He did not tell her that he remembered also that her eyes had glowed for an instant while they were flying to Chicago. He had never told anyone this. He believed that it was a reflection from something in the airplane, but it had disturbed him at the time because it had made Ella look like a child in a horror movie.

"Jare, don't just sit there. Tell me what you are thinking," pleaded Gloria.

"I'm just trying to take this all in and make sense of it, Glo. You have to admit, it is hard to believe all this."

"You don't have to believe it. I didn't expect you to, not really, but the spirit told me I had to tell you and that you would stand by me no matter what happens."

"Glo, you are really starting to freak me out. Of course I will always stand by you. I love you. But you are making everything sound so dire. Don't be insulted, but I think you should go back to counseling."

"Maybe I should," agreed Gloria, "I am totally overwhelmed by this and everything else that's been happening lately, but I don't think counseling will change anything about Ella. Sooner or later, you are going to have to accept that Ella was sent to us for a reason."

Jared went to cupboard and took out his good Scotch. He seldom drank it unless he was serving it to company. Gloria watched him from across the room. Maybe it was the Scotch, which Jared had downed in one gulp, but for a moment when he looked at her, he thought he saw an aura of light around her. He quickly dismissed that thought as new-age nonsense. Within a half hour Gloria and Jared had fallen exhaustedly into bed. Within an hour Gloria was up again, having soaked completely through her tampon, pad, underwear and pajamas. "Menopause is a fucking bitch," she said as she cleaned up the mess.

Once back in bed, she fell asleep immediately.

CHAPTER 27

My father was right about another drought coming. It was worse than the one before. But by then another local war had started and that made everything even worse. Things got so bad that my father and mother didn't try to hide it from me anymore. It was like everything was going wrong. My parents would look at pictures from their childhood when the earth still had some beautiful colors, and my mother would sometimes cry because the earth had turned to brown and grey. I didn't really know why she cried. I had never known the earth any other way.

My father said he wanted me to know what the earth had been like before the droughts and the wars. He told me that a place that I knew only as a dry brown patch of land had once been a lake, filled with clean water. He told me that the huge sandpit where my brother and I liked to play had once been a forest with many kinds of trees. He said when he was a very young boy, he could hear birds singing there. These things amazed me. I had never heard a real live bird sing. I imagined that it was a beautiful sound because my father missed it so much.

I am glad I have these memories of my father. I try to keep them in my mind when I think of him fighting in a war. I can't imagine my father killing someone, or raping a little girl. I will always believe that he never did any of those things, even though my mother told me that these are part of war. She told me that people have changed how wars are fought many times over the history of humanity, but that death and destruction and cruelty were always part of it. Even when people had rockets and missiles that could aim bombs at specific places, there was still widespread destruction and suffering. People used to think that technology could reduce the amount of suffering caused by war, but soon they discovered that the suffering was only reduced for the side using the technology.

My mother told me that humans have an incredible capacity for destruction, but also, an incredible capacity for creation. She said the worst combination was when people used their ability to create in bad ways, in ways that led to more destruction. She said that I should never look down on the people who did this because they believed they were doing it for good.

I asked her if she believed that it was good. She shook her head and said no. She said she hated for me to have to know these things, but it was important for this knowledge to be passed on, and maybe I would be a survivor. She wanted me to tell the other survivors.

She said that people had invented chemicals that could kill whole forests, and destroy whole farms. She said these chemicals would stay in the land, and that the people who lived there would not be able to use the lumber from the trees or to grow crops again. Sometimes, people would just burn huge areas of land so that the enemy could not inhabit it.

Another thing my mother told me was that there was a time when humans had great big wars with many countries, and during these wars whole cities were destroyed and hundreds of thousands of people died. She said that after these wars were over, people all over the world would vow to never have another huge war. But it never worked. She said sadly that throughout history people seemed to believe that war was an answer to conflict, even a way to improve lives. But she didn't think wars ever achieved those goals because a few years later there would be another war. She said it made her think that humans didn't really understand much about life at all. Once she told me that she thought animals understood more about how to live than humans did. My father disagreed with her, but he said he could see why she felt that way.

She said there was even a time when humans had developed a weapon that was so terrible that it could destroy whole cities and leave the people who survived with terrible diseases that would make the next generation sick too. She said that this weapon was so awful that many people thought just having it would mean there would be no more war. But it didn't work out that way.

Everyone wanted to have this weapon. It became so popular that many countries had it and to see if theirs worked as good as the other ones they would test them. She said there was a time when hundreds of these tests were done and the result was contamination of air and soil and water. But people didn't seem to care, she said, because they were more afraid of each other than they were of hurting the earth.

She said that during war, people made things to put in the ground and explode if someone stepped on them. She said that after some wars, many people were left without arms, or legs, or even eyes and faces. I couldn't believe this and I asked her why people didn't try to stop it. She said that some people tried, but that many people believed that war was necessary to make the world a better place and anything that would help their side to win was a good thing, no matter what harm it caused. She told me that sometimes people developed these things to protect themselves from people who were attacking them, and other times they developed them so that they could be the attackers.

She told me there had been so many different ways of waging wars; that people used clubs and swords and guns and bombs and sometimes even forced animals to participate too. She thought that was so sad. She said that in 200 years, there were so many serious wars that the earth was harmed in many ways. The destruction of forests and fertile soil caused erosion and the earth could not hold water as well, so droughts were worse and lasted longer and some of them caused famines.

But people weren't very smart, she said, because if the famine was in a different country, they would just thank God it wasn't happening to them. They didn't even notice when bigger parts of their own countries got drier and drier and they had less drinking water and less water for hydroelectric power. I didn't even know what she meant, but I understand now.

She said that people kept on doing all the things that hurt the earth and then they were surprised when the earth could not recover from the droughts. They started calling the drought that was going on when my father was taken away and my mother was murdered the Second Great Drought. The First Great Drought was when my father was a *young boy. He said it was very bad that these great droughts came so close together. There was no way the earth could recuperate in our lifetime, he said. But then he said that it probably didn't matter because most of us were going to die anyway.*

He said that in some of the cities that had been abandoned during the First Great Drought, desperate people had lived without sanitation, without clean drinking water and without a safe supply of food. Hemorrhagic fever was widespread in these devastated urban areas. If the fever didn't kill us first, our enemies would, unless we fought them mercilessly. The earth no longer could provide enough resources to support life for all of us. So, it was kill or be killed.

Now it was a different kind of war. Not country against country, but village against village. If it lasted long enough, he said, it would be family against family. He said that this is what the stupidity of the people in the 20th century left us with...a future of desperate struggle for survival that robbed us of our humanity in order to survive. He said there were droughts in the 20th century too, but people didn't pay attention.

I didn't understand a lot of what he talked about. There were things that people in the 20th and early 21st centuries had that I didn't really understand. My father talked about cars, vehicles that used oil to make them go. And electricity. Electricity sounded unbelievable to me. People could just flick a switch and light would come on, or they could watch a screen and see all sorts of shows; they had small devices that played music and told them about people all over the world. I couldn't imagine any of these things – he said they still existed in some places, but almost no one could afford them. And even the people who could afford them could not use them all the time the way the people in the early 21st century did. There just were not enough resources to support these things anymore.

It was hard for me to believe that less than a hundred years ago people had all these things. It seemed just like a fairy tale to me and my brother to think that people weren't always worried about wildfires and having enough food. But it didn't really make me sad, not the same sadness that I felt seeing the pictures of what the earth used to look like and all the different kinds of food people used to have to eat. There were so many choices all the time.

Once the war started, I didn't really think about any of these things. My brother and I would spend the day finding firewood to sell so that our family would have money and enough wood scraps so that my mother could boil water and cook. My father always came home with food to eat. I never knew where he got it, but sometimes we had feasts with meat and bread and sometimes we just had bread and once in awhile we would have a treat of fruit or even chocolate. I loved chocolate so much. I couldn't believe that little children used to have lots of chocolate.

Our life was hard during the war, but it was not terrible until they took my father away. That was the night when my life totally changed.

CHAPTER 28

When Gloria woke up she was in a state of total disbelief. She was totally disoriented and unable to accept what Earth Girl had recounted about her life. Earth Girl was from the future, not some dark and distant past. The difficult living conditions that she described were not from a time before electricity and running water; they were from a future time when people did not have these things anymore. She felt a sense of panic and dread. Was this the world that Ella would have been born into if she had survived Earth Girl's death? She desperately wanted to tell Jared about this dream. She wanted, no needed, him to believe it. She was sure that Ella's message must be about this future.

Maybe Ella was sent to help people prepare for what was to come, though Gloria couldn't even imagine how one could prepare for such a future. She wished she could put it all in a context that made sense to her. These Great Droughts. When would they happen? In her lifetime? In her children's or grand-children's?

Gloria ran to her computer. She started frantically searching on the internet. What should she look up? Climate change? Global Warming? Drought? She needed to know when all this would happen more than she had ever needed to know anything. Then she paused and took a deep breath. She willed herself not to believe her dreams.

Why am I so upset? Jared must be right. These are just dreams...the product of a really weird subconscious. I never knew my mind was such a scary place. It has all been dreams of my own making, except for Ella. Ella is real. Maybe I really was raped and that is why I dream about Earth Girl being raped. Only why does Ella have those eyes? Of course, that's it! I must have these dreams because of her eyes, to explain them to myself.

Still, Gloria could not stop searching the internet. She found a site published by the National Oceanic and Atmospheric Administration. She had never heard of this agency, but the site came up when she searched on "drought in the U.S." The page she found was created in September of 2011:

"An intense drought has gripped the southern tier of the United States for several months, accompanied by destructive wildfires, low water supplies, and failed crops. Dry conditions emerged as early as October of last year and culminated in one of the driest winter and spring seasons in the observed record for the region... At the peak of this year's drought in July, exceptional drought conditions were spread across nearly 12 percent of the U.S., from Arizona to Florida, reaching the highest recorded level of drought since the U.S. Drought Monitor began reporting conditions 12 years ago."

Could this be the beginning of the First Great Drought? *Get a grip, girl! Don't let some crazy dream make you think this stuff really matters. If this was really serious, the government, the scientists and politicians would be all over it. There is no way they would ignore this stuff.*

When Jared came into the room, he noticed that Gloria was perspiring and she had a worried expression on her face.

"What are you looking at on the computer?" he asked casually, trying to hide the degree of his curiosity.

"Here, come see it. It's an entry about drought from September 2011."

"Are you a meteorologist now?" he joked.

"Seriously, look at this, Jared, read it."

Jared quickly read the entry.

"Sounds like a bad drought. I don't remember hearing too much about it on the news, do you?"

"Not really, but we've missed a lot of news the past few years, trying to keep Ella from seeing it."

"True that. So tell me, what made you decide to look up droughts in the internet first thing this morning?"

"I hate to tell you. I had another dream and it was about drought and war and really bad living conditions, and then Earth Girl said it was about the end of the 21st century. She said that things had changed completely in just 100 years."

"And, of course, you believe this?"

"I'm not sure anymore. I can't believe that by the end of this century everything could possibly be that different. So it does make me think maybe my own weird mind is making all this stuff up."

"Gloria, I think that's the best thing I could ever hear you say."

"Really? Better than 'let's go back to bed and have a quickie before Ella wakes up?'"

"Actually, yes. But that would be the second best thing. Want to?"

"I don't think I should. My flow is ridiculously heavy."

"Yeh, I noticed the stain on the sheet. It's pretty big."

"Don't remind me. I think I better go to my gyno and see if she can give me something for this. I don't want to spend the next year like this. Months of no period, and then the world's worst period ever."

"Probably a good idea. No use suffering. Maybe losing all that blood is why you are so tired and pale."

"It's just 'cause I am so upset and confused about everything. If I'm not thinking about this stuff, I'm thinking about Mel, or Sheila. I can't just relax and chill out. My mind keeps racing. Like I woke up all freaked out about my dream, but now my mind is jumping to Melanie and RJ. I need to see them."

"Me too. When Ella wakes up, let's get some donuts and coffee and go over to there Surprise them with a treat."

"Sounds like a plan."

Gloria was trying to feel better. She tried to convince herself that everything was getting back to normal. She felt comfortable just dropping in on Melanie. Ella and RJ would get a chance to be together. Those crazy dreams were nothing more than dreams. Jared was right. Worrying about everything had made the dreams start up again.

Ella plodded out to kitchen, wiping the sleep from her eyes and holding her raggedy bunny.

"I had a sad dream last night."

"You did, baby? What was it?" asked Jared as he pulled Ella onto his knee.

"I dreamt that I had a different mommy and she died before I was even all the way born."

Gloria blanched and her heart started beating wildly. Jared looked visibly shaken, but tried to act as if the dream meant nothing.

"Well, that is a sad dream, sweetpea, but you don't have to stay sad because Mommy and I are both right here and we are both fine. It was just a bad dream."

"I know, but it scared me because in the beginning of the dream, my mommy was really poor and some man was being mean to her."

Gloria recognized parts of Earth Girl's story in Ella's dream. She knew that if Jared had paid attention years ago when she was pregnant and told him about the Earth Girl dream, he would recognize the similarity too. She looked at him. He looked very pale and his hands were shaking slightly.

"Let's forget all this bad dream stuff and get some donuts. We're going to visit RJ. I'll help you get dressed, Ella," Jared said with forced cheerfulness.

* * *

Ella ran to the door of Melanie and Roger's house. She was excited to see her aunt and uncle, and especially RJ. Gloria and Jared realized when Melanie answered the door in her robe and pajamas that they may have come too early. However, Roger was up and RJ was already dressed. Melanie looked surprised when she answered the door, but she welcomed them in. Ella handed Melanie the box of donuts and ran to see RJ. Roger thanked them and got out small plates and napkins. Both RJ and Ella were eager to pick a donut.

"Can we be first?" asked Ella.

"Sure you can. You and RJ pick what you want," Roger said affably.

As they chomped on their donuts, the two kids talked happily. The adults had taken their coffee into the living room and were just getting settled when Jared heard Ella tell RJ that Gloria was not her real mother.

"My real mother lived in a shack."

RJ was not to be outdone.

"My real mother lived in a jungle and had baboon friends."

Melanie heard this and rolled her eyes.

"Kids and their imaginations," she said.

Melanie walked into the kitchen to suggest that the kids go out to play. As she approached, they both started giggling.

"What's going on, kids?"

"We're pretending we're baboons and you are the mother baboon," Ella convulsed in laughter.

"Nice. Go out and play outside now. That's where baboons belong."

Within a few short minutes, Ella came in crying.

"What did RJ do to you?" Roger demanded.

RJ came in right behind Ella.

"I didn't do anything. Ella just started crying when I told her that my sand pile had a big puddle in it one year and then it never did again."

"Why on earth would that make you cry?" asked Melanie.

"Because it means the drought is coming, and then the famine and then we will all starve," cried Ella.

Melanie walked over to Ella and took her by the hand. She

was surprised at how protective she felt towards her.

"Here, sis, I want to show you something."

Melanie brought Ella into the kitchen and showed her the indoor herb garden that was on her windowsill. Then she grabbed the advertising section from the Sunday paper.

"Look at all the food that is for sale in the grocery stores. There's plenty of food. Think of all the restaurants Mom and Dad take you too. They never run out of food, do they?

"No."

"So see, there is nothing to worry about. There is plenty of food for everybody."

"Not for the starving kids in Africa," said Ella emphatically.

Melanie wasn't sure how to respond. She knew that in her attempt to console Ella, she was glossing over the real facts about food in the world. Just as Gloria had discovered, trying to explain the world food situation to a seven-year-old was not something she could do in a sentence or two. For that matter, she didn't have an in-depth understanding about it herself. But she knew it was a serious problem. Gloria joined them in the kitchen while Melanie was trying to come up with an answer for Ella.

"I have an idea, Ella. This might cheer you up. Daddy wants to take you and RJ to Playday today. You two haven't had a chance to go there together in a very long time. I bet it would be lots of fun!"

Gloria's tactic worked. Ella ran happily from the kitchen to find Jared and RJ. Gloria was relieved that she could still take Ella's mind off a subject by offering something different to think about. She wondered how much longer that ploy would work. She also wondered if Melanie would be angry about being trapped into letting RJ go somewhere with Ella. If Melanie was annoyed, she chose not to show it. Instead she returned to the living room with the rest of the donuts on a plate.

"Mom, Rog and I want to tell you something."

Gloria looked up from her plate expectantly.

"We've been talking and we think we might go to family counseling. The three of us together," said Melanie.

"I think that's a great idea, Melanie. I know it helped me and your father get through a really hard time. Every couple hits a rough patch, now and then," said Gloria encouragingly.

"Well, mostly we wanted to let you know because the counselor might think that a lot of our problems stem from you, Gloria, and all the issues with Ella," said Roger.

"Not that we blame you, Mom," Melanie added quickly. "Just, you know, in case the counselor wants to see you and Dad, or Ella. We thought we ought to warn you."

"No worries, you two. You know that Dad and I just want all of you to be happy. Whatever it takes, we'll do it," said Gloria. "I'm feeling a little tired now. I haven't been sleeping well lately. Can you give me a ride home?"

Gloria fell asleep during the brief ride.

"You weren't kidding about being tired, Mom. I can't believe you fell asleep in the car," said Melanie. "Are you feeling okay?

"Probably just fighting off virus, dear. Nothing to worry about."

Gloria meant exactly what she said. She had no time to worry about being tired. She needed to make sense of her latest dream. Although she thought she could dismiss it as nothing more than a far out dream, she was unable to do so. She was truly bewildered by the revelations in this dream. Somehow the whole Earth Girl story and even her bearing Earth Girl's child had seemed plausible, though very unlikely, to her because she believed Earth Girl was from the past. The unexplainable pregnancy and Ella's eyes had helped her to believe that what others considered preposterous was actually real. But it all fell apart for her when Earth Girl said she was living in the late 21st century. If that were the case then she had not even lived yet, so how in the world could Gloria give birth to Earth Girl's child?

When she had told Jared this, he thought that one story was

as hard to believe as the other. He was surprised that Gloria was able to accept such a totally incredible set of events if it happened in the past, but not in the future. He hoped that this meant her unconscious was beginning to come to grips with reality and that changing the story in a way that Gloria could not accept was her psyche's way of helping her let go of this fantasy. He made the decision not to share this supposition with Gloria, at least not yet.

What troubled him most was Ella. Whose child was she really? What was wrong with her eyes? Over the years, he had done research on the internet combing through medical journals and he had never found even one other case like this. It was disturbing. Even more so now that she had developed this obsession about famine and suffering. Plus he was worried about Gloria's health. She was so tired and her back was always aching. Was this her body's reaction to her mind finally beginning to accept the truth?

None of this was on his mind, however, as he watched RJ and Ella at Playday. He just enjoyed seeing them both appear so innocent and carefree. This had been a great idea. For both kids it provided a break from their problems and worries. For Jared it provided an opportunity to just enjoy being a father and a grand-father. He was glad that RJ and Ella were so close in age. It meant they would probably be close for their whole lives, even though they were being kept apart for awhile.

What Jared didn't know was at this moment both RJ and Ella felt more secure than they had in the last two months. Being separated had taken a toll on both of them, in ways that no one else could understand. All of the grown-ups in their world knew that Ella was dependent on RJ for companionship. He really was her only friend. But, they didn't realize that RJ had been feeling anxious and worried since he had been kept away from Ella. He was too young to put words to it, but he worried that maybe they would lose their closeness. His little-boy heart was breaking. It was true that being Ella's defender at school was hard on him and that sometimes he wished she wasn't around, but he loved her deeply. It would have been a surprise to Jared and the rest of the adults to know that RJ didn't really feel safe without Ella.

Ella loved RJ as a brother. She didn't actually need him to defend her. She didn't care too much what the other kids said about her. No one seemed to understand this. Her parents, aunts and uncles, and even RJ felt that she needed to be protected. She was young enough to accept whatever they did on her behalf. But it wouldn't be too long before what she wanted from all of them would be that they take her seriously.

After a few hours at Playday Ella said she wanted to go the park near the ocean. The young cousins' running, chasing and climbing was punctuated by laughter. Jared smiled at their exuberance.

"Daddy, I love the ocean!" Ella yelled from a few yards away. Jared joined her and stood looking out at the sparkling water. The sun was bouncing off the ripples made by the current, and it made the ocean luminously beautiful.

"Does everyone live near an ocean?"

"No, lots of people live far away from the ocean."

"That must make them sad."

"I don't think it makes them sad. They have other things to look at and enjoy, like mountains. The world is filled with beautiful things, lots of different things too."

"It would make me sad not to live near the ocean, no matter what I could look at. I always want to live near the ocean. I wish I could even live in it!"

"Well, maybe someday people will live in the ocean, but I doubt it."

"I'm tired of talking. Can we do something that's not so boring," pleaded RJ.

So Jared led them on a quest for seashells and sea glass, hoping that this would keep them both happy. He was beginning to appreciate the fact that he and Gloria had only raised one child at a time. At the very same time, Gloria was wishing that Ella and Melanie had been closer in age. She didn't know exactly why, but she felt it would be good for Ella to have an older sister living in the same house with her. Maybe if she had a sibling to play with she would not spend her time obsessing about problems that even adults could not solve. At least, that would be one less thing to worry about. All this worrying was truly exhausting. She had so much to do, but her eyes were heavy again. She leaned against the arm of the sofa. It was the perfect place for a cat nap. She was sure she would feel refreshed after a little sleep.

CHAPTER 29

I never knew what happened to my brother, but I liked to imagine that he was happy and living somewhere where there was no militia to join. It bothered me that every time I was being raped after My Friend left I thought of my brother. I thought that maybe he was going to become the kind of man who would do this too. But whenever I had that thought I would pray that God would keep him good and kind just like he was the last time I saw him.

When I was in the hospital listening to the other women talk about what had happened to them, I was surprised that some of them wanted the same thing to happen to the wives and daughters of their enemies. They said that in war, the only way to win was to do worse to the enemy than they did to you. One woman said that if our men raped and beat enough women, the women would beg their husbands to surrender. But another women said that was crazy because no one would surrender because of something like that. She said to remember what had happened to the women in Dafur. The war still went on for years even though most of the women and young girls had been raped.

Another woman said that rape is a weapon of war and whenever there is war there will be rape. She said we should not be ashamed that it happened to us. She said she thought it was good if our men did it to their women. She said we needed revenge. I remembered my mother talking about vengeance too after they took my father. But that didn't make any sense to me. I kept thinking that if everyone was trying to get vengeance, no one would be left after the war. I remembered asking my mother about our religion. I thought it taught us to forgive everyone who hurt us. But she said there were some things that were too hard to forgive. She said forgiving enemies is more than can be expected.

When I said that I knew the children of our enemies because we used to go to the same school, she said that they weren't our enemies then, but once the food and water got so scarce they became our enemies. She said the same thing happened over oil back when people had cars and electricity. I asked her if someone was your enemy because they had what you wanted. She said it shouldn't be that way, but it is.

I hoped that my baby would never be raped and that we could find a place to live where there were no enemies. I told the other women that I wanted to name her Orelia. A few of them laughed at me because they said I might have a boy instead. But I was sure that she was going to be a girl and I wanted to name her after the girl with the golden eyes that I had dreamt about.

I was so scared when I started to have birth pains. I knew it was too soon. The nurse told me not to be afraid, but I was. I was burning hot with fever and the nurse told me that I had an infection in my womb. She said it was probably from being raped. She told me not to worry about my baby. They said they would find a home for it, if it survived. She said I should not expect the baby to live because it would be too small.

I was so scared and delirious. I didn't even understand what she meant. I imagined they were going to kill my baby because I was raped. I screamed and cried and then it was over. Suddenly I wasn't there anymore. I knew I was dead and I knew my baby was dead too. I was scared, but then I saw my baby's golden eyes and I knew we would be part of the cosmos again.

CHAPTER 30

Gloria did not want to wake up. She didn't want to have to figure out what the dream meant. She remembered it in detail, but she wished she could forget it. She realized that she had forgotten about Earth Girl's brother. Why was he in the dream? She hoped, just as Earth Girl did, that his life was good and in a place of peace. She remembered the woman in the dream talking about the women in Darfur. She was sort of vaguely aware of the conflict in Darfur, but she really didn't know much about it. The part about all the women and girls being raped made her think it couldn't be true. Wouldn't people all over the world be doing everything they could to help those women if it were true?

Gloria realized she could look Darfur up on the internet. It occurred to her that the internet provided an amazingly easy way for people to stay informed. It also occurred to her that she seemed driven to go to it for information after almost every dream in the last few days. The one thing she didn't think to use it for was her own symptoms, fatigue, aching back, heavy bleeding.

Gloria typed "rape as a weapon of war." She was astonished by how many links there were. She clicked on a Wikipedia entry about the war in Darfur. She found a United Nations News Center article entitled "UNICEF advisers say rape in Darfur, Sudan continues with impunity." It was dated October 19, 2004. A surge of anger made her cheeks flush as she read:

"Armed militias in Sudan's strife-torn Darfur region are continuing to rape women and girls with impunity," an expert from the United Nations children's agency said today on her return from a mission to the region. Pamela Shifman, the UN Children's Fund (UNICEF) adviser on violence and sexual exploitation, said she heard dozens of harrowing accounts of sexual assaults, including numerous reports of gang rapes, when she visited internally displaced persons (IDPs) at one camp and another settlement in North Darfur last week. "Rape is used as a weapon to terrorize individual women and girls, and also to terrorize their families and to terrorize entire communities," she said in an interview with the UN News Service. "No woman or girl is safe."

In the same article Pamela Shifman was reported to have said that every woman or girl she spoke to had either endured sexual assault herself, or knew of someone who had been attacked, particularly when they left the relative safety of their IDP camp or settlement to find firewood.

Gloria felt weak. How could this possibly be true? It seemed like something that could not exist in this day and time. *Does Jared know about this? Melanie? Sheila and Joe? The people I work with? How many people actually know about this? And it's not just this war. It's every war!*

Gloria wanted to tell herself that the dreams were just a product of her imagination. But she had to admit, that even if the dreams were figments of her imagination they were leading her to truths about the world she lived in, here and now. Had she heard about these things on the news and ignored them because they were too awful to think about? Could these dreams be her subconscious' way of getting her to pay attention?

She wanted to call Melanie to ask her if she knew about what had happened in Darfur.

She remembered that about a year ago, Melanie had berated her for not knowing what was going on in the world. She had complained that ever since Ella was born, her parents had not paid attention to politics. Gloria had listened to Melanie talk about the threats to the EPA and the attempts to roll back environmental protections, but she usually dismissed Melanie's concerns over the environment in the same way that she had grown accustomed to ignoring Melanie's pacifism and distrust of politics. Melanie had often expressed frustration with politicians' tendency to think more about the next election than the good of the country.

Melanie had been a pacifist from the time she was very young. She followed the news, even as a middle-school child, and was openly critical about the U.S. incursion into Iraq. If anyone in the family knew about Darfur, it would probably be Melanie. But Gloria wasn't sure how to bring it up. She didn't want to tell her about the dream. Melanie had no tolerance for Gloria's dreams.

So Gloria was left to contemplate by herself, once again, what all of this really meant. Earth Girl had referred to an actual, verifiable historical fact in this dream. She also had described her own death. The whole dream had been grim and upsetting. Gloria did not feel refreshed in any way after this nap.

Jared and Ella arrived home just as the sun was setting. They found Gloria sitting in front of the window watching the sunset and crying.

"What's wrong? What happened? Did you get bad news?" Jared asked.

"Not really, but I just can't shake this feeling. I feel like I haven't really paid attention to what is going on in the world, like if bad things happen, part of it is my fault for not being more involved. I feel selfish."

"You are anything but selfish. You are a kind and loving wife and mother and grandmother. No reason to find things to blame yourself for. Most if it is completely out of our control anyway."

"Jared, do you know what happened in Darfur?"

"Well, sort of, I guess, not that kind of thing I would talk about right now," he said while tilting his head in the direction of Ella.

Gloria knew what he meant, but she continued.

"Almost all of the women were raped and all of them were in danger of being raped every single day."

Jared had a look of consternation on his face. He couldn't believe she was saying this in front of a seven-year-old, any seven-year-old, but especially Ella.

"What's rape?" asked Ella.

Gloria looked directly at Ella.

"It is when a…"

"It is something that you are too young to know about," said Jared. "Some things are for grown-ups to know, not children. Go on and wash up for dinner."

Ella left obediently, but she knew where the dictionary was, and she knew how to spell well enough to look up rape. The next day when Jared was not home, she told Gloria that she looked up rape in the dictionary, but she didn't know some of the words.

"Daddy didn't want you to know what it means because it is a very bad thing. He didn't want to upset you."

Gloria took Ella on her lap and put her arms around her before she continued.

"When someone forces someone to do things with their private parts that they don't want to do, that's rape. It's a very bad thing for anyone to do to anyone else."

Ella closed her eyes for a moment.

"When I had that sad dream about my real mommy, that's what the mean man was doing," she said.

Gloria wasn't sure that she had heard Ella correctly.

"What do you mean your real mommy?" she asked.

"My mommy who died before I was born. The mommy I had before I had you."

Gloria didn't try to convince that Ella that SHE was her real mommy. She was not convinced of that herself. But she wanted Ella to describe what she saw in her dream.

"What was the man doing to your mommy?" she asked gently.

"He was leaning against her and his pants were down around his knees and he was pushing against her again and again. Her skirt was up over her face. I think he was hurting her."

"Oh my, Ella, that was a very bad dream, wasn't it? No wonder you were sad. Are you still sad about it?"

"No, Daddy told me dreams aren't real and they don't come true. It was just a sad, scary dream."

"Daddy was right, sweetheart, just a sad, scary dream. Now go find your favorite book to read to me, and let's not talk about rape anymore. It hardly ever happens."

Gloria was not paying any attention as Ella read to her. She kept thinking about Ella's dream. It sounded just like what had happened to Earth Girl. *There is no way I could be making Ella have dreams that match with mine. My dreams must be real. Ella really is Earth Girl's child. She said as much herself. Even she knows that she had another mother before she had me.* Gloria couldn't imagine telling Jared all of this without making him extremely upset, and she didn't know how to face the future without telling him. *The only way he will ever believe this is if something happens that gives him proof.*

Gloria began to go over everything that had happened since she first started having the dreams. She wanted to remember every dream and everything about Ella as a baby, as a child, right up to the present. There must be something that she could use as proof. As she unconsciously rubbed her back, she had no way of knowing that the proof was right there.

The next morning when Gloria discovered that she was still flowing heavily and feeling rather weak, she made an appointment with her gynecologist. The outcome of the visit was disturbing to both Gloria and Jared. Her doctor was more concerned about the constant lower back pain and fatigue than he was about her excessive menstrual flow. He ordered a trans-vaginal ultrasound and blood work including a CA125. He told Gloria that there was a chance that she had ovarian cancer.

This news shook Jared to the core of his being. He could not, would not, believe that his wife had cancer. This was, he repeated to himself as if it were a mantra, nothing more than a false alarm. Much ado about nothing.

Gloria found it easier to believe, though equally alarming. She knew she had not been feeling well, but more convincing to her was the fact that the she had been told in her dream that she did not have much time. This was what the spirit voice meant. This was why she had to let Ella find the message. Gloria knew she was not going to see her little girl grow up.

Jared was frightened by Gloria's pessimism. First of all, she did not have an actual diagnosis yet. Secondly, even if it was cancer, not everyone dies from cancer. She should not just assume that her life was over. She needed to be positive, if not for herself, for him and for Ella.

Gloria began a frenzy of activity. So many things she felt she had to do before her treatment began. She had to get Melanie to promise to help Jared care for Ella. She and Jared had to let Sheila and Joe know, and she had to help Joe and Jared figure out a plan for Sheila, if she really did have Alzheimer's. Most of all, she needed to quit her job. There was no way she could keep it now. She actually felt pretty good about quitting. Maybe it would keep someone else from getting laid off.

Jared agreed that she should do all of these things. He figured that maybe with the pressure of everything removed, she might start feeling like her old self again. This was his fervent hope.

Gloria found it hard to call Melanie. First, she asked how things were going and gave Melanie a chance to talk at length about the counseling and how much better things were. Melanie sounded very optimistic about the future. Gloria decided to wait until she actually had a diagnosis, rather than create needless worry for Mel who was happier than she had seen her in years. She decided not to ruin that joy with bad news.

Sheila and Joe were a different story. They did not have good news at all. In the short time since Gloria had last spoken with her, Sheila had told Joe and they had seen a specialist. The doctor was pretty sure it was Alzheimer's and Sheila had sunk into a severe depression. The more Joe told her he would care for her, the worse her depression came. They weren't that old. Her dementia was progressing rapidly, but the rest of her body was healthy. She could last for years. The thought was devastating to her. She did not want to go on. Given this information, Gloria did not feel it was a good idea to tell Sheila and Joe that she might have cancer. Better to wait.

So she waited. Jared waited. The news came early one morning, less than a week after Gloria had seen her doctor. Her blood tests were consistent with ovarian cancer. The ultrasound showed a large mass on her ovary. They would do a biopsy and if it showed malignancy, a CT scan to see if the cancer had spread. Given the size of the mass, the prognosis was not good. But there was still the slight chance that it was not malignant.

When the biopsy confirmed malignancy both she and Jared cried. When the CT scan showed that the cancer had metastasized, they cried again. The oncologist laid out a plan of treatment and said that it would probably give her another year. Jared remained in a numbed state of shock for days. But Gloria began to plan. There was so much to accomplish in this year, and now having it confirmed by doctors that she did not have much time, she was convinced that everything in her dreams had been true. She needed to help Ella find the message and she needed to convince Jared to help Ella when the time came to spread the message.

Chapter 31

The following Monday was one of the hardest days of Jared's life. He had just brought Gloria for her first chemo treatment when he got a frantic call from Joe. He had just found Sheila unconscious on the bathroom floor. He suspected she had tried to kill herself. There was an empty bottle of Tylenol and three empty prescription medication jars on the floor next to her. Joe was waiting for the ambulance to arrive. Jared made an excuse to leave Glorias' side and rushed to Joe's house. By the time he got there, the ambulance was leaving. Joe and Jared followed them to the hospital. Sheila was pronounced dead on arrival. Joe collapsed into Jared's hug and sobbed violently.

"How could she leave me like this? She wasn't that bad yet. We still could have had time together. How could she do this? Did she think I didn't love her enough to take care of her?"

Jared had no answers. No words of wisdom, only compassion for his brother. Gloria's cancer seemed almost trivial at that moment. She still had hope. They still had time. But Sheila's death left no room for hope, no time to remember a life together, no chance for goodbyes. She was gone. It was over.

It was days later that Joe found the letter Sheila left. It helped him to understand why she chose to leave him that way, but it didn't ease the pain.

Dear Joe,
I know this will be hard for you and that it will seem unfair that I didn't even talk to you about it. But I am doing this now because I love you; because you still have your memory. I want you to have a good life while you still can. This might be many years for you, or it might be a few. We can never know these things. But I didn't want to take one good day away from you, and I know, Joe, that living with me, worrying about me, watching me decline would take away all your good days.

I know you love me and I know that you would probably sacrifice too much of yourself to care for me. I cannot stand that thought. I cannot stand to think of you feeding me and changing my diaper, even though I know you would be willing. I cannot stand to think that I would look at you and not know who you are; that I might want to answer you when you say you love me, but I would not be able to find the words inside my head. I cannot stand to think that those will be your last memories of me. I choose not to give you a chance to have those memories.

I want you to remember me as the girl you fell in love with and the woman who was your wife. It is okay to remember the hard times; that we could not have a child and that things were not always perfect. You can remember the sad days, but Joe, please, please mostly remember the happy days. Remember the time we got caught in the rain on the way to the prom. My gown was soaked and so was your tux. Remember how we decided not to go at all. We walked in the rain all the way to the beach and that was when we made love the very first time. Remember that day, Joe.

Remember the Christmas that you surprised me with the puppy; and the day we danced all night in our living room, just because we loved holding each other. Remember all those days and so many others, but don't remember this one.

Remember most of all how very much we loved each other no matter what. That is what is important. Not how long we had, but how much we loved. I will always love you. I will die loving you and I will always be with you and some day I will see you again in the glorious light of eternity.

Forever yours,

Sheila

p.s. It has taken me days to write this because I kept making so many mistakes, but I wanted it to be perfect for you.

Joe showed the letter to Jared and Gloria. All three of them cried as they read it.

"You know by leaving you that letter she left you with a piece of her," said Gloria. "Not everyone gets to have that."

Joe asked Gloria if she would read it at the funeral. She said she would be honored. On the day of the funeral, Jared stood by her side, helping to support her. The chemo treatments had made her very weak.

The next week, Gloria's strength returned and she felt that it was time to force Jared to see that her dreams were telling the truth about where Ella came from and why she was here. She began by asking him if he remembered that in her dream the voice had told that she did not have much time left. Jared admitted that he did remember that. She told him about the conversation that she had with Ella about the meaning of rape and what Ella had seen in her dream. He was annoyed that she had talked to Ella about rape, and he doubted that Ella really had dreamt about it, but he could see that Gloria needed him to believe. He wanted her to be at peace while she was undergoing the treatments. After he had witnessed Joe's losing Sheila so suddenly, he was more aware than he wanted to be that Gloria could be taken from him sooner than he was prepared for it.

So he listened and he promised her to be open to whatever came next. Gloria was desperate for more dreams because she felt that within the dreams she would find the answers that she needed to help Ella. Ella had not been told that Gloria had cancer, but she knew that her mother was sick. Strangely, she did not spend much time thinking about it. Her thoughts were focused on the news shows that she was now allowed to watch. It seemed to Jared that she had a hundred questions every day about what was going on in the world. Most of them Jared couldn't answer. Gloria spent a lot of her "feeling good" hours looking things up on the internet in order to answer Ella's questions.

Ella was particularly interested in learning about the

worldwide water shortage and she continued to dwell on the famines in various parts of the world. One day, after watching the news, she asked Jared, "How do cars eat corn?" Jared explained that corn was used to make a fuel that was added to gasoline so that cars would not use so much oil. Ella asked him if giving corn to cars meant that there would be less corn to give to poor people. Jared said he had never really thought about that before and that he didn't know the answer.

Gloria searched on the internet and found compelling arguments on both sides of the issue. She told Ella that some people believed using corn for fuel does take food out of the mouths of the hungry. But others believed that using corn for fuel will increase the market for poor farmers in other parts of the world and that will increase their standard of living.

Ella didn't like either answer. She wanted an answer that would ensure that there was enough food for everyone so that children wouldn't starve. So far, despite watching the news, reading magazine articles (with help from Gloria) and asking all the adults with whom she came in contact, no one could give her that answer. Ella approached the problem of famine with the simplicity of a child. Everyone should have enough to eat. No matter how many times the adults explained to her that it was far more complicated than she could understand, Ella insisted that there had to be a way for everyone to have enough food and water.

She heard on the news about the privatization of water, and again, went to the adults in her life for answers. Would this mean that more people had water, or fewer people? Would it be only the rich people? Again, the adults had no satisfactory answers for her questions. They explained to her that this, too, was a very complicated question and no one really knew how it would turn out.

Ella had not been a child who was prone to tantrums or defiance, but she became more and more angry as she listened to grown-ups admit that they had never really thought too much about such important things. What was the world going to be like when she had children if no one was thinking about these things? Only Melanie was willing to have these conversations with Ella. Once she realized that Gloria was helping her find information, Melanie started to tell Ella what she really thought about things. Melanie's opinion was that things would, someday in the future, get quite bad. Melanie said there were so many things harming the environment, that eventually it would be very hard to grow food, even in this country. She said that big giant farms didn't treat the soil well and that they used too much chemical fertilizer and toxic pesticides and herbicides. She said they used resources inefficiently. Ella listened, but as much as she wanted to, she didn't understand a lot of it. Melanie thought that giving Ella a specific example might help.

She told Ella about Meatless Mondays and showed her information on their website:

REDUCE YOUR CARBON FOOTPRINT. The United Nations' Food and Agriculture Organization estimates the meat industry generates nearly one-fifth of the man-made greenhouse gas emissions that are accelerating climate change worldwide...far more than transportation. And annual worldwide demand for meat continues to grow. Reining in meat consumption once a week can help slow this trend.

MINIMIZE WATER USAGE. The water needs of livestock are tremendous, far above those of vegetables or grains. An estimated 1800 to 2500 gallons of water go into a single pound of beef.

HELP REDUCE FOSSIL FUEL DEPENDENCE. On average, about 40 calories of fossil-fuel energy go into every calorie of feed lot beef in the U.S. Compare this to the 2.2 calories of fossil-fuel energy needed to produce one calorie of plant-based protein. Moderating meat consumption is a great way to cut fossil-fuel demand.

Ella did not understand most of the information, but one of the facts presented made her very excited. One pound of beef used up a whole lot of water! She finally felt like she had been given an answer she could understand. When she got home, Ella told Jared and Gloria that she thought they should have meatless Mondays. She had done the multiplication, and even if they only gave up two pounds of beef a week, they could save over 200,000 gallons of water in a year. Jared chuckled a little. What a sweet, smart little girl his Ella was, but she just didn't understand that 200,000 gallons of water was literally a drop in the bucket. When he told her this, Ella asked him how many people there were in the United States. She wanted him to multiply that number by 200,000. Gloria was amused and also proud of Ella's persistence. She said she thought they could easily manage meatless Mondays.

Ella continued on her quest to understand starvation. She knew that water was an important part of it. After Gloria allowed her to watch a documentary on the effects of war on agriculture, Ella could not be consoled. Jared felt that Gloria was going way overboard with her new approach. Letting Ella know what was on the news was one thing. He didn't really think it could hurt her too much. Most of it was about celebrities and politicians and the local weather. But finding documentaries about war, about geopolitical conflict over oil, food and water and the resulting impact on the lives of children...well, this was just way too much for a young child to handle. No one benefits from seeing human suffering, he argued, especially children.

Under different circumstances, Gloria would have completely agreed with him. She never would have wanted her little girl to be thinking about these things and she certainly would not help her find graphic pictures of starvation. But Gloria believed that these were not normal circumstances. Gloria's time was limited. She knew that. Even the doctors said that she only had about a year left. Yet, sometimes, when she saw how upset Ella would become, she questioned whether she was doing the right thing. What if her dreams were nothing more than dreams and she was subjecting her highly impressionable daughter to these images? She really needed another dream, but so far, her dreams were nothing more than vague abstract images of people and places. Nothing more than ordinary dreams.

Jared was trying to be, if not supportive, at least tolerant of Gloria's new approach to raising Ella. He wondered if he would have a lot to undo after Gloria's death. He talked this over with Melanie, hoping to find that she agreed Gloria should not be taking things so far. He was chagrined to find that Melanie actually was in favor of what Gloria was doing. Melanie told Jared she was beginning to believe that Ella was a special child due to Ella's intense interest in these topics. "Certainly not a child conceived in a dream," she added, "but maybe she is a little prophet just like those people thought when she was on *Oprah*." Jared was beginning to think all of the women in his family were going off the deep end. He needed to get a guy's perspective.

Joe was that guy. Since Sheila's death, Jared and Joe had seen more of each other. The trauma of Sheila's suicide had brought them closer. Jared could talk to Joe about his fear of losing Gloria and Joe could talk to Joe about how much he missed Sheila. They were both more open than they had been since their teen years. This openness made each more vulnerable. They needed each other in a way they never had imagined.

* * *

Melanie was taking care of Ella one Saturday so that Gloria could get some much-needed rest. Her most recent chemo treatment had really knocked her out. Melanie took out a scrapbook she had started when RJ and Ella were babies. It included news articles about Ella after she had appeared on the *Oprah Show*. She had never shown these articles to her family because Ella's brief notoriety had been so difficult for Jared and Gloria. But she thought Ella might like to see them. She also hoped that showing it to Ella might cause her to talk about her eyes and what she sees.

Ella looked at the scrapbook with great interest. When she got to the part about being on *Oprah* and saw pictures of people holding signs saying that she was a prophet, she asked Melanie what a prophet was. Melanie told her prophets were people who could see the future and tell other people about what they saw. She explained that some people had thought Ella was a prophet because of the things she said she saw when she was on *Oprah*. Ella closed her eyes for a few seconds.

"I remember what I saw. It was terrible. I hope I am not a prophet."

"You might not want to be a prophet, but you do want grown-ups to think about important things, right?"

"Yes. I wish Mommy and Daddy and my teachers would. You are the only one who does, Melly."

"I'm not the only one. There are lots of people who do, and to be honest, I don't think about these things as much as you do. I'm just like everyone else, really. I have a job and a family and after I take care of all my responsibilities, I don't really have much time or energy left to think about the really important things."

"That's what I don't understand. If you know they are really important, why don't you think about them, Melly? Why don't Mommy and Daddy? Doesn't anybody care?"

"I know you hate to hear that you are too young to under-stand, but sis, I think you might be. Right now you don't have any real responsibilities, except maybe going to school…"

"And setting the table and making my bed."

"Right, those too. But they don't take up all your time and no one depends on you, so you have time to think about these questions. For most of us, the bad things are happening far away to people we don't know, so we just kind of forget about them because we have so much to do just to take care of our own families."

"But that's stupid, Melanie, and not fair and mean. It's mean to let people starve and not care about it. And it's not fair to use up all the water and other stuff that people need because what will happen to the people in the future if we do?"

"That's a good question, Ella. It's the question none of us really want to think about."

Ella was quiet. She was staring at the picture of people holding signs. In a few minutes, she got up and went to RJ's bedroom. She lay on the bed staring at the ceiling. She appeared to be concentrating on an old water stain above the bed. Suddenly, Melanie heard the headboard rattling. She rushed into the room. Her heart skipped a beat when she saw that Ella was convulsing violently. She grabbed her cell phone and dialed 911.

Ella's seizure stopped before the ambulance arrived, but Melanie wanted them to take her to the hospital anyway. She called Jared and he dropped everything and headed for the hospital. Adrenaline was surging through his veins as he entered the ER. He felt as if fireworks were going off inside him. *Please! Please! Let her be okay.*

The ER doctor ordered an EEG and some blood tests. Everything came back normal. They kept her hospitalized one night for observation. She was sleepy, but other than that she appeared to be fine. Jared was weak with relief.

Gloria was profoundly relieved also. Melanie and her family had spent the night with Gloria so that she would not be home alone. Gloria wanted to know everything that had happened during the hours before the seizure. When Melanie told her about the scrapbook and their conversation, Gloria felt sure, again, that her dreams were definitely conveying reality...a reality that she could not understand, but reality nevertheless. Gloria had an intuition that Ella's seizure was caused by a vision from the future, from Earth Girl's time. She would not say this to Jared or Melanie, but when Ella was feeling better, she was going to ask her what she saw.

Melanie stayed to prepare a meal, ostensibly so that there would be something to eat when Jared and Ella arrived home from the hospital. She hoped that she could get Ella away from the rest of the family for a few minutes. She had been feeling guilty, wondering if the conversation about being on *Oprah* had triggered something for Ella. Melanie knew that the only other time Ella had a seizure was right before the *Oprah* appearance.

When they got home, Ella looked healthy as could be. Her cheeks were rosy and she was full of energy. Jared, however, looked like he was coming home from an all-night bender. He looked as if he had not eaten or slept at all. His clothes were crumpled. His hair was in disarray. He needed a shave and his eyes were bloodshot.

"Wow, Dad, did you get any sleep at all last night? You look awful. Why don't you go take a shower? I'll get lunch on the table."

Jared headed directly for the bedroom and lie down next to Gloria. His eyes filled with tears.

"That is the second time this child has scared me to death. I was so afraid that she was going to have another seizure during the night. I couldn't take my eyes off of her."

All of the emotion that Jared had hidden from Gloria since she began her cancer treatments came pouring out of him in tears and sobs. Gloria hugged him, and as they embraced they gently rocked themselves on the bed.

Melanie followed Ella into her room, eager to find out what she was thinking about before she had the seizure.

"What happened to you, sis? Did seeing the scrapbook upset

you?"

"No, but it reminded me of something and I had to figure out what it was."

"Did you figure it out, Ella?"

"I'm not sure yet. Melly, remember when I said I didn't want to be a prophet? I think I changed my mind."

Melanie was not sure how to respond.

"You want to be a prophet now? Why?"

"Because I want people to pay attention to me and stop saying I am just a dumb little girl and I am too young to understand things."

Melanie was reassured by Ella's answer.

"I don't blame you for that. But mostly people don't pay attention to prophets, especially now days."

Ella was undeterred. The next day she wrote a letter to the editor of the Newport Daily News.

DEAR EDITER,
I AM THE LITTLE GIRL WITH THE GOLD EYES WHO WAS ON OPRAH. I THINK I AM A PROPHET.
PLEASE WRITE ANOTHER STORY ABOUT ME SO THAT PEOPLE WILL PAY ATTENSHUN TO ME.
    LOVE,
    ELLA

Ella put the letter in the envelope and put a stamp on it. Before she put it in the mailbox at the edge of her yard, she kissed the envelope. "Now someone will listen to me," she said to herself.

Two days later, a reporter from the News called the house and asked for Ella. Gloria demanded to know who it was that wanted to talk to Ella and why. The reporter read the letter to Gloria. She didn't know whether to laugh or cry. She told the reporter that she would call back to let her know if she would allow her to interview Ella. She requested that she not make the letter public and that he not call the house again until she contacted him.

"Ella, Mommy wants to talk to you about something. Can you come sit beside me on my bed?"

"Sure, Mommy."

"Ella, sweetpea, did you write a letter to the newspaper?"

Ella nodded her head.

"Did you say that you are a prophet?"

Ella nodded her head again.

"Do you even know what a prophet is?

"Yes, Melly told me that a prophet can see the future."

"Do you think you really are a prophet, honey?"

Ella shook her head.

"Then why did you say that in your letter?"

"Because I want people to think about important things. The kind of things that everyone says I can't understand. I think grown-ups should think about them. When I was on television, people thought I was a prophet and they paid attention to me."

"I didn't know you remembered that."

"Melanie showed me pictures in her scrapbook."

"Oh...I didn't even know she had those pictures."

Gloria was surprised that Melanie had saved the articles. *Maybe Melanie will be the spark that Ella needs to find the message. Even though Melanie never believed me, maybe she will believe Ella.*

That night Gloria persuaded Jared to let the reporter interview Ella. She convinced him it would help Ella to feel good about herself and that it would give her a good memory from the months before her mother died. Jared looked stricken, but he too felt that Gloria was steadily losing ground in her fight against cancer.

When the reporter arrived she had a camera crew with her. They took a picture of Ella standing in front of the house with Jared, Roger, Melanie and RJ. This picture was Ella's idea. In another picture she was sitting between Gloria and Jared. Gloria was wearing sweat pants, sweatshirt and a bandana on her head.

Melanie had wanted her to dress better for the picture, but Gloria had neither the strength, nor the desire. The last picture was of Ella in her bedroom holding her old stuffed bunny.

Jared thought the pictures were silly and presented his little girl as a cliché – an emotionally needy child with dying mother, surrounded by loving relatives. But he didn't mind because he presumed this meant that fewer people would pay attention to the article.

The story appeared in the paper in the Features section on the following Sunday. The majority of the article recounted Ella's appearance on *Oprah* and the fleeting furor it had precipitated. It included a few details from the reports of the neurologists and ophthalmologists who had examined Ella when she was in kindergarten. Her letter to the editor was printed in its original form and her answers to the reporter's questions were interspersed throughout the story. The headline read: **"Prophet" of Newport Wants Grown-ups To Think about Important Things**. A sidebar entitled **Ella's Top Ten** listed the things she wanted grown-ups to think about:

starving children
famine
drought
privet water (sic)
things that are going to make it hard to grow food in the future
poleuschun (sic)
war
cars that eat corn
the future
my mommy getting better

Reporter's Note: This list was compiled by Ella during our interview. I asked her if they were in order if what she thinks about the most. She said she thinks about all of them together.

CHAPTER 32

The article got the results Ella was hoping for; the very same results that Jared was dreading. Ella was in the news again. The Associated Press and Reuters picked up the story. Bloggers wrote about it. Requests for Ella to appear on *Ellen, Anderson Cooper, Al Jazeera* and the *Today Show* arrived within a week. Jared turned them all down. He had allowed the newspaper interview. Ella got people to pay attention to her and he hoped that it would end right there.

Ella's teacher used the story as a writing prompt for her students. She told them to pick one topic off the list and draw a picture of it. Then they were to write three sentences about why it was important. Much to Gloria's surprise, Ella chose number 10. Perhaps, now that she had some people paying attention to her, Ella could return to the concerns of a little girl. Her three sentences were:

"It is important because I will miss her. It is important because Daddy will miss her. It is important because Melanie and Roger and RJ and Joe will miss her."

The National Association of Science Teachers asked middle-school and high-school science teachers to submit lesson plans based on Ella's top nine topics. A group of students at Salve Regina College planned a "War Is Bad for Children and Other Living Things" protest. They made posters listing some of the long-term environmental impacts of war:

Production and Testing of Nuclear Weapons=Radioactivity in Environment
423 atmospheric tests released radiation between 1945-1957.
1400 underground tests between 1957-1989 released radiation deep into earth's surface.
HOW MANY SECRET TESTS SINCE 1989??

Aerial and Naval Bombardment=DESTRUCTION
of forests, farms, transportation systems, irrigation systems,
sanitation systems.
Resulting in crop failure, erosion, dust storms, wildfires,
scarcity of clean water, famine, and widespread disease.

Landmines cause
Disruption of soil and water
destruction of plant life
disruption of natural ecosystems
Large-scale migration to avoid landmines leads to stress on
neighboring ecosystems, overfarming, water shortages and
speeds depletion of biodiversity.
Despoliation, Defoliation and Toxic Pollution

=

Deliberate Destruction of Environment

=

**Degradation of living conditions for 100,000's of humans and
animals
Is the future you want to pass on?
What are you going to do about it?
Ella wants an answer!**

Jared allowed Melanie to take Ella to the protests. One of the
students recognized her and asked if she wanted to say anything
to the crowd. All she could think of was "Thank you for paying
attention." The participants cheered for her. One of the
organizers of the event asked her to sign the Pledge Board they
had created. The pledge was simple: *I promise to pay attention
for the rest of my life. I will try to find answers. I will work to
pass on a better future.*

Students in other cities joined the movement, and within
months thousands of students had signed the pledge. WAR IS
NOT GOOD FOR CHILDREN AND OTHER LIVING THINGS

clubs popped up in schools and colleges across the country. Some of them were simply called ELLA CLUBS. Even Jared had to admit he was proud of Ella.

But Gloria knew that just paying attention was not enough. When she had the strength to sit at the computer, Gloria continued to research Ella's issues. The one that disturbed Gloria most was war. She knew that people could not control the weather, and that past environmental damage could not be undone, but if there was never another war, maybe the earth, and the people on it, could begin to heal.

Gloria felt an extreme sense of urgency. She didn't think she could tolerate much more chemo and there were things she wanted to figure out before she died. She wanted to understand why she had been chosen to be Ella's mother. She needed to know if there was more to the message. She felt sure that there was still something she was supposed to do with her limited time. Her preoccupation with finding the answers to these questions prompted her to remember the day she had thought of the holy unknown, who was wholly unknowable. She found comfort in the idea that some things could never be understood, not fully, not in this life. Yet, she wondered if the being who came to the world as Earth Girl and then returned to the cosmos could understand the holy unknown. She wanted to ask her.

Gloria's waking hours were fewer and fewer. She was declining more quickly than her oncologist had anticipated. Jared and Melanie took turns caring for her. Yet, when she was awake, Gloria was perfectly coherent and sometimes even energetic. She spent as much of that time as she could playing with Ella, or when Ella was at school, doing research on war.

Although Jared felt that a preoccupation with the causes and horrors of war was not really good for her, he recognized that it seemed to fill some sort of need. He had given up hope that Gloria would realize the story in her dreams was an illusion and that they would have closure about this before she died. He had accepted he would never know who Ella's biological father was, or the circumstances of her conception. So he turned his focus to keeping Gloria comfortable and as content as possible.

One afternoon, Gloria finally had the dream she had been waiting for throughout her whole ordeal with cancer.

CHAPTER 33

I am sorry you are suffering. Take comfort in knowing that suffering doesn't last. When you return to the cosmos, you will not remember the suffering. But you will remember the love. You will be love. Love is the holy unknown. Love is what gives us life. Love is eternal. On the earth, the completeness of love is still wholly unknowable. You see but a glimmer of it.

Do you remember the first time I spoke to you? I told you I would give you answers when you are ready. I didn't know you would fight it so; that you would try to convince yourself not to listen. I am here now because you are finally ready. I told you that I came to earth as the one who called herself Earth Girl, but that my life began before hers and continues beyond it. This is true of you too, Gloria. Humans experience their life on earth in the illusion of chronological time, so it is hard for you to understand that you exist in the reality of eternity.

I chose to come back to earth because the earth is an expression of infinite love. Yet, when I came back as a human, I came into a time when humans had lost their connection with love. It was a cruel time. Just staying alive was hard for most people. There was little joy in life, but there was, in the deep recesses of the human heart, the memory of love and the longing for the joy that their hearts knew was possible.

The time I came back was a time of widespread famine caused by war and by the harm that humans did to the earth in so many different ways. The earth was no longer beautiful. It had lost the colors of abundant life. The sky and the waters were brown and grey. There was little vegetation. But I had lived on earth before and I knew it didn't have to be that way.

When I came as Earth Girl, I had to struggle so hard to stay alive that I almost lost touch with my celestial life. I had glimpses of it, but I could not fully connect to it. But I knew that earthly life can be good because I had lived on earth before. That's why I knew that Orelia had to live, so that she could bring the message that the world Earth Girl was born into, didn't have to be that way.

While I lived in the world as Earth Girl, that was all I knew of the world. But my baby Orelia had not lived in that world yet, so she was not so far removed from celestial life. I wanted her to live to be able to tell people how good life on earth could be. I knew that she would have to be born into an earlier time, a time before it was too late. I wanted her to bring the message that the future can be changed.

I had a lesson for you that day. I do not know if you fully understood it. I am afraid that the difficulties you faced in your life might have kept you from understanding the message, so I will tell you again because I want you to share this message before you come back to your celestial life.

"Life on earth can never be fully understood. Life and all it holds is too big for humans to understand. There is the possibility for more joy than they can ever comprehend and there is the same possibility of pain and suffering. Humans have embraced pain and sorrow much more fully than they have embraced joy. This is why the world suffers. The earth was a beautiful place to live when I first took a body. Remember the joy. Seek the light. Orelia will be your guide."

Gloria, Orelia has been your guide even when you didn't know it and when you are gone, she will be Jared's guide. He will come to believe all that you have told him, but not in this life. You chose to come back to give Orelia life and you have been a good mother. Your work is done. She is ready and so are you.

Chapter 34

Gloria remembered her dream when she awoke, but she did not feel ready to go. Not yet. She had learned so much from Ella. Ella had taught her to think about the important things, but she had never had time to do anything to make a difference. She had never even figured out to live differently. She finally understood that Ella was coming with a message that people today were creating a horrible future without even knowing it. She wanted to figure out how she would have lived differently if she had understood Ella's message in time.

That night Ella had her second dream about Earth Girl. She dreamed that Earth Girl was from the future. In the dream, Earth Girl talked about the girl with the golden eyes and how she said to Earth Girl, "I have chosen you." Ella knew that she was the girl with the golden eyes, and she knew, without a doubt, that she had chosen Earth Girl to be her first mother. She had chosen to be born into that future, but Earth Girl had died, and so had she. She didn't understand it all yet, but she knew that in time she would. She was happy when she woke up.

Gloria really wanted to talk to Ella about the message in her dream. She wanted to see how much of it Ella understood already. Ella had the same desire.

"Mommy, can I get in bed with you for awhile?"

"Of course you can, sweetpea."

"I had a dream last night, Mommy, and I know I lived before, only it wasn't in the olden days. It was in the future."

"I think I had that same dream, Ella, that you really did have a mother before I became your mommy, and the dream took place in the future. I don't really understand it all, Ella, but I am so glad that I got to be your mommy this time."

"I am too, Mommy. I love you so much. I am going to be sad when you die, Mommy."

"I know you will, sweetie, and I will be sad to leave you. But

I will never, ever stop loving you, not ever."

"Me neither, Mommy."

"Ella, was there anything else in your dream?"

"I don't remember, except that there was a woman that my mother called My Friend. She took care of my mother. Mommy, she had your face."

Gloria was beyond being surprised by the revelations in the dreams. She thought for a moment, wondering if in another life...a life in the future...she had been the woman who had protected Earth Girl. She hoped that she would have at least one more dream that would give her the answer.

When Melanie came that afternoon, Gloria told her how much she wished she had starting paying attention to the important things sooner. She said that she knew Melanie had tried to tell her, but it was trying to find answers for Ella that had shifted how she saw the world. She didn't tell her that it also came from the dreams. She knew never to go there with Melanie.

"Mom, I tried to get you to watch the news. Not a biggy, really. But Ella wants us to think about what it all means and how we can make it different, better."

"I know she does. I am so proud of her. I have been trying to think of how I would live my life differently. I want to write it out. If it turns out good, maybe you could read it at my funeral."

"Mom, I don't even want to think about your funeral. But we can work on writing it if you want."

So Melanie sat at the computer as Gloria talked about how she would have lived differently. Melanie tried to organize the ideas and make them concise. As she completed her final version, she realized it would be hard for Gloria or anyone to live up to these ideals, but she also realized it would be worth trying. She wanted people to see it. Melanie wrote GLORIA'S NEW CREDO in large letters at the top of the page.

We share this planet with each other. None of us own it.

All of us are responsible for its survival.

We are all connected by our humanity.

I know that every other human being is no less valuable than I.

I believe that love can overcome hate, just as light overcomes darkness.

I believe in peace. I will work for peace.

I will try to:

Consider the impact of my actions on my fellow human beings and on the earth.

Engage in no activity that deliberately harms another human being.

Learn the impact of my choices on people in other parts of the world.

Seek nonviolent solutions to the problems we face.

Always recognize and protect the beauty of the earth.

Live with love in my heart.

"I know it is so easy for me to say this stuff now at the end of my life. I don't know if I really could live it, but I wish I would be around to try for awhile," said Gloria after reading Melanie's final version.

"Just by really thinking about it, Mom, you have already made a tiny difference and when people hear this at your funeral, who knows what an impact it will have. It is a beautiful legacy to leave us with. Besides, you're not dead yet. Start today."

Gloria smiled and eased herself under the covers.

"For now, I think I will just sleep. Please tell Dad to wake me up when he gets home."

* * *

"Hey, Glo, Melanie said you wanted me to wake you up."

"Yes, I did. Can you sit here with me, just the two of us for a few minutes."

"Sure I can. Are you doing okay?

"Yes, but I don't think I'm going to stick around much longer. I feel like I'm sort of drifting away. I'm not trying to die, but I'm not trying not too either."

"Oh, Glo, can't you try to hold on a little longer."

"Yes, but in case it happens, I want to say this before it is too late. Do you remember when your mother got sick and she said not to feel bad if she dies because the love lives on? She's right. I know for sure that she is right, and I want you to stay connected to that love and Ella and Mel and RJ and Roger and Joe especially. You need to remind Joe. You can stay connected to it and you won't be so sad."

"Do you mean like in heaven or something?" Jared asked. He knew that Gloria knew that he didn't believe in heaven.

"I don't know, Jare. I don't think it's heaven or a place. I just know that love is always there or here, everywhere. But you have to stay connected to it. Please promise me you will."

"I promise."

"It won't be easy, Jared. It's not easy to stay connected, especially when we are overwhelmed by pain or grief. I understand that more than ever now. I think some little part of me understood it before. Do you remember when I saw that Zelda Fitzgerald quote in calligraphy and I just had to buy it and hang it in our room? It was because some little piece of my heart knew that it would have to keep expanding to hold all the joy and all the sorrow that life can bring. But what I didn't get until now is that the heart CAN expand because it is always connected to the love, even when it doesn't know it."

Jared wasn't sure that he knew just what Gloria meant, but he clearly remembered the day Gloria spotted the small framed work of calligraphy. He remembered how tears came into her eyes when she read it. He didn't really understand it then. He looked at the wall next to Gloria's dresser. The small framed quote had hung there for so many years that he had long ago stopped noticing it.

"Nobody has ever measured, not even poets, how much the heart can hold."

He read it aloud. This time it brought tears to his eyes too. Jared lay down next to Gloria. He held her hand as she closed her eyes for the last time.

* * *

When family and close friends gathered at their house after Gloria's funeral, Ella said that she had a speech to make. Everyone sat expectantly, feeling pity for this little girl who had just lost her mother. They were not prepared at all for the words she spoke.

"I think I really am a prophet. I wasn't sure until today, but now that Gloria is dead, I know it for sure. "

A few of the adults were tempted to tell her that she should not refer to her mother by her first name, but they also thought she was young enough to feel that this was somehow appropriate because she was now without a mother.

"I am from the future and so was my first mother," Ella continued.

"Ella, sweetpea, this is not the time for nonsense. We just got back from your mother's funeral," interrupted Jared.

"I know that, Daddy, and I am sad that Mommy died. I wasn't sad when my first mother died because I didn't even have a chance to be born."

"Ella, honey, you aren't making any sense," said Melanie.

"I am so. My first mother lived in the future and she died while I was being born. So I decided to come to earth in a better time so that I could be born and live in a place where I could grow up."

"Ella, what on earth are you talking about?" one of the neighbors said. "I think you're very upset and confused. Melanie, maybe you should take her to her room and get her ready for a nap."

"I don't want to go to bed. Mommy wants me to tell you this. She wants you to know that she was the woman who took care of my first mother after her parents were killed by the marauders. She couldn't remember it while she was alive because she could only remember this life. But she was in her celestial life when my first mother died and she knew I had to be born, so she chose to come here now and live. But when she got here, she forgot. She lost her connection to her celestial life. That's why she had all those dreams. So she could know."

Most of the people in the room looked embarrassed. They made sure that they did not make eye contact with Jared and Melanie. They felt so sorry for Jared. He just lost his wife and now his daughter seemed to be showing signs of mental illness.

"I lost my connection to the celestial life too, but when Mommy died I saw it all. I saw that I appeared to my first mother in dreams and I told her that I chose her. She loved the dreams about me, the girl with the golden eyes, but she didn't understand them. When I said in the dreams that I chose her, she thought I meant that I chose her to do something. All I meant was that I chose her to love me."

Melanie took Ella by the hand and said it was time to go change her clothes.

"But I don't want to go bed now."

"No, not for bed, sis. Just to get you out of that room. All that stuff you are saying is upsetting people."

"But it's true."

"I'm sure you believe it is. But, Ella, people don't come from the future and live in the present. Nothing in the future even exists yet."

"I know, Melanie, that's why it's so important," said Ella

excitedly. "They can still make the future better, but they have to change things now."

"Ella, you got all those college students and lots of other people to pay attention to you and you developed a reputation as a very wise little girl, but no one can believe this and I want you to stop talking about it while the guests are here. You are embarrassing Dad and making him sadder."

"Poor Daddy, he doesn't understand." Ella was completely dejected.

After the guests left, Joe stuck around to keep Jared company. He was still in deep grief over Sheila's death, but he knew that Jared would be in bad shape.

"That Ella has quite the imagination. Making all that up like that. I guess it must help her get through losing her mom," said Joe.

"Joe, remember the night we went out to dinner and Gloria told you guys about her dream about Earth Girl and being pregnant. It's the same story. I don't know whether Gloria told her that story against my wishes, or if Ella actually did dream it. But either way, it freaks me out."

"It would freak me out too, bro. I don't want to make things worse for you right now, but maybe you should consider that Gloria had periods of psychosis...you know breaks from reality, and maybe Ella inherited the tendency."

"Maybe...I don't think so, but even if that were the case, she couldn't inherit the same delusions. Joe, I don't even want to think about it anymore tonight. Let's just drop it for now."

"Okay, bro. Consider it dropped. You want another beer?"

Chapter 35

The days after Gloria's death turned to weeks and the weeks turned to months and the months turned to years. Roger and Melanie abandoned the idea of keeping Ella and RJ apart shortly after Gloria's death. Their hearts were broken for Ella and they knew that RJ was her only real friend. As Ella and RJ progressed from childhood to their teens, their relationship grew closer and closer. People who didn't know their families sometimes mistook them for twins.

Ella never changed her story. When asked, she insisted she was from the future and was here to urge people to change what they were doing so that the future would not be horrible. Most people stopped asking her. Despite this apparent break from reality, Ella excelled in school. Her favorite subjects were science and history. When she could get someone to listen, she loved to talk about how science determined history. She was often met with blank stares, even from her teachers.

By their senior year, Ella had the highest average in her class, giving her the honor of delivering the valedictory speech. Ella approached the podium with confidence and a sense of purpose. RJ sat on the stage with the rest of the graduating class. He hoped that Ella would not say anything too weird. He wanted to enjoy his graduation without any complications.

Ella positioned herself behind the microphone, cleared her throat and began:

"My mother died ten years ago. I mark everything in my life from that day. Before my mother died, she began to understand that how we live now matters for the future. She hoped our generation could change things.

"We have been children for the last ten years, but now we go into the world as adults. We must look at what has happened during those ten years. During that time, we have continued to pollute the air and water, deplete the soil, and increase the emissions of greenhouse gases. We have also continued to wage war. We have contributed to the suffering of thousands, if not millions, now and in the future. We are ten years closer to a future more bleak and disastrous for society than you can imagine. I know because I have seen that time. I have come to you from that time to plead with you not to let that future come to be.

"You may not believe me. That is alright. You do not need to believe me to understand my message. You may not think that what happens in the future matters. But those of you who sit here today will have grandchildren living in that time. You may not think you can do anything, but you can.

"When I was a little girl, I begged grown-ups to pay attention to important things. Now I am begging you. We must learn how to save the future. The information is at our fingertips. It has been there for years. What has been lacking is the will. Let us be the generation that brings that will.

"It is our time. Let us make the most of it."

Jared and Melanie held hands nervously during the speech. Roger sat next to Melanie and held her other hand. They were all worried about what she might say. Just like RJ, they hoped that graduation would be a happy experience, not a vehicle for Ella to create controversy.

"That wasn't too bad, Dad. She didn't mention coming from the future that much. If you weren't listening closely, you probably wouldn't even notice it."

"Yeah, all in all, I think we got lucky here."

That night during her graduation party, Ella made another speech. It was brief, but alarming.

"Mom wants me to tell you to look for the golden orbs of light."

Jared and Melanie exchanged worried looks. RJ took Ella by

the hand and led her away from the guests.

"Look, Ella, I know you believe everything you say and I think you are right about caring about the future, but you have to stop saying weird stuff like that. It freaks people out. You aren't going to have me around to defend you when you go to college."

"I know, RJ. I am going to miss you so much. You are my very best friend...you always have been."

Ella gave RJ a long embrace.

"I'm sorry I made things so hard for you by being your weirdo aunt who is in the same grade as you. It's probably good that we are going to different colleges. You will finally get to have a life of your own without me."

Tears began to form in Ella's eyes. RJ noticed with some discomfort that they glistened gold as they dropped onto her cheeks.

"I really can't imagine being away from you," said RJ softly. "I needed you as much as you needed me."

Ella smiled through her tears.

"Look, Ella, I have something for you. It's kind of a good luck charm for you to keep with you when you're away at college."

He placed a ring in her hand. She folded her hand tightly around it. She didn't tell RJ, but for some reason holding the ring made her think about Earth Girl. It made her feel more connected to her than she ever had before. She knew she would always keep it with her.

"Where did you get this? It looks like an antique."

"I found it when I was digging in the yard when I was a little kid. It was buried in that sand pile that I played in. For some reason I always felt like I was meant to find it. But it's really a woman's ring, so now I want you to have it."

"RJ, let's make promises on this ring. I want you to promise that if you ever have to fight in a war, you won't seek vengeance."

"Ella, I don't think I even know what you mean. Do you mean I won't kill the enemy?"

"Not exactly, RJ. I mean that you won't give in to hate and that if you ever have to kill, you will do it with deep love and respect for that person."

"That doesn't even make sense to me. How could I love and respect someone I am trying to kill?"

"You could love and respect his humanity. You could remember that the person you see as an enemy has a family...parents who will miss him or her, maybe a spouse and children who will be devastated...that as far as the universe is concerned this person has as much right to live as you do. So if you have to kill, you would do it with respect and never try to inflict extra pain or humiliation and never try to get even by raping or hurting people. You would realize that you are taking a human life and that the person you see as an enemy probably considers him or herself a good person fighting for a just cause. Just like you do. That's what I mean. I want you to promise me that you won't let love for your country make you hate people from another country. I don't want you to change; to lose yourself to hate. Please, promise me."

"If soldiers thought of all those things, they would never be able to kill anyone," said RJ.

"I wish that were true," said Ella. "Please, just promise, okay?"

"I promise that I will try to remember all this if I ever am in that position," said RJ, with an eerie feeling, almost like deja vu, that once he had been in that position.

"More than try, please, say you won't change; that you will stay sweet and kind like you are now."

"Geez, Ella...sweet? I'm not sweet."

"To me you are. You always have been. You always looked out for me and made sure I was never alone at school. You were always kind to me. Please promise," she pleaded.

"Okay, okay, I promise. Can we end this conversation now?

"But what do you want me to promise, RJ?"

"I don't know. I guess you could promise that for the rest of the summer you will stop talking about things that freak our parents out."

"I promise."

"Somehow, I think that will be a hard promise for you to keep."

Ella frowned at him.

"I said I promise. My prophetic lips are sealed for the rest of the summer. I will only talk about TV shows and the Red Sox this summer. Does that make me normal enough for my family?" asked Ella in a haughty voice.

"Well, kid, it's a start," laughed RJ.

"Let's get back to the party. You can watch the new conventional me in action. By the way, who are the Red Sox playing this week?"

* * *

Jared spent as much time as possible with Ella before she went off to Washington, D.C. for a summer internship with a nonprofit environmental and social justice advocacy group. She hoped that working with this group would help her decide on her college major. She had chosen Clark University in Worcester because they were allowing her to design her own major, but she had to figure out what her concentration should be. Environmental Sustainability, Social Justice, or Nonviolent Conflict Resolution? She knew that each of these areas was vital to the creation of a better future. She just wasn't sure where she would focus her energy and talent.

She was going to spend six weeks in D.C, and then have two more at home before freshmen orientation. She couldn't wait to begin the internship. She felt as if she would finally be working with people who shared her hopes for the future. She, RJ and Melanie sat in the back seat of the car on the way to the airport.

Jared and Roger were in the front.

Jared pretended to be interested in Roger's discussion of the recent stock-market upswing, but his thoughts were really focused on the fact that this would be Ella's first time away from home. He couldn't help but worry about how she would be received. *What will her co-workers think when they see her for the first time? Will she begin to tell stories of her mother from the future and totally alienate her colleagues? Will she make any friends without RJ there to run interference for her?* His stomach was in knots by the time they approached the exit for the airport. He struggled to hold back tears as Ella entered the security line at the airport. Melanie, Roger, and RJ stood next to him. They assured him that she would be fine.

"Well, I am encouraged by the change I saw in the last few weeks. I think she is really maturing. She hasn't said any of her 'back from the future' stuff since graduation."

RJ smiled. "You can thank me for that. I made her promise not to."

Melanie looked at him quizzically.

"How did you get her to promise that?"

"I agreed to promise that I would never seek vengeance in a war."

"Gotta love that little sister of mine," said Melanie.

Jared just shook his head.

CHAPTER 36

Jared need not have worried about how Ella would be accepted. Everyone that she would be working with already knew all about her. In fact, she had been chosen for the internship because they wanted to capitalize on her notoriety. They hoped that Ella could influence people on behalf of their causes just as she had when she was Ella, the child prophet. Although most of them had seen the newspaper pictures of her, they were still surprised at what she looked like in person. Her orb-like golden eyes were both mesmerizing and disturbing. Within a few days, however, all of her colleagues got used to her appearance.

Ella arrived filled with energy and enthusiasm. She was excited about all that she could learn during her six weeks in D.C. Her mentor, Susan Fernandes, was an older woman who had devoted most of her life to environmental causes. Short in stature, with greying hair and about twenty extra pounds, Fernandes was known for her no-nonsense approach to politics. She knew her way around Capitol Hill and she was eager to share her knowledge with Ella.

After a week of orientation, Ella was given her first assignment. She was to deliver a presentation to high-school students attending a leadership conference. Her goal was to convince the audience that young people could have a profound role in saving the rainforests if they understood the social and political issues related to deforestation. This was to be the first of a series of appearances Ella would make, all with the goal of getting young people to understand the dangers to the environment and the role that they could play in solving the problems.

After a few minutes, Ella deviated from her prepared presentation. She told the audience about the visions she had as a young girl; about seeing the earth as a dry, barren landscape where starvation was the norm. She talked about this as the inevitable future if they did not do something to change it. Not when they were adults, but now. She urged them to talk to their parents, their teachers, and their friends. Many of the young people were moved by her passionate plea. Some raised their hands to ask questions, but the moderator took the microphone, saying that Ella had already gone over the time allotted for her presentation. Ella glanced at her watch. She still had six minutes left to speak. Ms. Fernandes confronted Ella immediately after the panel presentation.

"You've got a lot to learn about working in a political environment. You can't go off script like that. You'll lose all of your credibility if you keep telling stories about dreams. That audience definitely did not understand the metaphor you were trying to use."

"I wasn't using a metaphor," replied Ella. "I really did have those visions in my dreams. It's not a story I made up to make the presentation more interesting."

"Listen, Ella. It's one thing to use your notoriety as a precocious child who had some influence for a while. That helps us get gigs. But if you really want to make a difference and influence people to take action to protect the environment, you can't say things that make people thing you are crazy," said Fernandes.

"They didn't act like they thought I was crazy," retorted Ella. "They were raising their hands to ask questions."

"First lesson in real politics, honey...you have no idea if those questions were going to be in your favor...you know what I mean...questions that would move our cause along. They just might have wanted to ask things to embarrass you."

"Like what?" asked Ella.

"Like if you were on drugs when you had those visions," answered Fernandes. "We don't need to discuss this anymore. Stay on script."

Ella felt embarrassed and deflated. *I thought this would finally be the place where I could be myself. I don't want to censor everything*

I say to make it politically acceptable. This was not what she signed up for.

That night, Ella went to RJ's Facebook page. She missed him and she wanted to see what he was doing. She didn't message him because she had told herself that she should give him space this summer. She had barely begun scrolling down his timeline when she came across a You Tube video someone had posted on his page. The comment above it said, "Your cousin is getting famous. 2900 hits already."

She clicked on the video and saw a slightly fuzzy image of herself giving her speech at graduation. *Who put that on YouTube? I wonder if Dad and Melanie know about it yet? I should probably warn them.*

Before she could make the call, one of her fellow summer interns entered her room. Brendan Nugent was the only other intern from New England. He and Ella had been paired together during orientation. The first time she saw him, his appearance made her think of the hippies she had seen in the old movie, *Woodstock*. His hair was longer than hers and he wore bell-bottom jeans. By the end of the first day, she knew that he was a vegan and that he loved oldies music. By the end of the second day, she knew that he liked her. She had finally found a friend.

Brendan looked intently at the screen on his phone.

"Hey, Ella, I think there's a video of you on YouTube. Is this you?"

Ella's face flushed.

"Yeah, it's me. It's my graduation speech. I don't know who put it up."

"It's already got 4789 hits," he said.

"Really? That's way more than a few minutes ago!"

"I think you should show Ms. Fernandes. Maybe you can use some of this in your presentation."

"I doubt that. I'm in hot water with her for going off script today."

"But it's good, Ella. I think it's inspiring."

Ella blushed. She had never really had attention from a male before.

"I guess I'll think about it. I have to call my dad and warn him about it. He hates it when I get publicity. Makes him really uncomfortable."

"That's weird. I think he should be proud of you."

"He is, but nervous too. Anyway, I'll see you at breakfast tomorrow. I'm anxious to call him."

"Okay. G'night."

Brendan closed the door behind him. Ella decided to watch the video one more time before calling home. It had 6,021 hits. *Maybe Brendan is right. People seem to like it.* She had trouble sleeping that night. Her thoughts turned to her mothers, the one she had never known and her beloved Gloria. She missed Gloria so much. Her death had caused a void that no one could fill. But during this night, Ella longed to know her mother from the future; the one who wanted her to be born in this time so that she could bring a message that would save the future. Although she did not understand how she could be from the future, she had believed it ever since dreaming about it before Gloria's death. *I don't have to understand it to know that it is true.*

She remembered how she felt while she wrote her graduation speech. She had tried to express her message in a way that people could accept. Now it was going viral on YouTube. *Did I express it clearly enough? Do people really get it? Are we going to do something to save the future? What more can I do?*

Her heart was beating rapidly. She felt like time was running out. Less than 100 years from now, people would be struggling to stay alive; the earth would be dying, and its inhabitants would be warring over the most basic of resources. Food and water. Somehow she had to get people to pay attention.

Ella was full of energy the next morning. She had a plan. She couldn't wait to tell Brendan. Maybe he would even want to help her. She fiddled with her notebook nervously, while waiting for him to show up for breakfast. They had eaten together every morning since the first day. Her cheeks went pink with excitement when she finally saw him approaching the table.

"Brendan, I have an idea. You know how my speech is going viral. I think I can use it to really get people to do something to save the world and bring lasting peace."

"Well, that's a modest goal. How much coffee have you had?" he quipped.

"None. I'm serious," she answered. "We are running out of time. We have less than 100 years before things get really bad."

"I'm not sure environmental scientists agree with that timeframe," he said.

"Check it out, then, Brendan," she said. "I did. Almost all of them have changed their predictions of how long it is before we do irreparable damage to the environment."

"If you tell people that, they will think it is hopeless," countered Brendan.

"No, that's just the point," insisted Ella. "If we can slow it down, humans can find ways to adjust to it; they can plan for a future with fewer resources of some kinds, but more resources of other kinds. There are lots of ways to make the future better for everyone, if we act now."

Brendan listened without commenting.

"Just like I said when I was a kid, people need to pay attention. We can fix this, but not if we ignore it because it is too scary!" she concluded.

Brendan was moved by her passion.

"So what's your idea?" he asked.

"I think I can make another video and link it to this one. In the new one I will say that I need everyone's help to save my mother. I can tell them about what happened to her. What I saw in my dreams and what my mom told me before she died. I will make it sound like it is happening to her now. I can say how I need help to save her before she gets raped and dies," she said excitedly.

"Wait, Ella. I don't get it. You are going to tell people you need help to save your mother, but your mother has been dead since you were a little girl."

Ella frowned. She looked down for a moment and then reached for Brendan's hand embarrassedly. She had never held a boy's hand before, other than RJ's and that didn't count.

"Remember those dreams I told you about? The ones I had right before my mother died? I didn't tell you everything. If I did you would understand," she said.

"Then tell me now," he said. "I want to know what you are talking about. If it makes sense to me, maybe I can help you."

Ella noticed how tentative he sounded, but she didn't care. She hoped he would help, but it would not deter her if he chose not to do so. She told him the details of the dreams and the conversations with Gloria. She told him that she was convinced that she had first been conceived by Earth Girl.

Brendan was silent for what seemed like a long time to Ella. Way too long. She pulled her hand back.

"It's okay. You don't have to believe me. No one else does," she said.

Why am I noticing how gorgeous his eyes are right now? He thinks I am nuts just like everyone else who ever heard the story. My own family thought Mom and me were both crazy. Whatever. He's just the first guy to ever act like he likes me. No biggy.

Brendan reached for Ella's hand.

"Don't pull away. I'm just trying to process all this. It's a lot to think about," he said.

"I know," she answered. "But it is all true and I know that I was sent with a message to save the world. I just realized last night that I can't wait until I graduate from college. I have to do something NOW. Something that will get people to pay attention, even if they DO think I am crazy."

"Ella, I do want to know more, but I just don't know how the video would convince people to pay attention to the environment, or war, even?"

Ella explained that if she could get people to care about her mother; to want to save her from imminent danger of starvation and rape, that video would go viral too. She figured that after there was a big uproar about it, maybe even news stories, she could explain that she means Earth Girl, her mother from the future. She could tell people what kind of life Earth Girl is destined to have in the future if people don't make changes now.

"I know how much you care about this," Brendan said tenderly. "But I don't think this plan will work. It's way out there."

"I know it is, but maybe that will help it get attention. I don't care if people think I am crazy. Once a few people start checking out what is going on with droughts and farming practices and starvation, and the environmental impact of wars, and everything else that goes along with it...and they see that everything I say could happen...well, I just think that it will gain more and more attention. If a few people in every country believe it, and they get passionate about it, maybe then others will and protests will start and governments will begin to notice. I can't NOT do it. I have to try. I really have to," she concluded with a vehemence that surprised Brendan.

Ella was talking so fast that Brendan could hardly keep up with it. He wondered for a brief instant if she was on speed. Yet he could feel himself being influenced by her.

Before he could respond, she continued.

"Besides," she said quietly, "I know you can't understand this, but I really do want to save my other mother. I care about Earth Girl. I even love her. I want to save her from that life."

Brendan was torn between believing his mind and believing his heart. His mind told him that it was a crazy, futile idea and not to get involved. His heart, however, was already committed to helping.

"What can I do to help?" he asked.

Ella leapt out of her chair and hugged him before she even realized what she was doing.

"Just don't tell people you doubt me," she answered. "It's okay if you doubt my dreams, but if you are going to help me, you can never admit that you have doubts. Okay?"

"Okay."

No matter what she was doing during the next few days, Ella could not stop thinking about her plan. She was pretty sure she and Brendan would have to resign from their internships once they posted her new video on YouTube. She didn't care. She hoped that Brendan would not care either. *I can't believe I have a crush on someone at this point in my life. How weird! But how wonderful!*

Brendan found it all pretty weird too. This was not his first crush, not by a long shot, but he was pretty sure that it would be his last. *I think I am falling in love with the strangest person I have ever met. Scary thought.*

As Ella had predicted, her new video went viral. Hundreds of people posted comments asking her how they could help. When Melanie showed it to Jared, he erupted in anger. Melanie had not seen him this angry since the day Gloria had told them that she did not know how she became pregnant. His anger was surpassed only by his disappointment. His worst fear had been realized. Ella had gone into the real world on her own and had succumbed to some sort of psychosis. *She can't be allowed to live on her own.*

Both Ella and Brendan were asked to resign from their internships. Brendan's parents were furious. They demanded that he return home immediately and they insisted that he cut off all contact with Ella. When he told Ella, they both cried. As they hugged each other, their tears mingled together making a salty river of pain that dripped off each of their cheeks.

Brendan was the first to stop. He wiped the tears from Ella's cheeks.

"I should have known my parents would freak," he said sadly.

"Me too. I'm sorry. I didn't mean to ruin everything for you."

"You didn't ruin everything for me. I don't care that much about this internship anymore. But you ruined one thing. I won't be able to see you anymore, at least not with my parents knowing about it.'

"I know. My dad is furious too. He said if I don't make a reservation for a flight home today, he will. He's even talking about not letting me go to Clark," said Ella.

"He would keep you from going to college?" asked Brendan incredulously.

"It doesn't really matter," answered Ella. "I won't stop what I'm doing. We need to make one more video before we leave. This is the final one. The one that will tell people that I am talking about Earth Girl, and that they can save her by doing things to save the environment and to end war."

"You need to tell them that when they save Earth Girl, they will be saving an entire generation, not just her," said Brendan. "They will be saving their own mother too. Mother Earth."

"That's perfect!" said Ella excitedly. "I knew you would get it!"

That night, after making the video, Ella and Brendan left their dorm at American University and started walking. It was an unusually comfortable summer night for Washington, D. C. Not too hot, not too humid, a slight breeze, few clouds and a beautiful full moon. They walked past the White House and Ellipse, stopping frequently to embrace and kiss.

Ella had never felt this mixture of emotions before; love and desire blended in with a sense of purpose and a shared goal. It was exhilarating. They were in love; they shared a lofty goal; and they had even gotten in trouble together. When Brendan tentatively reached inside her blouse, Ella took his hand and placed it on her breast.

They found a secluded spot in Potomac Park. Lying under the stars, they said little, but Ella felt that Brendan was sharing in her every thought. She desperately wanted him to make love to her. She knew she might never see him again. *This might be the only man who ever loves me.* She leaned over him and kissed him gently. She was new at all this and wasn't sure what to do. But her life as a solitary teen had left her plenty of time for reading...love stories...as well as science, history and environmental research. She hoped he would understand the meaning of that gentle kiss, as she lay down onto her back.

He took her hand in his and squeezed it gently. Then he gently traced his fingers from her cheek, down to the tips of her fingers. Her pulse quickened as he leaned toward her and unbuttoned the first button on her blouse. He kissed her once on the forehead. Softly, gently.

After the second button, he kissed both of her eyelids.

"Open your eyes for me, Ella. Look at me with your beautiful golden eyes."

After the third button, he kissed the tip of her nose. After the fourth, he kissed her lips. With the fifth, he kissed her neck. His breath was warm and tantalizing. Ella hoped he would continue.

"Ella, is this okay? Do you want this?" he whispered.

"Yes, yes, I do," she whispered her answer.

When the sun rose the next morning, Ella and Brendan were still in each other's embrace. Ella was happier than she had ever been. Yet, she knew that when she boarded the plane for Providence, she would be terribly unhappy. She was afraid she would never see Brendan again. She knew they would talk, and Skype and maybe even write to each other over the coming months. But she also knew that when their latest video was posted, things might spin out of control. Brendan might choose to back away from her if the publicity got too negative. She would have to risk that. Changing the future was still the most important thing. *It will be my life's work. No matter what it takes.*

CHAPTER 37

Melanie insisted on accompanying Jared to the airport to pick up Ella. She hoped she could use the time it took to drive from TF Greene Airport to Newport to mediate what she expected to be an angry exchange between her father and her baby sister. On the way to the airport, they heard on the radio that there had been a major airline disaster involving a flight from Washington, D.C. The plane had plummeted into the ocean off the coast of New Jersey. By the time they arrived at the airport it had been confirmed that it was Ella's flight. There were no survivors.

Ella's funeral was attended by over a thousand people. Although most of them did not know her, they had been inspired by her. Some of them remembered that, at the age of seven, she made her plea for people to pay attention to the important things. It had changed the way they lived. Others knew her from her videos. They had only recently been affected by her plea for people to pay attention to what was happening to the mother we all share.

Jared received letters that recounted changes, big and small, that people made because of Ella. Melanie, Jared and Joe were astounded by the impact Ella had on people of all ages from all parts of the world. They had no idea that her message had been heard by so many people.

Despite the outpouring of sympathy after Ella's death, Jared was lonesome and depressed. He found himself struggling to understand Ella's life and his role in it. He still missed Gloria deeply and Ella's death made life even more unbearable. He found the news depressing and seldom watched it. He began to isolate himself from the world around him.

One night Jared had a dream. Ella and Gloria were both in it. They were pleading with him to believe everything they had told him about the future. They said they would send a sign to prove that the dreams had been real and that people could change the future. They told him he would see Ella's eyes again.

Jared was deeply disturbed by the dream. There was no way he would ever see Ella's eyes again. How could he? They had not even been able to recover her remains from the plane wreck. She was gone. Just like Gloria was gone. They were both gone forever and he had to figure out how to live the rest of his life without them.

"Stay connected to the love. You will find us there."

Who said that? It sounded just like Gloria. Now his mind was playing tricks on him. *Maybe I am hearing her voice in my head because I miss her so much, because I want to believe that we are still connected to each other.*

But he didn't want to believe the rest of it. He didn't want to believe that his wife and his daughter had come from the future to try to change it. He didn't want to believe that their warning about the bleak future in store for humanity was true. He didn't want to believe that Ella's golden eyes really were the eyes of a prophet. He just wanted his wife and daughter to be alive. He wanted to bask in the warmth of their love once again.

The more Jared thought about the dream, the more dismayed he was. If Gloria and Ella were both from the future, well then, who was he? Did he have some sort of role to play in saving the future? Was he supposed to spread a message he did not even believe? Why had he ended up with Gloria?

He struggled to maintain a normal life. His job was a lifesaver. It forced him to get up each day; to make decisions; and most of all, to communicate with other people. He had no desire to socialize anymore. During his free time, he took long solitary walks, often passing by the Athenaeum and resting in Touro Park. He felt close to Gloria there. It had been one of her favorite places in Newport.

One Saturday, as he sat looking at passersby, Gloria's homeless friend sat down beside him. Jared didn't recognize him. He hadn't seen him since Roger had chased him off their lawn after Ella's appearance on TV.

"You the man. You the one," said the homeless man.

Jared moved as far to the end of the bench as he could. *Just ignore him. He probably wants money. He'll go away if I don't look at him.*

"I know who you are, man. You're the next one. You are part of the plan, man. You don't even know it, I looked through a window and I saw your face, clear as day. You're next, man."

Jared got up and walked away without looking back. *Part of the plan? The next one? Sure thing, if I looked at him he'd ask for money. I'd be the next one to give him money. Not me.* Jared felt a little ashamed. He knew that Gloria would have wanted him to be kind to this panhandler. That's the kind of person she was. She never judged people. He remembered her telling him that we all have something to learn from everyone we encounter. He didn't agree with her, but that didn't keep his heart from aching for her.

When he got home, he called Joe and broke down on the phone. He told him that he didn't think he could go on without Ella. He was trying hard, but he could not seem to get over his terrible sadness. Joe, more than anyone else he could talk to, understood. He convinced him that they should take a vacation together. They could spend a few weeks driving, camping, and fishing; make it an old-fashioned road trip, the kind most people could no longer afford to take. They would leave behind their everyday life and all of the things that reminded them of their lost loved ones. Joe described it as a retreat into the simple joys of nature. His enthusiasm for the trip convinced Jared to go along.

After a week of isolation, on the shore of a remote lake, Joe checked the news on his car radio. He had wanted to do so every day of the trip, but never had out of respect for Jared's desire to get away from it all. He was shocked to learn that an asteroid was supposed to be heading towards earth at an alarming rate. If it stayed on the same trajectory, it would just barely miss the earth. However, in the last few hours, NASA's telescopes had picked up two smaller objects accompanying the asteroid. They appeared to be veering off of the trajectory and were headed for earth.

For those who were not in the direct path of their descent, it was predicted to be an amazing, once-in-a-lifetime light show. The problem was, the further away from the asteroid they were, the more erratic was their movement. It was going to be impossible to predict where they would land.

Joe told Jared that they needed to decide whether to go in search of shelter. Either that or make the ultimate gamble. Maybe dying or maybe seeing the most amazing light show ever. They chose to take their chances. They couldn't wait to look at the night sky. It was the first time Jared had felt enthusiasm about anything since Ella's death. Although pollution blocked the view of most of the stars, the moon still shone brightly.

Joe pulled out the sleeping bags while Jared called Melanie to make sure she and Roger knew what was going on. He got her on her cell phone. She was just heading into a municipal building built to withstand hurricanes and tornadoes. They briefly wished each other luck and said how much they loved each other. Neither one really thought it would be the last time they would speak.

Joe and Jared lay on their backs next to each other. They stared at the sky for over an hour. Then gradually, a small light, the size of a star came into view. In an instant, a second one was visible.

"That must be them!"

"I wonder which way they are going."

The two specks of light grew larger and larger. They seemed to be coming directly toward them. As they got closer, the whole sky was illuminated and the lake below became a luminous pool of blue. Suddenly, Jared felt Gloria and Ella's presence. If he had time to describe it he would have said that he felt he was basking in the light of their love.

"Ohmigod, they're coming right at us."

Jared grabbed Joe's hand tightly.

"I guess this is it for us...the end!" Joe gasped.

"Or maybe, the beginning," said Joe as two golden orbs landed in the blue waters of the lake.

Soul Rocks is a fresh list that takes the search for soul and spirit mainstream. Chick-lit, young adult, cult, fashionable fiction & non-fiction with a fierce twist